MORE PRAISE FOR

The Glass Kingdom

"A master of the literary thriller." —*Fodors*

"Showing Osborne at the height of his powers, *The Glass Kingdom* upends the Western reader's most basic assumptions about the human world. Slyly, almost imperceptibly, but quite relentlessly, Osborne subverts crime fiction as a genre and the worldview of its readers. As you turn the pages of this stylish and disquieting tale, you will find your fictions of choice and autonomy crumbling along with the Kingdom."

—John Gray, *New Statesman*

"Bangkok is the star of this accomplished novel. Its denizens are aliens to themselves, glittering on the horizon of their own lives, moving—restless and rootless and afraid—through a cityscape that has more stories than they know."

—Hilary Mantel, Booker Prize–winning author
of *Wolf Hall* and *Bring Up the Bodies*

"Osborne is among the finest pure writers at work today."

—*CrimeReads*

"Exceptional descriptive skills fuel an overwhelming sense of menace: It is no mean feat to make the ending of a novel truly shocking. . . . The next day you will still be thinking of Sarah's fate with horror."

—*The New York Times Book Review*

"Osborne, a journalist and novelist, [who] distinguished himself in 2018 with *Only to Sleep* . . . brings the same canny way with displaced characters to a politically turbulent, monsoon-drenched Bangkok in this unhurried but beautifully textured tale."

—*The Washington Post*

"Riveting . . . There's an ominous sense of foreboding from the first page, and the tension ratchets up to a terrifying pitch before the horrifying and brutal conclusion. . . . A gripping read."

—*Booklist* (starred review)

"Masterfully drawn, mesmerizing . . . A seductive, darkly atmospheric thriller with a spine-tingling climax."

—*Kirkus Reviews* (starred review)

"A guilt-ridden exploration of the clash between cosmopolitanism and rootedness, between the wealthy who wander and the poor who belong."

—*London Review of Books*

"If you're looking for an escape from the ordinary, *The Glass Kingdom* fits the bill."

—*The Christian Science Monitor*

"Gripping...a horror-satire of globalised capital in which money might buy you idle time or the semblance of power, but it also makes you a target." —*i* (UK)

"Oozing menace...wonderfully atmospheric and deeply macabre." —*Daily Mail* (UK)

The Glass Kingdom

THE GLASS KINGDOM

A Novel

LAWRENCE OSBORNE

HOGARTH

London New York

2021 Hogarth Trade Paperback Edition

Published in the United States by Hogarth, an imprint of Random House, a division of Penguin Random House LLC, New York.

HOGARTH is a trademark of the Random House Group Limited, and the H colophon is a trademark of Penguin Random House LLC.

Originally published in hardcover in the United States by Hogarth, an imprint of Random House, a division of Penguin Random House LLC, in 2020.

Library of Congress Cataloging-in-Publication Data

Names: Osborne, Lawrence, 1958–
Title: The Glass Kingdom: a novel / Lawrence Osborne.
Description: First edition. | London; New York: Hogarth, [2020]
Identifiers: LCCN 2020002452 (print) | LCCN 2020002453 (ebook) |
ISBN 9781984824318 (paperback) | ISBN 9781984824325 (ebook)
Subjects: LCSH: Psychological fiction. | GSAFD: Mystery fiction.
Classification: LCC PR6065.S23 K56 2020 (print) | LCC PR6065.S23 (ebook)
DDC 823/.914—dc23
LC record available at https://lccn.loc.gov/2020002452
LC ebook record available at https://lccn.loc.gov/2020002453

Printed in the United States of America on acid-free paper

randomhousebooks.com

9 8 7 6 5 4 3 2 1

Book design by Fritz Metsch

Kwam lub mai mee nai loke
There are no secrets in the world

—THAI PROVERB

The Glass Kingdom

ONE

On the upper floors of the Kingdom, as the first winds of the monsoon picked up, the rains swept in just before first light. The cannons of a storm sounded in the distance. In Sarah's apartment, where she kept the tall sliding windows open, she felt the gusts even in her sleep, the geckos hunting on her walls scattering, moving toward the ceiling and its deeper shadow. She dreamed that she was swimming in an indoor pool back in New York, at the old YWCA near Fifty-Third Street, alone and chilled, until a siren wailed in the distance and the pool disintegrated. Her eyes opened, the equator returned, and the sweat on her back failed to dry. She panicked for a moment and felt for the edge of her mattress to situate herself. What day was it? Koel birds called out across the city, whooping laments, and at once she remembered the waste lots of jungle below her windows with their listing flame trees alongside the ruined tobacco warehouses that had stood there since the Japanese occupation. A faint hum came from the stormy Saen Saep Canal nearby, its black water churning with dawn commuter boats. She was alone among the flies, and the moon was still high above the dirty white skyscrapers of Bangkok.

The construction sites that surrounded the Kingdom had not yet stirred to life. But now storklike figures in gumboots picked their way through the pools, squatting under awnings and smoking their morning pipes while rain collected in the cement craters around them. They seemed to work night and day, dark Khmer men in *chams* who sometimes came out into the stifling air and looked across at the aristocrats in their vertical kingdom. There was nothing in their eyes, no recognition, just as she imagined there was nothing in hers. She drank a pot of French press coffee at her garden table and heated up half a defrosted croissant. The hour before six A.M. was the only time of the day when she felt safe, the hour she imagined when even the policemen here slept for a brief interlude, distracted from their own enormous indifference to crimes and punishments.

Gradually, the first low rays hit the hundreds of towers. In the gardens fifteen floors below, the maids had emerged with their carpet beaters. The villas lay all around her, with their high walls and fan palms, and in a sheltered pool within one of them an old woman lay on her back with a small dog on her stomach, a virtuoso balancing act. The sluggish fountains came back to life, breakfast was served in summerhouses, and men in black suits departed in limousines. She had chosen her spot carefully. It was a corner of upper-class affluence hidden within a forgotten ruin.

She had been in her new apartment for a few days and had purposely met no one, apart from the eccentric Thai grandee who was her landlady, Mrs. Lim. It was how Sarah wanted to keep it. Most of the seven rooms in her apartment were still unfurnished and did not yet feel familiar. In the sitting room her three suitcases still lay open on the floor, clothes spilling out of them. She was too listless to unpack them properly, and was still uncertain whether she might have to decamp as suddenly as she had arrived. Therefore she left the cotton blinds permanently down against both the sun and other tenants. Inside, there were parquet floors and a long kitchen like a ship's galley with a chessboard floor and an American fridge with steel doors. There was a feeling of estrangement and isolation about it, though the previous tenant had been a Thai designer who had painted all the walls ocher and dark green, which might have been colors of luck and fortunate karma for all she knew. The cabinets were made of old teak, a wood now illegal, and there was a stained-glass window in the kitchen. Now that she thought about it, she was fortunate that the class-conscious landlady had not asked to see a passport. She had impressed Mrs. Lim with her aura of good breeding, and it appeared that the august American name Talbot rang a little silver bell even here. In reality, she had chosen the name Sarah Talbot Jennings merely to be forgettable.

Each morning began with an idle swim in the shared pool. For this she went down in the elevator in her swimsuit and a bathrobe, wearing spa slippers and carrying a thermos of more freshly brewed coffee. But before that, and facing her bathroom mirror, she pulled her newly dyed white-blond hair up into a tight ponytail, and inserted the colored contacts that changed her eyes from green to blue. She had found them in a Thai supermarket, a line called Alcon FreshLook. It was not a complicated operation, and she was learning to do it a little faster every day. When she was done, she put on her bathing suit and calculated all the moves she would make that day. Mere repetitions calculated to pass the time, to make her appear ordinary, because an unplanned day is more difficult to organize than a planned one. Since she had no job, it was an unexpectedly difficult problem she had to solve anew every morning. She was in the city purely to make herself invisible for a while, to turn herself into a living ghost in one of the few places where a solitary white woman would be little noticed, sexually or otherwise. When eventually the day was completely mapped out in her head, she sortied out in her bathrobe with her thermos and stepped onto her private landing, where the elevator awaited.

The Kingdom consisted of four towers, each with twenty-one floors, each connected to the others by closed-off landings whose glass doors could be opened only with the security key each tenant possessed. They were thus entirely private. The first and second floors of the building, however, were public spaces. On the lower of these two floors was a replica of a French formal garden, with shrubberies dying in the heat and two-story villas around it, a grander form of lodging offered by the Kingdom. The patios were filled with Chinese lions and plaster Germanic milkmaids with wide-brimmed bonnets pinned onto walls of plastic ivy.

A flight of steps connected the decaying garden with a large pool on the floor above it, itself surrounded by trellises of untamed foliage and Chinese box trees with their aroma of crushed almonds, looking out over abandoned tobacco warehouses. This kind of building had once been fashionable. It was a long-outmoded idea of luxurious living built in the heady days of the early '90s, the Asian boom that had come and gone and come back again. Now-bankrupt tycoons had built European-style fantasies up and down the street, with turrets, portcullises, and topiary, but they had faded and peeled in a heat that didn't suit them. The little canals, the *klongs*, which once gave the illusion of lordly moats, had filled with toxins and monitor lizards.

In the elevator Sarah found herself reflected in a full-length mirror. She glanced up at the security camera in the corner, knowing that the men at reception were watching her at all times, and as she did the camera's eye seemed to blink. On the fourth floor, a middle-aged woman dressed in a housecoat and slippers got in with her Pomeranian, and in an instant the elevator was claustrophobic. The woman, unable to speak English, had one hand gripped around a leash studded with glass diamonds. The elevator doors at last opened to the first floor, where Burmese maids were already gathered with their masters' own little Pomeranians and toy poodles. There was a sound of carpets being beaten in the surrounding obscurity. Sarah walked past them, climbed the single flight of steps up to the pool, and slipped into the water.

The children had not yet arrived with their inflatable dolphins and flamingos, and the maids high up in the windows paused to stare down at the white girl resting in the shallows. How did she appear to them? As she looked back at them that morning, another early-morning swimmer made her way toward the pool. A woman of about Sarah's age, thirty more or less, in the black one-piece of a serious amateur lap racer. The newcomer didn't even notice Sarah at first and was under the trellis, throwing aside her towel, when she finally did so. She had not yet drawn her goggles down over her eyes when a brief smile came to her lips, and she wished Sarah a good morning. She was Thai or Eurasian; it was hard to tell, though there was little that was European about her.

Sarah returned the greeting. She then edged away to give herself a little more space. The woman positioned herself carefully, delicately self-conscious, and then sprang into a slick front crawl that propelled her to the far side of the pool in seconds. She did ten laps before she stopped at the shallow end, whereupon she raised her goggles and looked over at Sarah.

"Did I disturb you?"

She spoke in British-inflected English, the accent regionally indistinct. Instinctively, Sarah decided that she was wholly Thai after all. She had learned her English at a good school, that was all.

"Me? No. I'm not really here to swim. I just come to cool off and waste time."

The girl slapped the water with both hands. As if obeying her signal, the clouds parted above the surrounding towers, and a shaft of sunlight shot down into the gardens and hit a corner of the pool. It was a different heat from the air's humidity.

The girl went on, "Well, it's as good a reason as any to be in a pool. But I haven't seen you here before."

Sarah said that she had just moved into her apartment. It was on the fifteenth floor, in the southeast tower—Tower B.

"I'm on the floor below you—floor fourteen, in Tower A," the girl said. "I'm Mali, by the way. But my nickname is View."

"*View?*"

"Yes. It's a Thai thing—we give our children these odd little names. I know the English don't do that." The newcomer's voice was pitched in the English way, but its sensuality felt slightly rehearsed to Sarah's ear.

"I wouldn't know, I'm an American."

"You here alone?" she asked.

Sarah paused for a moment before answering. "Yes."

The girl cast a cool and unforgiving eye over the looming towers above them.

"It's quite a place to be alone."

With that, she pulled herself out of the water and walked over to the towel draped across the back of her lounger. Her back was scooped and subtly muscular, the arms toned without being overdeveloped. There was a dark blue *sak yant* Buddhist tattoo on her left shoulder, a fashionable accessory these days. It carried a calculated element of *sprezzatura*. She walked with a poise that had been fine-tuned over the years. Like a dancer, Sarah thought, who never quite made it. She had a touch of recklessness about her, her perfectly cut hair reaching down to the small of the back, where it curled gently upward in a wave produced by tongs. An expensive cut. She had a thermos as well, Sarah now noticed. Mali unscrewed the top of hers and drank.

"Would you like some?"

"No, thank you, I have one," Sarah said, pointing to her own on the lounger.

"This isn't coffee."

Sarah swung herself out of the pool as well and sat in the rapidly disappearing segment of sunlight.

"What is it?"

The girl came over and handed her the thermos. It was gin and tonic, and Sarah spat it out.

"It gets me going," the girl said, ignoring the spit, and leaned back on her elbows with a smile. "Maybe you don't need anything to get you going. Let me guess—you're a teacher or something? Don't take that the wrong way."

Sarah said that she was a writer, of sorts.

"Of sorts?"

"I'm just starting out."

"Do writers start out?"

"I guess they do." Sarah felt herself tense, wanting to change the subject. "And you? Not a teacher, I'm guessing."

"I'm an assistant to a financial manager. A British guy." Mali's tone was vague, as if she were making it up. "Do I look like one?"

"No, you very much don't."

And for a moment Sarah's hand instinctively went up to touch her hair. She was sure that the girl had given it a questioning look.

The pool could be seen easily from hundreds of windows above it. Yet the Kingdom itself rarely cast a shadow over the water. Like an Egyptian temple, it had been designed with the movements of the sun in mind. Profiting from this, Sarah and Mali lay on the loungers looking up not at the rows of windows, many dusty and half-opened, but at the thickening monsoon clouds above them. There was a drumroll of thunder from far off, a single muted flicker of lightning. The first drops of rain on the trellis and on the surface of the pool.

"I hate *naa fon*," Mali said at last. "The rainy season."

"It's my first one."

"Oh, you'll hate it too."

Mali stretched out on her lounger, and it seemed to Sarah that she was in no hurry whatsoever to get to work.

"Soon we'll be living on an island. The street outside floods almost immediately. Some of the residents have little dinghies that they use to get to the main road. Two hours of rain and we'll have a foot of canal water up to our knees. But if you don't have to go to an office every morning then you won't care."

"No, I'll be here."

Breezing along with a lie she had prepared in advance, Sarah said that she was here to take an extended leave from her life in New York while writing a few freelance lifestyle pieces for *Town & Country* to keep herself occupied. It was enough for her to get by.

Mali smiled at her. "Lucky girl. How long have you been in the city?"

Sarah was vague: a few days. She had been traveling around Asia for a while, probing and experimenting, keeping her savings close to her chest.

"You're one of those, then." Mali sighed, sinking back and sucking on the thermos.

"One of what?"

"Trust-fund babies. The building is full of them."

Mali's eyes lit up with mischief, which in turn made Sarah smile, despite herself. In some way—Sarah thought—it was obvious that she didn't need to work and it was amusing to think that she could so easily have been caught out.

"You got me there."

The conversation rolled on. Mali revealed that she wasn't married, nor did she have a boyfriend. She guessed Sarah was the same. Mali had had an inheritance but she had spent it all on disillusioning herself through her own pleasures, which was why she now had to work as a personal assistant. Her firm was

nearby in the Interchange Building—a well-known office building a few blocks away on Soi 23—and she walked there every
morning. Her clients were all high-society psychopaths. She
then said, changing the topic, that she had two other friends in
the Kingdom and that they sometimes played cards together after work. One was a chef, the other a hotel manager. Perhaps
Sarah would like to join them one night?

"How kind," Sarah said, pretending to think it over while
wanting nothing more than to distance herself from this early-
morning gin-drinking woman who struck her as a loose cannon.

She had been about to politely refuse, but something had
shifted in her mind: perhaps a few acquaintances in the building might be expedient after all. Even after only a few days—she
had to admit to herself—she was already lonely, and with that,
distinctly bored. The distractions of the city had not yet penetrated her solitude, if they ever would, and each evening, not
knowing quite what to do with herself, she would sit on her balcony and listen to the student dances lighting up the night in the
university campus on the far side of the street. She grew aware
of how completely they excluded her and how isolated she was
likely to remain.

"Come," Mali insisted. "You can play poker?"

"I haven't played in years. But you can refresh my memory."

"Done. We also drink a lot—so I hope you're not a teetotaler.
We can't have one of those in our midst."

"I drink once in a while. Not much."

"It's usually yadong and rum—a toxic but fun combination.
What else is there to do on Tuesday nights?"

Or on any other night, Sarah thought, recalling her monoto-
nous evenings.

"I can tell you're a little shy," Mali said. "But don't be. Come hang out with us—we'll bring you out of your shell, I promise."

Was the shell so obvious? Sarah felt her jaws tighten against each other, and yet she made the effort to be nonchalant, as she thought someone of Mali's class would be. Very subtly, however, she felt herself being tugged by the other woman into admitting things that she didn't necessarily feel. She admitted that she was a little "alienated" by the city, when in reality she was merely uncertain of it. It was a strange reaction. It was, she decided in that moment, Mali's openness, the softness of her voice, which rolled out even blunt phrases as if they were silk carpets—and the dancing playfulness behind it—that persuaded her. It was as if Sarah needed to surrender a secret opinion in the interest of true honesty, a secret that her own deficiencies had kept withheld, and was now being pried from her by a touch of charm. Some people have that gift—to get you talking more than you ought. Mali then got up without any haste, shot Sarah a smile, and said that she was late for work. "I'm in Unit Seventy-Four. You?"

"Eighty-Six."

"I'll drop a reminder under your door. Oh, and you have to bring a bottle of something. Wine doesn't count."

"Whiskey?"

"Whatever makes you crazy. Whatever makes us sane."

Mali made an exit similar to her entry, clogs swishing against the tiles, deliberately impervious to everything, her thermos of gin and tonic dangling from one wrist by a rubber band. There was something Old Hollywood about her, as if she had been studying those films for years. The way Bette Davis might enter and leave a room, using a cigarette as a wand, signifying authority. But then, Sarah had finally met one of her neighbors. It had left her with the distinct feeling that her defenses had been breached. A little distractedly, but amused, she went back to her apartment and ran a hot bath in order to think it over. Sarah hardly needed a new friend, but she did need a new social life, as she put it to herself. Mali was faintly preposterous but she had a charm, a slink to her. Or else she would prove a distraction while Sarah passed a few months waiting for her disappearance from New York to become less significant. Perhaps Mali and her friends could be just that: light entertainment while time passed, like the music and champagne between the acts of a tedious play.

From the bathroom the skyline could be seen, towers adorned with crests like samurai helmets, by neon letters and hanging gardens, a demented free-for-all created by generations of developers. It could be Bogotá, São Paulo, any city near the equator that she had not seen. Even though she had been looking at it every day since she had got here it was no less incomprehensible. It was a landscape created purely by money and autocracy. At night a host of flashing red lights would come on to warn tycoons in helicopters away from the rooftops, and men on distant balconies would fly drones that dipped between the towers along with the shrilling swallows. But now it was morning. The construction site had finally come to life, and the crane at its center moved through a humid onslaught of rain. The endless mania to build luxury condominiums that would remain mostly empty, their Chinese buyers perpetually absent. Even the recently completed towers were dark at night. As each tower went up, banners offering discounts to new buyers appeared within a month, but the sad little units remained unclaimed. Around this site lay muddy pits with excavator machines clawing away at the soil where rods and cement pillars were beginning to emerge from the chaos. The noise was distracting, and she had to wear earplugs all day long until nightfall, when the machines finally went silent.

She sometimes glimpsed a neighbor or two. An old lady watering her plants in Chinese pajamas or a man in a string vest doing his tai chi in front of the TV. Figures from an antediluvian age, from before the flood that had destroyed their world. At seven that evening a piano began playing in the unit above hers, a rendering of what sounded like an old Thai tune. This had been going on ever since she'd arrived at the Kingdom, but she was convinced that it was becoming louder and more frequent. It sounded like a child doing her exercises. She hoped that this time the mangled tune wouldn't go on for hours. After fifteen minutes it stopped, and she heard light footsteps padding around the balcony above hers.

In the half-light, white cattle egrets floated around the golden rain trees that surrounded the Kingdom and proliferated both in the gardens of the wealthy villas and in the undeveloped parcels of land around them. It was only beyond their plumage that the streets of the city could be seen, shining in the rain as the headlights of cars passed along them. The land around the Kingdom glittered with *saan jaoti*—the spirit houses where little figures of the dead sat on thrones next to miniature zebras and rotting apples. In these shrines sat the previous occupants of the land on which the modern buildings now stood. During Sarah's initial meeting with Mrs. Lim, the formidable landlady explained to her that her family had once owned all the land of the Kingdom, and that her grandparents had lived in a gracious mansion that had been torn down after their deaths during the tuberculosis epidemic of 1942. Her forebears sat there still on their tiny thrones while their souls voyaged onward through their unknowable reincarnations. Among the offerings that surrounded them were bottles of red Fanta, distinct from the green Fantas that were normally offered in most of the stores, and she, Mrs. Lim, had heard that while the green Fantas were meant to evoke the sacred color of the god Indra, what made the red ones significant in the context of the supernatural was that their color was similar to the blood of demons.

As for the Kingdom itself, its portcullis-style gate and the moat that surrounded it revealed an ancestry distantly rooted in the Disney castles of the 1940s. Its pointed blue roofs rose above a labyrinth of old lanes filled with tin shacks and old condo buildings that spilled down toward the Khlong Saen Saep, an artery that cut through the city with a trade in water taxis. But equally close to it were other winding alleys where, as she had noted, the rich hid their villas. These two worlds almost touched. The land around the Kingdom had tripled in value since it was built in the 1990s. And as more modern towers had risen around it, its themes now seemed out of place at the end of Soi Sawatdi, which ran along one edge of the Srinakharinwirot University campus, filled with towering fig trees. The portcullis gate was the only entrance to the darkened interior, and its guard post was staffed by thin men from the slums in pale cappuccino uniforms who wore their Buddhist talismans discreetly.

The alley outside housed student dormitories. When Sarah walked along it, the students were usually at the cafés in their pressed white shirts. The girls looked at her with an imperious cool; the boys had a half-smile for her. The Kingdom was known in the neighborhood for its foreign inhabitants and for the high-society families who had snapped up the grand apartments when they had first come on the market.

In May, with the start of the monsoon, the street flowed with water every afternoon, and the cicadas were roused by the electricity in the air as the lightning began, roaring in the high trees. Even from inside the Kingdom, in the long and dark parking lot that led from the portcullis to the reception lobby, she could hear them rasping in the tall grass and the dipterocarpus trees nearby. Instantly familiar with her from day one, the guards in their peaked caps saluted Sarah and asked her how she found the weather. *Too hot, mai?* But the lobby was always cool. It rose into a twenty-four-story atrium in the John Portman style and winds rushed through it, scattering dust and pieces of paper that the staff chased with useless brooms. Undoubtedly it would have been chic thirty years earlier. Loftily imposing, it sucked up all the surrounding noise and turned it into murmurs and echoes. Gold-painted Egyptian lotus cornices decorated its four corners while a dim glass roof with patterns of emerald peacocks covered its summit.

On the nights of violent weather, you could hear the glass being battered by the rain, the echoes spiraling downward back to the lobby. During the nights of *paa yuu*, the monsoon storms, even the old hands who had been there since the building was first built felt unease and a touch of fear. The staff, too, became subdued. In the lobby, there were long silk-upholstered sofas with traditional cushions, a glass table with an urn for flowers, and the four doors—locked to visitors—that led to the elevators of the four towers. When Sarah came in with her soaked umbrella, they bowed to her, but their eyes didn't connect with hers. Perhaps it was what the tenants wanted: a feeling of discretion and avoidance. Higher up, the corridors that connected the four towers were open to the air, and charged with an atmosphere of secrecy. They ran past the inner windows of all the apartments, and yet the tenants didn't seem to care about being observed. Most of them didn't even have blinds. Walking along her corridor on the fifteenth floor as she took out the trash, Sarah couldn't help looking through these portals into other people's lives. She peered into kitchens and bedrooms and front rooms filled with cheap Buddhas and candlelit shrines with flowerpots. There were hundreds of tenants in the Kingdom, and the building itself connected them in unexpected ways, but that didn't mean they knew one another by sight. Although Sarah didn't yet know it, this honeycomb was ruled by a rigid order that no one needed to articulate because it was so pervasive: it subdued every mind and made them bearable to others.

Even so, soon after she had moved in, she could no longer remember why she had chosen the Kingdom in the first place. She had gone to see five other apartments in the same area, but none of them had struck her as homely or quirky enough. They were too modern, too designed, and the rooms were too small. None had the old sense of comfortable family living, of large spaces and multiple rooms, but also of secrecy and abandon. The Kingdom came from a different age, and that was what she liked—the small signs of decay everywhere reassured her that here she would be removed from the world's radar. The entire city was filled with these tower blocks slowly sinking into their own twilight.

One of the freedoms of New York was that you were allowed to be evasive. A week earlier she had left the city without anyone noticing, as subtle in her absence as she had been in her presence. The small Air Force town in the California desert where she was born had never been explained to anyone; but then no one had ever asked about it. You didn't move to New York to talk about your past. You went there to shed it. Even during those years when she was working as a personal assistant to a famous novelist, nobody she knew ever suspected that she had grown up near a base north of El Centro. The Mexican border was somewhere that became material only in photographs published in *The New York Times*. The military personnel, the migrant workers, the mixed-race farmers of Imperial Valley with their lettuce businesses and their strawberry profits, the owners of the saltworks out in the desert: how could they be of interest?

Sarah Mullins was strikingly dark, somber in character, enigmatic enough to intrigue people even from afar. She had completed three years at San Diego State, where she majored in English, after which she was almost entirely adrift in a landscape that she had known since childhood. Her father had given her a dusty, secondhand Toyota, and she drove home to El Centro every weekend. She made no friends, reading around the clock until she found the heroes she craved.

One of them was April Laverty, a novelist of the 1970s whose books described the struggles of provincial women: women whose backgrounds very much resembled Sarah's. For an impoverished girl from a broken home living in a run-down room in Mission Hills like herself, Laverty's books became a refuge, a safe haven. From a distance she followed the eighty-five-year-old Manhattan writer's career in literary magazines and online gossip, learning minute details about her with a careful eye to meeting her one day, if circumstances ever permitted. It was a one-sided voyeurism she felt gave her an advantage. Armed with expertise in such a singular subject, Sarah was never entirely conscious as to why she had given herself such an obscure mission.

In her summers, meanwhile, she worked in El Centro bars and saved up for her graduation, after which she planned to leave for New York and look for work. Her move was meticulously planned, each step thought out over months so that real events would follow a logical sequence: a job, a small studio in Queens, the patient saving week by week until she could move on to the next step. Within a year she had rented a room in the Paris Building on West End Avenue, a short walk from where Laverty lived on Riverside Drive. She already knew that Laverty, still able to walk vigorously with a cane, liked to slog her way up West Ninety-Fifth Street to either the Broadway Diner or a place called La Nueva Victoria, where she liked to work alone with gallons of iced tea. In her purpled hair and button boots, she was a known entity to the staff, and therefore to Sarah Mullins. It was there that Sarah ran into April Laverty, in a meeting that was as carefully staged as an event in a Kabuki play.

It was never clear to Laverty's old friends whether the young writer, who may have been nothing of the sort, had chosen the Paris Building deliberately in order to be close to the woman she idolized from a distance; it could also have been a coincidence, which Laverty herself was prepared to overlook, or which she found charming precisely because it was so strange. They didn't know and they couldn't guess.

The friendship between the young woman and the elder luminary had caught them by surprise. There didn't at first seem to be any substance in the relationship. But soon the closeness between the two assumed, to their eyes, a familiar pattern: the famous but slightly insecure old writer anxious about her legacy and, hovering at the glittering edges of that fame, the young, fanatically devoted acolyte who promised much for the future of her name while flattering her in the present.

Sarah appeared so nervous and genuine that the doyenne—that fateful afternoon when Sarah had walked up to her table and announced herself as a fan—was taken aback and invited her to sit. She was fabulously rustic and charming. Sarah didn't know what oolong tea was. It turned out, as Laverty told her friends with relish, that the hayseed was the bookish daughter of a traveling preacher in South Dakota, something like Robert Mitchum in *The Night of the Hunter*, but that she had read practically everything, especially the complete works of April Laverty. The girl proceeded to give her a lecture about her own work. Seduction complete.

To Laverty, the girl seemed vaguely familiar. Had she seen her at one of her readings? It was possible. As she had told her friends, Sarah was not timid when it came to confessing her admiration for Laverty's novels. They began to meet regularly and exchange their feelings about books, and many other things. Laverty believed it with only a slight misgiving—her instincts were still sharply discerning. Sarah was undeniably raw. She used her fork as a stabbing weapon and had the air of someone who had spent too much time in the company of books rather than people; the learning worn heavily on her sleeve. But she was wonderfully direct. "She's so *frontal*," Laverty would say to others. "That even if she was lying you wouldn't doubt her." To the old woman she was like a girl from the '60s, wild at the core and unafraid to say what she thought.

This was how Laverty came to ask Sarah if she would like to

be her assistant. It would be a small wage, she explained grandly, but a large experience. For Laverty there was a sweet thrill of nostalgia in asking such a person to be close to her. The '60s, yes—the new world of Frank O'Hara that she had inhabited for a while and that was now compressed into a brittle idea whose time had come and gone. No one among her contemporaries, and certainly no one among the generations that had appeared since, had quite lived up to the raving poems of that era. But she had not forgotten the atmosphere—when, to borrow a phrase from a poet in her inner circle, she was still first-rate and the day came fat with an apple in its mouth. No, it was no use worrying about that time or its lost promises, but still the predictable disappointments of growing old could be offset now by the glow of a young and erudite savage. Enter Sarah Mullins.

She would walk every morning to Laverty's prewar apartment, taking the iron elevator up to the top floor with doughnuts and coffee, and often stay late into the night taking dictation, answering emails for Laverty, helping plan dinners with other writers, and after eight P.M. reading to her employer while the latter lay in bed with a shot of brandy and a hot water bottle. With time, Sarah came to run much of the household. She was known as Laverty's secretary and factotum, and was said to assist in the writing-down of the current work-in-progress. But her own life was kept away from prying eyes, conducted in total solitude in a single room ten feet by fifteen with a washbasin in one corner and a hot plate that she rarely used. She was careful never to let anyone see it or to enter any relationships. Her master plan was so delicate that it was easy to ruin.

When Laverty had to attend a function, Sarah went with her to hold her arm and keep her reassured. She helped her at the rare readings she gave and even accompanied her to a dinner party or two, sitting at her side and saying as little as possible. It was noticed as a curious relationship. Within a year, as Laverty's health and mental clarity declined, Sarah had assumed most of the running of her complex literary enterprise. She corresponded with libraries and foundations, with prize committees and sponsors, with publishers and private collectors of manuscripts.

Collectors were especially interested in paying for Laverty's letters and private documents, including manuscripts that the author was inclined to sell. There was a market for these in unexpected corners of the world. Millionaires and universities in Seoul, Paris, and Hong Kong wrote every month inquiring about the availability of this or that handwritten set of papers, and the former paid more. It had become a matter of prestige to collect the papers of famous writers as a bored Croesus might collect rare wines or paintings. Sarah had become the go-between in these transactions, the one who wrote to the collectors and asked their price. Sometimes they were not even aware that it was not Laverty writing to them. Since the writer insisted on handwritten notes herself so that everything could be verified later while remaining cheerfully personal, Sarah took to learning her handwriting and carrying on the correspondence by herself. She had access to everything in Laverty's desks so she could take existing letters and patiently, week after week, rehearse forming the words in exactly the same way as Laverty would have done herself. In the end, and to her own surprise, she found that she had a gift for it. Day by day, she slowly mastered the frail script of her employer while noticing that the old lady had begun to stop asking Sarah questions about her correspondence as her health deteriorated. So Sarah had continued for another year, mastering Laverty's hand almost completely. It was a life she had suspected she might fall into all along: scholarly in its way, reclusive, focused and unsensual. She had no friends and she was content not to have acquired them.

In her second winter on the job, Sarah received an offer from a private collector and property developer in Hong Kong by the name of William Chan. He was particularly interested in a cache of Laverty's letters from the time of the Vietnam War that were available for sale. A few had gone to the University of Washington, and Chan was interested in acquiring the remainder, provided that they were to and from celebrities. These might prove to be a worthy investment, especially if Laverty were to win a certain major international prize, as rumors on the literary grapevine had led him to believe. Chan was a man of bookish tastes, and owned two of the largest private libraries in Hong Kong, one of which was housed in his father's old mansion on the Peak. He revered Laverty, and as such was prepared to pay well above what others had paid up till then. When Sarah discussed it with Laverty, the writer intimated that Sarah should conduct the negotiation and, if she wanted, take the letters herself to Hong Kong for delivery, as Chan had requested. The billionaire made no offer to fly to New York. He expected Sarah to do the traveling.

Sarah agreed. Without expectation, the submissive provincial from Westmorland was suddenly in charge of the exchange of large sums of money in a city eight thousand miles away. When she departed for Hong Kong with twenty-eight genuine letters from between 1965 and 1970, when the young Laverty was in the prime of her political rages, she also carried forty letters that she had patiently forged herself, most of them only a few lines long.

She had learned to replicate each letter of the alphabet as idiosyncratically rendered by the writer and then to string them like beads along whole sentences, all on the same stationery that Laverty had stocked for decades. The fictitious correspondents included Angela Davis, Diana Vreeland, and Candice Bergen, all of whom had known Laverty in her heyday, and Sarah had calculated how much to ask for them when she met Chan in person. Everything would be in line with what she was asking for the genuine articles. With whom would he verify?

Sarah had left her apartment at the Paris Building as it was, with no sign of any intention not to return, nor did she steal anything directly from Laverty herself. She slipped away, and nothing more.

It was the first international flight she had ever taken. In Hong Kong, a place she knew nothing about, on a continent she had never visited, she checked into the Upper House on Pacific Place in Wan Chai, where Chan had arranged her accommodation. For three days she stayed inside the hotel at night, staring out at mountains as green as those of Bolivia in her imagination. Everything about it was unsettling. The thin and rakish towers, the basketball courts embedded into the hillsides, and the winding roads glistening with typhoon rain. She thought about Laverty, and even called her on her first night there, afflicted with misgivings about the sleight of hand she was about to execute. But Laverty herself merely asked where she was, clearly unaware that she was no longer in New York. The old grandee was sliding into dementia. When Sarah went to Chan's office on Pacific Place, she had been surprised to find a man much younger than she had imagined. He had offered her a proper drink, a "house cocktail," and offered her the seat opposite his desk.

"So you came all the way from New York to deliver the papers," he said, then asked what she thought of his view, the green tumbledown mountains behind Wan Chai. "It was very gracious of you to make such an effort."

The cash was prepared in a suitcase and handed to her without any further questions. There was concern about her handling such a large sum by herself, and an escort to her hotel was offered. She accepted it. She told them she would be depositing it herself at HSBC the following day. It was an odd arrangement, but Laverty was known to be on the eccentric side when it came to money matters. The writer kept an offshore account in Hong Kong for tax reasons, which she'd had for many years— plenty of writers quietly did the same. Martini socialists who discreetly paid less taxes than little Sarah Mullins. She would transfer the sums that Chan had paid for the real letters openly to this account and there would be nothing irregular about the deposit apart from its large size. After this it was only the money paid for the forgeries that Sarah would keep for herself: a figure close to $200,000.

She walked out into the Hong Kong heat and took a taxi with the escort back to the Upper House. She left the suitcase of money in the room during her stay, a five-star hotel not being a risk, and spent two days dining out on the Laverty dime. Transaction completed. It was a question of how long it would take for Chan and the estate to compare notes. There was no obvious reason for them to do so, though it was normal procedure to double-check. But with Laverty's decline the estate was in disorder and it was possible the sale would go overlooked for some time. How long—a week, two weeks? She didn't know. For two days, however, she decided to keep up appearances and show herself at the Café Gray Deluxe on the top floor of the hotel, perching herself for dinner at a table for one next to the windows that overlooked Victoria Harbour and the fairground lights of Tsim Sha Tsui. For the first time in her life she felt in control of her world. Anonymous, professionally dressed, with money at hand: a forger with a future price on her head.

The morning after she had deposited the fee to the estate she walked down Causeway Bay and found a hairdresser she had researched online. It was a small salon on Paterson Street opposite the Kam Lun Dispensary and a Fossil store, specializing in turning even the darkest manes of Chinese hair to the lightest shades of blond. The small white-brick place was lined with glamour photos of Caucasian heads sporting heads of platinum-blond hair. There she asked to go down to the palest blond they could possibly muster, and even had the hairdresser cut her some bangs, which framed her face and made it look narrower. She was sure, meanwhile, that no one there would remember her.

Back at the hotel she inspected her new look, adjusting the bangs slightly with a pair of scissors. That evening, as she passed the receptionists on the ground floor of the Upper House, whose real lobby was higher up, they did not appear to recognize her. The disguise was effectively simple. By the time she crossed passport control in whatever city she chose to run to, she would have assumed a different name. She decided she would pack the money from her forgeries in her checked luggage—a dangerous gamble, but less dangerous than having it on her person. It was the one risk she was forced to take.

She had chosen Bangkok for muddled and emotional reasons. The city conformed to her idea of a lawless and chaotic environment in which it would be remarkably easy to slip into anonymity. It would be like a slipstream that carried one along. There would be no surveillance of the serious kind, only the incompetent kind. The police would be porous and ambiguous and remarkably laissez-faire, and the large population of dubious whites would enable her to go unnoticed—more than anywhere else in the region, perhaps even the world. It seemed from a distance to be a perfect refuge.

When she arrived there, she took a room at a hotel called Two Three in the Asoke area and went on visits with real estate agents for a week. As soon as she saw the Kingdom's shabby exterior, she knew it was the right place for her to go to ground. It was set back from any major streets and possessed an air of decaying reserve. She had also liked the neighborhood itself. There were yoga studios and espresso bars, restaurants open late and Japanese cocktail joints, dry cleaners and health-food stores. The paraphernalia of the hipster age. It was convenient and secluded. It had an air of affable stability. It was here that she would wait and see what happened in New York, but her assumption was that the estate would send a private investigator to find her, and it was only surprising that he had so far failed to show up.

To herself, she considered the money well earned. She had already jumped the low hurdle of her own guilt, and in her own eyes it was no more of an immorality than telling Laverty that her father was a preacher. What did it matter? It was a war between herself and the moneyed classes, and in that war all ruses were legitimate, all feints justified.

TWO

The girl who opened the door of Unit 94 on Tuesday night was dressed in yoga pants and a chef's white jacket with her name monogrammed onto the chest pocket. *Ximena Hernandez.* Her narrow face, covered with freckles, reached its greatest intensity in the eyes, which were the color of damp moss. She was about thirty, Sarah would have said, thirty and full of life, as opposed to thirty and on the edge of the precipice.

"Ximena," the girl said, taking Sarah's hand for a moment and searching her out with her eyes. "You're Sarah?"

It was obvious to the American that Mali had already described her to Ximena, and that she had already formed opinions about her. Sarah was already nervous, therefore, and after kicking off her flip-flops, hesitated before entering Ximena's apartment. It was differently laid out from her own. The Thai owners all had wildly varying tastes and configured their units accordingly. Ximena led her into a large front room decorated with Tibetan and Thai Buddhist paintings. The gold *apsaras* of weekend markets and airport lounges. There were no sofas or chairs, just large cushions on the floor. The deck was lit up with tea lights, and because the apartment faced east the view was also different from Sarah's: overlooking the Avani Atrium Hotel that stood opposite, tumultuous freeways and yellow cranes, and the *gorfas* of a small tiled temple. The other two had not yet arrived there, but Sarah had her votive bottle of Yamazaki, which she set down on the coffee table.

"Make yourself comfortable," Ximena said, leading her outside to a table set with four chairs. "Mali and Nat will be along in a bit. Would you like to smoke a joint?"

There was a bowl of guacamole and chips and shot glasses with a bottle of the yadong that Mali had mentioned. Sarah was about to tell Ximena that she didn't smoke weed, but at the last minute changed her mind and accepted the joint. They had a first glass of yadong. It was a strange choice for four women. People talked of it as a raw man's drink.

"You're in Unit Eighty-Six, aren't you?" Ximena said. "Are you renting from the Lims?" The Lims were the overall owners of the Kingdom and over the years the other buyers had purchased from them.

"I met the mother when I moved in," Sarah said. "She owns my unit. How about yours?"

"I rent from an American. She lives in Los Angeles. How do you like it here so far?"

"It's quiet."

"Yeah, in its way."

"I'm not familiar with it yet, to be honest—it feels a little unreal."

"It's a bit of a haunted castle, isn't it?"

Sarah smiled. Yes, it was.

She said, "Your place is beautiful. How long have you been here?"

"Two years. My restaurant is nearby. Maybe you know it? It's called Eiffel—it's a French place on Soi Thirty-One. It's supposed to be one of the best in the city, which means it's actually one of the worst. I live here because I can walk there every shift. I hate the place, but it's a job."

"Eiffel?"

"You know it?"

Sarah shook her head.

"So you're one of those people who doesn't go out much?" Ximena teased.

She didn't quite mean it, and yet it had already occurred to her that there *was* something etiolated and sun-starved about this odd American. She looked like she had been indoors not for days but for years, perhaps even decades.

Sarah felt the tension coming.

"It's not that. I'm just unfamiliar—"

"There's nothing to be familiar with. It's a city like all cities."

"Is it?"

"Not really."

Ximena sucked on the joint and her head tilted back. With a courtly and slightly elaborate gesture she handed the joint to Sarah. The American was trying so hard to maintain her façade—a façade of what?—that Ximena felt obligated to at least crack it. Amused, she watched Sarah grapple with the joint and then begin to enjoy it. At least she was more familiar with joints than she had let on. She wanted them to relax together into a state that might be conducive to gossip. Ximena told her that Mali had described their meeting in the pool.

"She said you were very attractive and very shy. She was right about both. What did you make of Mali? A firecracker, no?"

Sarah remembered the thermos of gin at the pool.

"You could say that."

"I've known her for a few months. But I can't say I know her all that well yet. We've played poker a few times. I think she's been having these poker evenings for a while. But I gather that her boyfriend doesn't approve. From what I understand, he's a bit older than her. Sometimes he calls up when we're playing and shouts at her."

Sarah was sure Mali had said she was single; she didn't seem like the kind of girl who liked to be tied down.

"She likes unwinding with us," Ximena went on, "so now we do it regularly. I don't know why she doesn't do it at her place. Nat says it must be because it's a mess. It's just the floor below yours . . ."

Sarah handed back the joint and lifted the glass of yadong.

"I probably shouldn't be drinking this stuff," she said quietly. "Does it have snakes in it?"

"We wish."

They touched glasses, shot the burning rice liquor back.

"Jesus Christ." Sarah snorted.

"Yeah, it's brutal. It was Mali's idea to begin with—her father makes the stuff up-country. Or his slaves do."

"Slaves?"

"They might as well be slaves. She's from a wealthy family. I wish I was. Then I could quit and go study sashimi in Tokyo."

Ximena slammed the glass back down on the table and let out a whoop. She took a long drag on the joint.

"How about you? Mali said you're a writer. That's a fine thing to be. But how do you make any money?"

It was a brusque question that momentarily rattled Sarah, but she brushed it off without being impolite. Instead she answered it according to her prepared narrative.

"I don't. My parents died a while back and I inherited everything. I'm an only child." Sarah saw Ximena's eyebrows furrow, and indeed the other woman had sensed a tall tale, an effortlessly smooth exaggeration. "I guess you think that makes me sort of spoiled?"

Instead of repelling Ximena, the false note in Sarah's voice intrigued her. Sometimes a person's unconscious falsity was more interesting than their conscious virtues. The chef could tell that she wasn't born rich; that was something you could smell on a person, something almost hormonal on the skin. Ximena spent all her time around the moneyed classes and she knew the difference.

"Don't be so hard on yourself," she said after a pause. "None of it is your fault. And we're all spoiled in one way or another. Isn't everyone guilty of privilege now? It's all I ever hear. We're all supposed to be wearing our hair shirts round the clock."

"I guess." Sarah sighed. "My parents didn't feel guilty about anything. They just pretended to." Sarah threw back her shoulders and sucked in a long drag, the sudden relaxation a little dramatic.

"What did your father do?" Ximena said.

"He was in pharma. He owned his own company. We lived in Vancouver for a long time and then London. Have you ever been to Vancouver? It's a desirable city; we should have stayed there but we didn't. My father was impulsive."

"Were you close?"

"Not especially . . ." Sarah trailed off before gathering herself. "I suppose you're wondering what happened to them. They died in a traffic accident."

"Oh," said Ximena, surprised by Sarah's bluntness.

"In Mexico," Sarah continued. "My father wasn't driving. They were in a chauffeured car."

"How long ago?"

"I was ten. So you see—I'm pretty used to it."

Ximena didn't press the matter further. They slipped into a gentle *gan-chaa* high, striated swallows wheeling around the darkening towers of the Kingdom and synchronizing with their mood. The traffic was stationary in the small *soi* far below, as it always was at this hour, and the smell of warm rain was already in the air. Between the towering trees along the alleys they could see girls in crisp white shirts walking with stately unhurry, umbrellas already flexed. Ximena felt a calm contentment, the repose of the early evening magnified by the ganja's hit. She found herself enjoying the idea that this slightly preposterous American girl, with her cultivated persona, was in reality a fluid and practiced liar. Yet the lie had gone down well, Sarah herself was certain, and her confidence rose. She began to talk more brazenly, inhabiting the persona that was taking shape, evolving sentence by sentence. She said how carelessly she had chosen Bangkok as a place to live for a while—though this much was true—and how the pressures of life in New York had brought her to a boiling point that now needed to be released. She had been working as a fact-checker for a magazine for years, though she was reluctant to say which one, and had been conducting a volatile and unhappy relationship with a man working in finance. She called him Peter and invented his biography on the spur of the moment, inspired by the ganja. She gave him houses, suits from Cifonelli in Paris, enormous wealth. They were all things that Ximena could not cross-check. But, she went on, all had collapsed, her heart had been bruised, and she had decided to take a sabbatical from her own life.

"That's a bit tragic," Ximena had to say.

"No, it's not tragic exactly. It's just an experiment. Did you never have the urge to pack up and leave, walk out the door?"

"Every midnight."

"So you know what I mean."

Ximena wondered. When Sarah asked Ximena what had brought her to Bangkok, she was reticent to answer at first because she couldn't quite collect her reasons. She was from a middle-class family in Santiago, her father was a famous architect, her mother was a journalist. She had grown up there and in Geneva, where she had gone to school, and then university in Madrid. She had lived all over the world working in kitchens, one of the hordes by her own admission inspired by Anthony Bourdain, and she had come to Bangkok purely because of the job opening at Eiffel. It was easier to get into a good kitchen here than in a Western capital, and once you did so the life was easier. Rent was lower, the scene more fluid. The local food was more interesting to her than the French and the Italian, which she already knew; moreover there were many Westerners doing what she was doing; they had a small community. Her employer had found her the apartment in the Kingdom—apparently the Lims were regular guests at Eiffel—and she had a deal on the rent that was favorable to a bohemian existence centered on enjoying the twilight of youth. She had wanted to break out of the Western restaurant scene anyway. Too many male egos, too many hierarchies, too much bureaucracy. But maybe it was also resignation combined with hedonistic indolence that made her stay. As a known chef, she was often invited to the city's elegant tables and it kept her distracted. The week before, for example, she had been invited to a chef's dinner hosted by a famous chef from Moscow, where psilocybin mushrooms were served in truffles at the end of the meal. She had ended the night in someone's room, with no idea whose or how she had gotten there. This, she said, was the only way her solitude was ever shattered.

"So, Vladimir Muhin was shuffling three kinds of caviar in little dishes like a card trick and none of us could follow them with our eyes. I got to eat trout caviar while high on psilocybin."

She had a lot of time to herself. She had taken to walking around the city alone at night looking for novel things to eat. It was what all real chefs did. She herself liked to wander around the streets of Lat Phrao, the dormitory of the city, and especially the old market on Chok Chai 4. It was a long, gently curving street of little trees and white tenements, and at its base there spread a covered market filled with shrines. Off Chok Chai 4 lay a darker side street called Sangkhom Songkhro, where the street-lamps looked as if they had been abandoned to their fate before the Vietnam War. From here an even smaller alley, Soi Samakhom 1, led to a garden restaurant at a corner where time itself had gone off duty. It was a sukiyaki-style place with a pool and fairy lights, and in the garden old men sat with their papers and lemonade, prolonging, so she thought, the last moment of the '60s, when they had been young. Here Ximena also sat smoking her *gan-chaa* and thinking over her various menus until, in fits of inspiration derived from the sukiyaki, she cracked them.

Ximena enjoyed those older neighborhoods. Their fading innocence, their streets that shouldn't exist. The past that had already been condemned for the simple crime of being the past. It was what was still beautiful about Bangkok—the avenues like disordered reliquary shops, the decay that held a dark human nectar inside it. The neighborhoods where the illuminations after dark didn't stun the eyes and where the people moving through them looked as if they had belonged there for centuries. They hadn't, but they had been there long enough to give off the illusion. Soon they would all be bulldozed and the city would be turned into the new Singapore. But there were a few years of life left; life without order for its own sake.

When she was bored at the Kingdom, in similar spirit, she would take her motorbike and ride around the back streets nearby. The capillaries superior to the arteries, as she thought of them. Behind the Kingdom, Soi 31 wound its way through small outdoor malls and condo towers until it passed grander villas from another time and then melted into the mesh of alleys behind Thong Lor. It became Soi 39 and then 49, but without any logic, and the junctions became claustrophobic and chaotic. But at night it was returned to the quietness of a past age. Pressing on, she followed the road until it swung to the left, past little clubs and restaurants she had never heard of, and then ran for a kilometer toward its cul-de-sac end: an airy mosque and its courtyard, a Muslim village with the songbirds of the deep south hung in bamboo cages and the guesthouses garish with rod lights where some of her staff might well have lived. So close to the noise and glamour of Thong Lor and yet a thousand miles away in spirit. There she would sit on the steps of the closed mosque eating pickles from a plastic bag. The birds on their verandas sang even louder in the early hours.

So, she told Sarah, she might stay here for a while. Her parents were still in Chile, and she never thought about going back there. There was an entire class of people now who could not return to their points of origin. She supposed aloud that she was the only one of them who wasn't a semi-millionaire, but even if she had been, she would have stayed in Bangkok. Her patron kept raising her salary. "I think he's in love with me."

"Is he French?"

"French and fat. It's how I like them."

"What's his name?"

"Gregoire, if you can believe it."

The two women laughed.

"And what about Nat?"

"Natalie?" Ximena handed back the joint that she had hoarded for a while. "What about her? She's a hotel manager, but her money is independent. She's married to a perfect jackass, though. He's a lawyer. Have you ever met one who wasn't a jackass?"

Sarah took a slow drag and began to feel it overwhelming her completely.

"I'm sure they never have sex," Ximena went on. "I see him in the elevator but he never says hello to me."

"Which floor are they on?"

"The twenty-first, in one of the penthouses. They have some serious money. I'd much rather play poker on *her* balcony but the husband makes it into such a drama."

"So she never brings him?"

"To our girls' night? No. I think she's relieved to get away from him for a little late-night fun."

"All the same," Sarah thought aloud, "maybe not having sex is a good basis for a marriage."

At that moment the doorbell rang.

It was Mali bearing a bottle of sake and dressed in a black skirt two inches above the knee hemmed with matching brocade. She looked as if she had just returned from dancing on a table at a club. Her face was flushed with the corridor's heat, and when she saw Sarah she let out a long and welcoming cry. Though the rain outside had not yet started, her hair sparkled with intact water drops, and her skin was misted as if sprayed, like the surfaces of supermarket peaches, Ximena thought, not yet knowing how to decode the physical details of the Thai girl from the fourteenth floor. She had given the newcomer the impression that she knew Mali quite well, but that was not at all the case. To her, Mali was as novel as she surely was to Sarah. The Thai girl's slow, wary eyes were still surprising, her affected English still curious.

"So, you two have been chatting," Mali said as she came in her bare feet out onto the deck. "Are you friends yet? How are you getting on?"

"Like a house on fire, by arson," Ximena said, "and almost burned to the ground."

Sarah was by now pleasantly high. She looked up to see an indolent moon hanging just out of reach of the city's glare, moving in and out of rolling clouds as they dispersed slowly around a starless zenith, their edges flickering with lightning. In the immense rain trees swarms of bats swooped around the towers as if disoriented.

Inside, they rolled another joint and Mali sat with her feet curled underneath her while they drank another round of the yadong from cut-glass tumblers. She told them about her trip to the gold markets in Chinatown to buy T rings. It was a popular form of investing here. Sarah thought she was just as swaggering—if that was the word—as she had been the first time they met. Like something rolling downhill at high speed but with no end in sight. They ate some lasagna that Ximena had made, and waited for Natalie to show up before breaking out the cards.

It was ten o'clock before she did. And then in strode a tall and shaky-looking British woman of about forty carrying a black leather tote bag, thin and fleshless, with a large nose that made her ponderous and melancholy-looking. *A stork*, Sarah thought at once, even as she regretted the cruelty of the thought.

Natalie saw the newcomer at once and made a beeline for her, one hand extended, a little cold: "I'm Natalie."

"Sarah."

She was in hotel-manager gear: black tights and shoes, a dark green silk skirt with a matching jacket. She was drenched with rain and sweat, and after the handshake she went to the bathroom to towel herself dry. When she came back, she appeared brighter and less tense. They dealt the cards, lit up a third joint, and began to play a round of poker. Natalie, having taken her place, unfurled her long legs under the table and her foot brushed against Sarah's calf. Their eyes met. The bottle of yadong was soon half empty and they were on their fourth, then fifth joint. The ganja seemed to be inexhaustible. Ximena's supplier, it turned out, was Mali, who had family connections in the north and could get Green Demon, the best leaf from the hills north of Chiang Rai.

"So you're new here," Nat said to Sarah as they were making a toast. "I think I saw you on the street the other day."

Her eyes contained a strange hint of vendetta, Sarah thought to herself.

"No one knows anything about Sarah," Mali said with a smile. "She's the most mysterious tenant in the Kingdom. She's renting directly from the Lims."

"Who was in your place before?" Nat asked. She turned to Ximena. "It was that Japanese couple, no?"

"I can't remember."

"I'm sure I remember them. I wonder if the Lims had an exorcism after they left."

"Why?" Sarah asked. "What was wrong with them?"

"Nothing at all," Ximena said. "The Lims are just famous for having exorcisms. They're superstitious. Or so I've been told. They're the richest landowners in the city, or one of the richest. The great-grandfather was a Chinese tax collector back in the day. They made their money in pharmaceuticals later, and then tobacco. Now they're a decaying dynasty. The children are all wastrels and known to the nightclubs." Natalie threw back her head and laughed.

They went on playing their cards. Out of the darkness came a chorus of tree frogs, their lowing like tiny cows that got on Sarah's nerves. She was thinking faster than she talked, listening carefully to the others and trying to interpret them. Were they just bored foreigners with Mali as an extra?

It was unclear what they thought of her. She controlled her

rising tension and tried to enjoy herself for a change and forget about Laverty, the letters, and the nagging guilt that inevitably came with contemplating them. She let her legs stretch themselves. The lightning on the horizon had become more neurotic, one part of the sky silently flaring for a moment, and a second later a different part. The flashes lit up random buildings in the distance, towers that she hadn't noticed before. And then haggard trees, forgotten walls, temple spires that didn't seem to exist in daylight, dogs in the streets shuddering and moving away. The great shaggy mulberry trees around the Australian School shivered in the same way.

It was at these moments, which came upon her with stealth, that she realized how unknown this spiritual landscape was to her, how little she spoke its languages or understood its symbols. All she knew was its weather. She told herself that a city like Bangkok was full of interlopers, con men, professional strangers and wanderers. But unlike most of them she had enough money to buy herself a perch that would probably keep her safe for a while. Like them, however, she was still an escapee. And like them she had slipped out of a class system that had bedeviled her all her life, shadowing her, keeping her in line.

As Sarah lost game after game, Nat amused them all with a story about a private detective who had come to her hotel to ask for her cooperation in an adultery case. It was a businessman who booked his mistress into the Marriott on Tuesday afternoons.

He'd been taking her to the same room for years. A man of about fifty. Same room, same time. But now a detective wanted her to help him spy on the man. As a private operator, he was in a position to bribe her. She declined, then threatened to call the police. But he managed to talk her out of it. In the end, she had agreed to take him up to the room herself.

"Did you hear them doing it?" Mali asked without looking up.

"Yes. It was pretty wild. But the investigator seemed to enjoy it. I wasn't sure what he wanted. Did he mean for me to open the door for him?"

"Did you?"

Nat shrugged and denied it. Of course she hadn't. But the detective had offered $100 cash in hand.

Now Mali looked up, her cards dropping to the table. "Did you take it?"

"You want the truth?"

"If you lie I'll find out!"

"All right, I took it."

They laughed. Ximena's eyes went sly.

"You took it for the hell of it?"

"Absolutely. I thought, all right, you filthy little man, if you're offering it I'll take it and I'll go to the spa after work. That's just for not reporting you to the police."

"The police wouldn't do anything anyway," Mali said, rolling her eyes.

"I know. But I went to the spa anyway."

Nat crossed her legs with satisfaction. Had she told her husband? Ximena asked.

"Roland would make me give it back at once. He's so Dutch about those things."

"Is he Dutch?"

"His father's Dutch. That's enough."

"Then don't tell him," Mali said.

"I didn't. Who knows when the staff will report to me that *he's* doing the same thing?"

"Here's to bribes, then." Mali raised her shot glass.

Sarah joined the toast, and her eye caught Mali's. Something conspiratorial immediately transpired between them and Sarah felt a sudden liking for her. Though she was obviously born to the country, the girl was not wholly of one race or the other. She was bilingual, and slipped between what seemed to be two backgrounds. Probably her father was English, Sarah reasoned, or some such. Although Sarah didn't know it, there were many like her in the city, the children of mixed marriages. In Thai, they were called *luk khrueng*. She was the most refined of them. And she was now telling them some Kingdom gossip that Ximena and Nat already knew, or had gotten a whiff of from either the maids or the staff. The retelling was for the benefit of Sarah.

"Last month, the Lim father died in the penthouse upstairs. Did anyone tell you? He was ninety-one, but it wasn't a normal heart attack. He shot himself in the head after an argument with his daughter. You might have seen her in the elevator, their place is in your tower. Her name's Narisa but they call her Cherry; she's known in the society magazines. Her father had apparently asked her to stop dating foreigners—or so people are saying. But probably they were arguing about money and property. The argument got out of hand and he went up to his bedroom and shot himself with a small pistol. It was going to be a scandal, but they managed to control the damage. The staff say the body was removed in the middle of the night via the service elevator. A car was waiting to take the body to the morgue and the staff were sworn to silence about it. That's how it works here: if no one saw it, it didn't happen. The family waited two days and then made a bland announcement to the press about him passing away. The press took the bait and there was no mention in the media about a suicide. They probably paid off a fair number of people too. They then went ahead with a normal temple cremation. I suppose you must have met his wife, Wendy, when you signed the contract for the apartment."

Yes, Sarah remembered her. A quietly elegant woman of about sixty-five decked out in malachite and gold and curious about her new tenant. They had stood for a while together on the deck and watched the workers playing *tagraew* below.

"I'm very proud of that sport," the older woman had said wistfully. "I'd like to see it played at the Olympics."

She had gone on to lecture Sarah about the benefits of alternative medicine and the hospitals in the neighborhood. She recommended Samitivej for fatigue.

"Are you alone in life?" she had asked Sarah with a faint smile.

Sarah felt herself being measured, intuitively diagnosed. It could be done with a mere glance. For Chinese families, being alone in life was an inconceivable condition. When Sarah said that she had no significant other, Mrs. Lim sighed a little and asked her if she was going to be all right living alone in such a large building. Sarah had reassured her that all she needed was a room, a balcony, and a pool—the necessary antidotes to get over her New York–induced exhaustion.

"Are you really exhausted?" Mrs. Lim had asked.

Mrs. Lim's generation had little sympathy for such fragilities. They thought that Sarah's generation was weak, when it came down to it. *Mere moderns.* But one doesn't say so to a tenant.

"She's the real power behind the family," Mali went on. "They say Bangkok is run by Chinese women, and it's true. Don't ever cross them or you might as well leave and never come back."

Though one inevitably gets to that point anyway, Sarah thought.

"So they cremated the old man?" Ximena asked. "And the monks went along with it?"

"Yes—they then had an exorcism for the spirit of the suicide. But they had it at night so fewer people would notice. The staff were terrified and still are. They say that Mr. Lim's spirit is now bound to return to the building despite the exorcism. They can't be talked out of it."

"I've heard it a thousand times before," Nat said.

Mali went on: "To me it wouldn't matter if his spirit did return. What harm would it do? The idea doesn't scare me."

"Nor me," Ximena said.

"What do you think, Sarah?" Mali asked.

Sarah felt their eyes upon her, not with curiosity but with sarcasm.

"I don't know. I've never thought of things like that before. I don't believe in ghosts anyway."

"You don't?"

"I'm not against the thought, I just don't believe in it."

Eventually Ximena brought out a lemon cake she had made at work and cut it up on a paper plate. It was professionally, deliciously tart. They ate it with the Yamazaki that Sarah had brought.

"We have to make a toast," Mali said. "Or if we're too drunk and stoned, we can just shout *Chaiyo*."

So they shouted, "*Chaiyo!*"—the Thai toast—and Sarah

steadied herself discreetly on the arm of her chair and forced her mind to stay clear. From below she caught the violent sawing of the cicadas, roused again by the approach of rain. Along Asoke, just visible between the gleaming towers, the torrent of cars had resumed like an immense funeral cortege. Ximena was describing her day at her pompous and stuffy high-society restaurant, which felt to her like a tomb repurposed for the living.

"I don't know how those people can eat there. I know Mrs. Lim stops by, and last week I saw her daughter as well with her *farang* toy-boys. The girl did coke in the bathroom one night. There were even a few lines left on the toilet cistern. I was kind of glad—it made the place a bit more alive. I thought of putting some in the soufflés that night. I wonder if anyone would have passed out."

"They both eat there?" Nat said.

"Yeah, they come in separately, though. It's the nearest haute cuisine to the Kingdom and they can walk home. Well, cuisine anyway."

"I doubt they walk anywhere."

"Who does Mrs. Lim eat with?"

"Before, with Mr. Lim. Now she comes in with her son. And the former prime minister sometimes."

"She gets around."

"She orders lobster and steak Rossini. Yes, we actually have steak Rossini. It's like the 1950s never happened. It's like the *twentieth century* never happened."

"I'd love to eat that now," Nat sighed. "Steak Rossini. And then more of this delicious cake."

"Where is your restaurant?" Sarah said to Ximena. "I'll stop by one evening."

"Here's my card."

Ximena slid it across the table to her and Sarah saw the word EIFFEL with an image of the tower and the smaller words *fine dining*.

"I'll make you an orange salad with psilocybin. How's that?"

"I can't wait."

Then, deftly switching the subject, Mali asked Sarah if she had found a maid yet. She hadn't? A maid was a critical question in the Kingdom. Remaining maidless was almost a statement of intended anarchy. They all shared the same one. If Sarah wanted, this Thai woman named Goi could do her apartment as well. The maid herself would be happy to, since she lived in the Kingdom with Nat and Roland, and the more clients she had, the better for her. She was a freelancer not merely confined to her duties with the couple in the penthouse. Nat had encouraged her to take on extra work to supplement her income. Goi was reliable and spoke English well enough. Fifteen dollars for four hours was the going rate. Nat could call her right then and arrange it.

"I don't know," Sarah said. "I'm not sure I need a maid."

Although she couldn't quite say it openly, it was a terrible idea from her perspective. But she felt that to refuse it would seem churlish or even suspicious. She was cornered for a moment and had to make a split-second decision. Mali went on, "Everyone here employs Goi. She's like family. Drop the guilt."

"It's not that—"

But it was something worse. She thought of her money stored in the suitcase in the spare room and knew if there was a maid coming on a weekly basis she would have to hide it with great care. She thought it over. It would be undeniably inconvenient, but in the end it would make her appear normal to the other residents. Perhaps it was better to blend in and not make herself even subtly suspicious by raising an objection to a generous offer that she couldn't justify on the spot.

"All right," she said, disguising her uncertainty. "I suppose I could try it."

Mali called Goi and it took all of a minute to set up. She was most free on Tuesdays and Wednesdays. So Sarah could choose either day. Sarah took the Wednesday, and Mali said, "She's a discreet old woman and you'll love her. She'll make you meals, too, if you pay her extra."

They rolled yet another joint of the Green Demon as Sarah asked Mali about her family. Her father was indeed English, as Sarah had guessed. He ran a high-end travel agency for the well-heeled called Elite Excursions. "Bespoke travel" to "unknown Asia," which meant travel, in other words, to an Asia that was entirely and depressingly known. Her mother belonged to a prominent family who carried the ancient name of Na Ayud-haya. Mali had inherited her apartment at the Kingdom from her maternal uncle but otherwise she rarely saw any of them unless it was an official family occasion that was strictly obligatory. She alone among them now seemed—to Sarah—completely unaffected by the Green Demon. The immunity raised an interesting question. Her body's on speed anyway, Sarah thought. She's high and flying, the only real one among us.

Mali had gone to school in England, some miserable place in Northumberland. Many high-society Thai children were packed off to such schools in Britain, France, and Switzerland. But her job was not as clear-cut as she had intimated earlier. She went to the office every day, but the head of the firm was a friend of her mother's and so he cut her a lot of slack. She went out for long lunches with her friends, she took afternoons off, and came in late when she had a hangover. She was spoiled, she admitted, but she wasn't going to give up a good thing. Being a personal assistant was an unserious sinecure by its very definition, and she was using it to bide her time while she figured out what to do with her life.

"I can't exactly criticize you," Sarah said. "I'm the last person to judge—"

"You don't have to be ashamed of having money. No one here is ashamed of it—that's a Western affectation. And not earning it gets you respect here. You can just roll with it."

"Believe me," Nat said, "if my husband wasn't rich—"

The whiskey was by now exhausted and, exasperated, they finally switched to a bottle of hardcore Chinese Kaoliang.

"I can't drink anymore," Sarah murmured, and glanced at her watch. She didn't want to leave and yet she had to. It was past midnight and she wanted to keep to her routine. It was an important matter to her, the keeping of a schedule that did not vary from day to day by more than an hour. A routine that served no purpose except keeping her sane, which made it all the more necessary. Without it, she didn't trust herself not to go off the rails.

"Just one sip," Mali said, and filled her glass a quarter inch. "Just a small one."

"All right, just one." Sarah relented.

"*Chaiyo.*"

The wind picked up and the chimes on the balcony began to sing. They looked up. Dust and grit in the air, the rain trees seeth-

ing in the dark. *Soi* dogs scattered around the craters of the building site.

"It's going to rain in an hour," Mali said. "I can feel it."

Ximena also looked at her watch, but the time meant nothing
to her. She didn't have to get up until eleven the next day. Her
shopping lists and menus for the day were already worked out
and all she had to do was show up.

"Next week," Mali said, "maybe we'll do this at a restaurant.
What do you say?"

"Fine with me," Nat agreed.

Ximena reached out and brushed the back of her hand
against Sarah's bare shoulder.

"Did you know there's a chef living right opposite you on
your floor? His name is Choi. He's fat and cooks naked in front
of his window. I dare you to go have a look."

"Oh God."

"He'll invite you in and make you something Chinese, you
better watch out!"

Sarah laughed and covered her eyes.

"Right, I'm going to bed," she said, standing up and smooth-
ing down her slacks. "I'm toast."

Sarah said her goodbyes, took the elevator one floor down to
the fifteenth, and walked out onto the open-air bridge that connected the towers.

She stopped for a moment halfway across it, holding herself
firm by the parapet while her inner balance returned and the
heat stabbed at her face. A few of the windows were still lit.
Looking up, she could see the great atrium roof near where the
Lims had their penthouse. The stained glass with its images of
flowers and amorous peafowls was dimmed by accumulations

of dust. Below, frozen in its own unease, the table in the lobby could be seen with its urn of marigolds and one of the guards fast asleep in a rattan chair. On the other side she calculated which windows must belong to Mali, the unit in the opposite tower one floor down on the fourteenth. That it was Unit 74 was a matter of simple deduction. She stood opposite those three windows and saw that they were screened by white Venetian blinds with no glimmer of light behind them. So Mali did live alone. Or perhaps there was a boyfriend already asleep in bed. Sarah walked on until she was at her landing, lit by a sour bulb clogged with dead mosquitoes, and the apartment opposite hers on the fifteenth floor came into view. Its lobby area was dark yellow and filled with Thai antiques set with pieces of glass that shone in the half-light. Through the windows she saw a kitchen with a night lamp standing on a steel counter, but no one there. There stood an elaborate shrine to the recently deceased King Bhumibol in the middle of an empty room with incense sticks and offerings, decades' worth of images from press cuttings and affectionate prayers. So that was where the other chef lived, with his beloved monarch in a room of his own. Yet another unknown inhabitant of the Kingdom enclosed inside his own shabby life and determined to live it the way he wanted.

THREE

During the flooded mornings Mali and Sarah sat under the swimming-pool trellis, which was reinforced by a plastic sheet, and drank coffee and gin and tonic and forgot about their swims. Around the tobacco warehouses that surrounded them, glistening pools formed and the idle workers sat under tarpaulins playing cards. Sometimes Mali brought croissants and fig jam and it would be nine o'clock before they went their separate ways. Mali was tactful and curious in a measured way, and Sarah noticed the quiet change in register; she talked about her family and her work for the most part, and Sarah listened, grateful not to be asked any questions. As they lay there gossiping about the building, a lopsided, heavily tanned Englishman would sometimes get into the pool for his daily swim, regardless of the rain, and Mali told her that he was named Tom Gifford, and had made millions designing software for the Post Office, now retired to the Land of Smiles. He had married a mentally unstable Thai soap opera star, and the wall nearby covered with plastic German shepherdesses was theirs. He swam his lengths entirely underwater, with a great gasp at either end. So these were the neighbors. Sarah glanced up at the hundreds of windows and felt herself grow cold. It was like a lunatic asylum when you looked at it from the pool. A vertical realm made of glass, every inhabitant partially visible to his or her neighbors, squandered and guttering lives piled on top of one another in anonymity.

At nine Sarah walked to a yoga class at the top of their street, in a small office tower where the escalators never worked, and there she worked ineptly on her positions until the end of the morning. On the ground floor there was a café and chocolate shop called Duc de Praslin, which made its own Belgian chocolate. She sat there by a large window watching crowds pouring through the heat with their umbrellas and the glassless blue buses crashing through waterlogged potholes until by midday she felt lost. She wondered what Mali was doing in her office— the Interchange was only a short walk away. She could have called her but chose not to. She didn't want to be pushy or seem desperate for company. But in the end, and within a few days, it was Mali who called Sarah as she sat at the Duc de Praslin with her hot chocolate and asked her if she wanted to go for lunch.

Mali asked to meet inside the Emporium Mall on Sukhumvit Road. "Let's splash out on an expensive tea. There's a place I have in mind that I want to take you." And Sarah accepted immediately, since she had nothing else to do and, in truth, it was a call she had been waiting for. She wanted to stay out of the gloomy building for a few more hours.

She strolled there with her umbrella, her yoga mat rolled and slung over her shoulder, through the broken sidewalks choked with tourists, ducking under the power cables. An unfamiliar excitement quickened her steps. She had been alone in her isolated anguish, waiting for some consequence from her fraud to catch up with her, small torments that racked her by the hour, and now the doors to the real world were opening once more to include her. It was normal life, but for a moment she shrank from it. *Lunch.* In the end, the thrill of this simple invitation propelled her down the street. Yet as she was passing an optician's shop, she had a moment of irrational fear walking by its window display. A foreign man standing there looking at Ray-Bans glanced up at her and smiled as she came into his field of vision. He was dressed in a summer suit and seemed to have been waiting for her—or so she thought for a second. But a moment later she recovered her senses and scolded herself. She had already formed the shadowy idea that she was being followed, but it was weakness to succumb to it so easily.

The mall lay on both sides of the Phrom Phong Skytrain station, which loomed over the street. The left side was the EmQuartier, its smooth, white walls soaring into a jumbled and adolescent skyline, filled with hanging gardens set among waterfalls. On the artificial rocks sat two equally artificial peacocks, and this was the view from the terrace of the TWG teahouse, where Mali had suggested they meet.

As soon as she arrived, she saw Mali sitting alone with a gold pot of tea as if she had already been there for some time. The room was filled with hundreds of gold-colored tin canisters of rare tea, among them colored ones with the names of blends. *Weekend in Saint Tropez. Weekend in Shanghai.* A place for rich Japanese girls and men discussing money.

"Do you like it?" Mali asked when Sarah reached the table.

She had to say that she did, and it was true that she felt calmed by the starched napkin laid in her lap by a waiter.

"What's in the pot?" she asked.

Mali's tea was dark, orange at the edges. "It's Winter Palace Tea. Shall I get you some too?"

"Why not."

"My father loves this place," Mali went on. "He says it serves the only decent Earl Grey in the world. But he hasn't been here in years. Anyway, I wanted to say something to you . . ."

"What?"

"It's nice to see you outside of that building. Somewhere bright and *alive*. Or younger anyway. By the way, don't you love their white shirts with the matching white ties?" She motioned to the waiters as they bustled past. "And they play *Phantom of the Opera* all day. What could be better? It's so kitsch it makes me want to break into song."

They talked as they nibbled their way through an afternoon tea. Outside, the ornamental waterfalls tumbled from terrace to terrace in a mist of spray and heat while the neons of an H&M store sign above them shone through the drizzle. It was like twilight in a rain-forest glade. Even on the cool side of the glass they could feel the sticky humidity pressing against it. The people outside struggled through this heat with mortified expressions, disoriented in their delectable maze, and Sarah felt a tightening of the thorax just as she would have inside a jungle beginning to darken. Yet it was midday. The fountains sparkled in slanted sunlight. There was an elegant horror to it, a mindless prettiness. She lost focus, then regained it as Mali talked, tuning in at the moment when she said that she wanted to know more about Sarah. She had the sense that Sarah was very alone in the world. As for men, it was good, she said offhandedly, to do without them for a while. It was good to do without them for a *long* while. But even if she had agreed with this sentiment, Sarah had no feelings about it. She had to keep up an appearance of caring, of making her tone convincing.

"I keep feeling," Sarah said, though not knowing how intimate to be with someone she didn't know very well, "that the last year was my final chance in some way to find a partner. Maybe one always feels like that. No one walked through the door, as it happens. But even if someone had, I would still be here. I don't feel the lack yet. No one is right for you all the way. It's just a question of how much wrong and how much right."

"Me? I could accept twenty/eighty, wrong/right."

"You're pragmatic; I'm not. We Americans are indoctrinated with this idea of soulmates."

"Maybe, but I was never married either. I've had the families of boyfriends say that I'm unworthy of consideration. Fuck them."

Sarah then asked Mali if she was seeing anybody. Given her own divulgences, it didn't seem a bold question.

"Nobody serious," came the reply. "I met a Japanese guy at a bar a short while ago. He's older, works for a Japanese company of some kind."

"A bank?"

Mali shrugged. "No, but finance of some kind. I know what you're thinking—a finance guy. But I promise you, he's not one of them. He's nice. He just bought me a puppy!"

"He did?"

"He bought it for me last week. It's a teacup poodle, like a toy. We named it Whiskey. Not every man buys you a Whiskey."

She laughed a little too loud, and the aloof ladyboy waiters cocked their heads, penciled eyebrows bestirred.

"I don't think I'm going to be alone forever," Sarah said. "That's not my thing. It's more a matter of circumstance."

"No. It's not really my thing either. All the same, I wake up sometimes and I forget the dog is there in the apartment with me. I see her and get a shock. A living thing in my space. It's the first living thing I've ever had to look after."

"What's the man's name?"

Mali looked away for a moment and her mouth tensed.

"It doesn't matter. He won't stick around. All the Thai girls want to be with Japanese men, so they have their pick of us. He even has a driver. He picks me up when we go to dinner. The Japanese here are a different world. They have their own rules."

Looking at Mali's cobalt-blue Pucci dress, Sarah wondered if the nameless Japanese man with his own rules also bought dresses for her. It wasn't unlikely. Then she realized why Mali was taking her afternoons off. It was probably when they had their trysts.

"You're lucky. You have a man who doesn't want to control you and who leaves you alone at night."

But Mali twisted in her seat, as if rattled.

"Oh, I didn't say anything about that. He's *very* controlling. My mother used to say it was a sign of a man caring. It isn't, but it is. Anyway, no one controls me."

Across two gold pots of Winter Palace, they were assessing each other more carefully. To Mali, the American girl was unhealthy-looking. She was already scheming up ways to improve her. Sarah didn't seem to know what she wanted in life; she was a dilettante looking for a way to turn her fortune to something worthy without having found the key to do so. She was badly dressed because she had not thought about such things seriously before, but then wealthy Americans were often like this. Their puritanism lived on inside them unconsciously. They were ashamed of their money, but they didn't give all of it away to charity. They admired the idea of poverty, but they loathed being poor. They romanticized the poor, but they loathed being around them. In the end, it wasn't a complicated paradox.

But at the same time a parallel idea had already occurred to Mali: that Sarah had not left her country simply because she was exhausted or disappointed by unnamed events. She was making herself up day by day and had perhaps left for a more specific reason. And maybe she wasn't a rich kid either. That would explain her gaucheness. A pathless wanderer who had lost one social class and not yet found another.

Sarah, for her part, was dazzled by the other girl's confidence. Mali looked after herself in a way Sarah hadn't seen before—not maniacally or obviously, but thoroughly and calmly. They were about the same age, but when she looked down at her own hands, she noticed for the first time that they looked strangely shopworn. But before she could feel annoyed about it Mali said, "What are you doing now? I've decided I'm taking the afternoon off. Let me just call my office and clear it with them. I wanted to go buy some books—why don't you come with me?"

The Kinokuniya bookstore lay on the floor above the teahouse, lit like a large private library, and they spent an hour there browsing through the shelves, going their separate ways for a while. Alone in the aisles of books Sarah thought for a moment of leaving quietly by herself and making an excuse later on. She felt trapped by Mali and by the bookstore, and by the afternoon itself, and she wondered if it had been a good idea to come out so offhandedly. But before she could decide, Mali was behind her, tapping her shoulder and whispering that it was time to move on. And so, just as aimlessly, they wandered through the mall's labyrinth until Mali expressed her considered opinion that Sarah really should buy some new clothes.

The American was looking a little "tired" in that department. Tired and unkempt. Surprised, and a little stung, Sarah tried to laugh off the observation, but then almost as quickly she admitted to herself that it was about right. Tired and unkempt was precisely what she had become. She had neglected her appearance over the last few months. But come to that, she had never much cared about clothes; there had never been any need for them and shabbiness had felt comfortable to her, a disguise in some way. It made people trust her when she wanted them to trust her. It was a manipulation. Now, however, when she saw herself in the plate-glass windows she realized that next to Mali she looked like a beg-packer, as poor whites begging to finance their travels were known in the city. There was an objective side to her appearance that she hadn't considered before. A person could resemble a piece of furniture that had been worn down by neglect and made to look tarnished and humiliated. That was her. It insulted her pride and she slid almost instantly into a countervailing mood of lavish determination. *Spend*, she thought, reminding herself that her bag was filled with Chan's money. They were in front of a Vilebrequin store. Mali dragged her inside to buy a flowery summer shirt or two and eventually she bought three, along with some pale-pink beach shorts. Satisfied with these, they moved to another store, where she bought a short black evening dress. These were the things one needed. Sarah wondered why this had not occurred to her before: clothes as eye-deflecting armor.

Mali said that she would take Sarah to a spa called Divana, which her mother used, just to disengage with the city at their own pace. It was one of those rituals that women here took seriously, in her opinion, and with which Sarah ought to become acquainted. They went back outside into the street, where the sun had created a ten-minute illusion of an English summer afternoon. There stood the mototaxi stand that the shoppers used. The pressure-cooked air made her skin flinch. But the elements in Sarah's chemistry now quickly realigned and her whole personality—she felt—began to list deliciously to one side, a loss of gravity that induced new feelings, which at first simply corresponded to what she thought was happiness. And as she mounted the bike behind her driver a monumental idea came to her: that this was her first taste of that condition.

Moving into the back alleys, they wove through vegetating traffic until they were moving at high speed along a walled *soi* where Japanese restaurants were turning on their outdoor lanterns for dusk. The towers turned bronze as the sun slipped away behind them and cast enormous shadows across the gardens. The city switching from its brutal daylight chaos to its sweeter nocturnal order. The acacias brimmed with little excited birds collectively capable of creating a continuous roar, and above the whitewashed walls fan palms and bougainvillea suddenly stood out with a dark and formidable glamour. A whiff of wet jasmine came from nowhere, and in those same high and outlandish towers the lights came on, suggesting something optimistic and homely to the viewer in the street below.

The Divana was an old Thai house with a garden made up of fig trees draped with creepers, giving the illusion of a rain forest mutilated by the city. The past surviving, as it sometimes did here, as untouchable trees inhabited by spirits. One such spirit was the female Nang Ta-khian, whose presence was marked by ribbons wound around the boles of takian trees, which was said to decide the outcomes of lottery tickets and pregnancies. After their massages the two women lingered in the garden and talked. Unsurprisingly, Mali said as they lay on sofas with cups of lemongrass tea and bowls of sliced banana drizzled with honey, Nang Ta-khian also draws in passing men with melancholy songs and devours them. It was predictable. She was the spirit inside takian trees where they lie near water.

The weather had changed. Rain now cascaded down through those takians and the staff in traditional silk *sampot* wandered along wooden pathways with umbrellas, skirting the pools that must have been inviting to the spirit. Mali lay on her side, picking at her rounds of banana with a dainty wooden pick. Her eyes didn't leave Sarah for a moment, their focus quietly inescapable. The puzzle of Sarah, she was thinking, was beginning to fall into place, just as Sarah was thinking that the puzzle of Mali was becoming more intractable.

"It's good to come here," she was saying as Sarah laid herself out full-length on the divan and the odd raindrop splashed into their saucers. There was no other sound but the outbursts of tree frogs. "No one uses their phones—it's a miracle. Out there it's like the whole population of the world is working round the clock at a giant hotel switchboard. Don't you think?"

"I've almost stopped using mine."

"I'm the same. I don't want to be a slave at the switchboard. I'm glad we have that in common. I come here after work almost every day and read. We all need a place that no one we know ever goes to. This is mine. I'd stay longer now but I have to go—I have an appointment, I'm afraid."

"That's all right. I'm going to bed early tonight."

"You'll sleep in a different way. In the meantime, I was also going to ask you a favor. I know it's short notice, but I was wondering if you'd take the puppy for me for a couple of nights. My beau might be taking me away for the weekend. If you don't want to, it's fine. I can ask someone else. Ximena and Nat can't do it because of their work hours. I thought of you because you're at home all day. What do you think?"

Sarah was too surprised by the request to answer at first.

"The puppy?"

"She's really no trouble. All she does is roll around and sleep. You might even enjoy her. She's extra adorable."

"I don't know, I—"

"You'll fall in love with her, I promise. But like I said, if you can't do it I understand."

"No, it's not that. I just have to think." As with the maid, Sarah hesitated.

"Just two nights?"

"Tomorrow and Saturday. We'll be back on Sunday evening."

"Where are you going?"

"The beach somewhere."

"And you'll prepare all the dog food?"

"She doesn't eat gourmet, Sarah honey. It's just biscuits and a protein drink."

Sarah found herself giving in. It was possible that it might be comforting to entertain a puppy for the weekend. But better than that, it was a favor that Mali would not forget. Caught between two opposing instincts—for safety and anonymity on the one hand and for social warmth on the other—she faltered before accepting. But since the decision had to be instantaneous, and since she needed to appear natural in order to maintain her cover, she forced herself to accept the request with a veneer of lightheartedness. She said that she would do it. In response, Mali rolled over onto her back and looked up into the tops of the trees and their spiderweb canopy. She said quietly that in the first place she was grateful and secondly that she would stay here while Sarah went home because her beau was picking her up at the Divana. As for the following day, she would deliver the puppy at Sarah's preferred time. Her tone implied a sly awareness that Sarah's schedule was not exactly overwhelmed during those drawn-out monsoon days, but it was accurate.

"I think you'll enjoy it. When I get back I'll take you around the city a bit, if you like?"

"I would."

"You can wear that dress we bought. You needn't worry—no one looks at white women here. You're invisible."

Mali caught the quick aversion of the American's eyes.

You're not used to being looked at anyway, Mali's look seemed to say. *Here Thais call you a* yaksha *behind your back, a plodding, clumsy white.* Instead, she touched Sarah's shoulder lightly and said, "Till tomorrow, then." It was the evening's kiss farewell.

After she had put her shoes back on, Sarah was escorted down to the gate by one of the staff. The *soi* outside was in darkness and long pools had formed in the uneven surface. She walked to the top, where it met Sukhumvit, and stood for a moment trying to hail a taxi. There a black limo sat waiting, its engine idling. The driver was in uniform, with a peaked cap, and he was reading a newspaper laid against the wheel. After a minute she gave up and walked down toward Soi 23 and the thumping noise of its nightlife. She came to a statue of Shiva housed in a pillared gazebo, and there she turned and looked back at the limo, which she sensed was waiting for Mali. There were few other people it could have been there for.

She walked home in the rain along Soi 23, where the bars were filling with foreign men, the small massage shops with the girls grabbing at passing arms in an imitation of five-second courtships. Outside a place called Crazy House on the main *soi*, girls in kimonos and clogs sat at high barstools eating noodles, and they noticed the foreign woman's half-smile as Sarah passed them. As she turned to them for a moment they cried out "*Kwam yin dii!*": a phrase that meant congratulations but included the word for smile.

But even if she had understood the phrase, she would not have known what she was being congratulated for. For being an alien alone in the street? For being burnished by a spa scrub? And for a vivid moment she remembered the man in the optician's shop earlier in the day who had smiled at her through the window. He had been on her mind all day. Perhaps his smile proved that he was not a spy or an investigator after all. She wouldn't see the man who was really following her anyway. Even now, as she turned right as Soi 23 split into two separate streets, she would not sense a professional on her trail. The street became quieter while its gutters gushed with turbulent black water. A few Japanese men smoking intently among themselves as they paced past her, their faces drenched but absorbed in prospects of sexual release.

Soon she could hear birds in the trees of a small plaza next to a palatial club called the Pegasus, insolent with white columns, sculpted trees, and a vast portrait of the new king. The birds seemed to have gathered in the foliage around it, as if mating by night. She stopped for a second time to take in the topiary and the grand staircase, behind which gold and vulgarity loomed under fairy chandeliers. The birds calmed her. Men were getting out of limousines and buttoning their jackets as they made for the doors, which opened for them with diligent bows, and she realized that for the first time in her life she was no longer visible to any of them, just as Mali had predicted. She realized that she had chosen her city well, because it was a place that had instantly rendered her sexless, and being sexless she would go unnoticed. Being unnoticed, she would blossom.

But as she took the long, straight street that led back to Sri-nakharinwirot University her mood turned once again and she kept stopping to cast glances behind herself. The overhead lamps threw down intervals of light and in the patches of gloom a lone dog could be seen following her at a distance.

At the campus the metal barrier had been closed for the night and a guard in a folding chair sat fast asleep surrounded by cats. She had to scatter them and wake him up, paying him 100 baht to let her through into the shortcut that led to the Kingdom. As he escorted her with his flashlight, complaining about the disturbance and his pay, she noticed students lying as if asleep among the trees and all over the open grass playing field. They seemed to have fallen where they played as if by a collective trance. They came to the second metal barrier, where there was a guard post and a man in a fanciful blue uniform. Behind her the dog, which had followed through the first barrier, now stopped and moved sideways into the shadows along the walls. The men had dropped the habitual friendliness with which they had greeted her before, but it was clear that they were preoccupied by other matters. The students strangely asleep in the open, tensions that, as an outsider, did not concern her. She paid them another 100 baht.

The dog could not follow her into the back alley that led to Soi Sawatdi, where the canal lay alongside the Kingdom, and so she returned to the portcullis alone. There, too, the guards were peacefully asleep and they didn't sense her presence as she cast a last look back at the sunken-looking alley where she felt someone had been following her. The canal flowed between a grass bank and a rail that extended alongside the street, and it was there, above the poisoned water with its scum of cigarette butts and plastic bottles, that she felt her tormentor waited, maliciously discreet, holding himself back so that for a few seconds she was forced to question the quietness of her own nerves.

FOUR

That night she slept badly. From out in the dark, at around
three in the morning, there was what sounded like gunshot,
which echoed with an ominous arrogance and then, a moment later, seemed impossible. A gunshot to kill a dog, or a man
playing with a gun in his garden: but it could not be either. She
lay awake sweating, her pulse rising to the backs of her eyes. No
siren came to investigate the shot; there was only the wind howling around her half-decayed windows. Unable to go back to sleep,
she turned on the lights and went to the second bedroom, where
she kept the suitcase filled with cash. She took it out of the closet,
laid it flat, and opened it, a ritual of self-reassurance she had been
meaning to perform for a while now.

The $200,000 in bricks was wrapped in $10,000 units, each
neatly enveloped in opaque white plastic that she had chosen
herself. She had learned online that drug dealers moved cash
around in this way, a method seemingly more risky to themselves than any other. But one had to remember that risks come

with conveniences. Now, day by day, she unobtrusively exchanged the dollars five hundred at a time at a tourist exchange in Nana. The Thai baht she kept in a separate room. She had considered buying a safe, but caution drove all her calculations: would it be noticed? She now slept with the money as if it were her principal companion in life. She closed up the suitcase, replaced it in the closet, and went back to the main room, turning off all the lights. Now she possessed all the small reflexes of a fugitive. She lay on her futon and smoked to still her heart. What kept her up was the way the building appeared to be awake on its own terms. There were little stirrings coming from the building's interior. Footfalls, the whir of the service elevator, moths beating against the landing lights as they died voluntarily. Together they formed a vitality greater than themselves. She thought about who could be using the elevator so late at night and why the students were lying like cadavers among the trees.

The following afternoon Mali came to the door with her apricot-colored toy poodle. She set her down on the floor and the toy dog, stirred into mechanical motion, waddled inside Sarah's apartment and disappeared into one of the back rooms. Mali handed over a bag of prepared meals with written instructions and gave Sarah a lingering hug. She was dressed up for a weekend at the Four Seasons on Koh Samui, as she explained, and from there she would not call in.

"Ryo liked it there," Mali had said, and it was then, out of the blue, that the man's name fell between them like a small charm that has slipped carelessly out of a wallet.

"Just make sure Whiskey doesn't escape into the corridors; she'll try and find her way home. She might be a bit temperamental at first, but she'll calm down."

There was a tiny yap from inside the apartment, and Sarah turned. The dog had jumped up onto her sofa and rolled onto her side. The ease and trust had come without any effort on her part. Mali ventured to kiss her cheek, as if Sarah had earned it, and just as she had appeared out of nowhere a few moments before, she disappeared back into the building. Sarah went to the sofa, fondled the dog's velvet ears, and let the animal tumble over her lap while she came out of a momentary confusion. The dog appeared to be starved of affection rather than spoiled, as she had expected, and Sarah herself felt a little used. It was a bit much to dump your pet on someone you hardly knew. There was something undisclosed in Mali's behavior. Perhaps it was Ryo, the now-named beau, who had told her to do the dumping. Either way, she was slightly offended. To brush off the feeling she leashed the dog and took her down in the elevator to the first-floor public gardens, where gazebos and swings stood exposed to the wind but protected from the rain.

As it always was, the floor was taken up by the building's maids and their masters' dogs. Sarah sat a little apart from them on one of the swings, rocking herself to cool her temper, and kept an eye on rushes of small dogs around the gardens, which formed little whirlwinds on their own. She was watching a middle-aged but sprightly Japanese gentleman in an immaculate black suit practice his golf swings with real balls, hurling them loudly against one of the cement walls opposite the warehouses. His hips were slightly off-kilter as he swung his club, as if his right leg was not quite functional. After a while she got up and wandered around the gardens to stretch her legs. Across from the Kingdom lay the empty shells of the Lim family's tobacco warehouses, each entangled by the roots of rain trees. On the

Kingdom's side, the walls by the elevators were covered with posters edged in black that announced, at last, the death of the elder Mr. Lim. Beside them were others that announced a meeting of the shareholders in the ground-floor conference room to discuss the "succession" of the eldest Lim son to the throne of the Lim Enterprises Company. The tenants were also welcome to attend if they wished. As she stood there reading, she sensed one of the middle-aged groundsmen who did odd jobs around the Kingdom watching her.

He was sitting on one of the white iron benches with his legs crossed and smoking a rolled cigarette. The staff called him Pop, and the receptionist had once explained to her that it came from the Thai word *pop-hen*, meaning "to find," because when something went missing in the complex labyrinth of the Kingdom he was the one who could always retrieve it. But it was a nickname mainly for the foreigners because they knew that it also meant Daddy. Pop, meanwhile, was the oldest of the staff members. She saw him almost every day in the entrance parking lot washing expensive cars to make some extra money. He always wore a sleeveless singlet and heavy gold rings, and *sak yant* tattoos covered parts of his shoulders. His amulets were complex and could not be deciphered—neither she nor he could know that they were faddish ornaments derived from votive tablets placed in temples to revive the Dharma if Buddhism were ever to fade from the world. Images of the god Jatukham cast in candy-colored resins. When she turned, he said, "Hello Khun Sarah!" and raised the hand in which his cigarette was lodged. She smiled back, but she never knew what to say to him, nor how he had come to know her name in the first place. He must have made a point of learning every tenant's name. So she turned back to the warehouses just as the puppy came scampering back to her and circled around her legs. Then, seeing Pop, the puppy rushed over to him and did the same.

He picked her up and let her lick his glass rings, and then took her to the wall where Sarah was standing. He spoke some English and there was rarely a moment when he wasn't smiling, when a quiet softness wasn't in his voice, although the smiling was merely a permanent gesture, without any feeling behind it. He walked with a slight limp, and yet his whole body was packed with muscle and power.

"This is not your dog," he said, handing Whiskey to her.

"It belongs to Khun Mali. You know, from the fourteenth floor. She went to the beach for the weekend."

"You're looking after, *na?*"

The dog was now whining because he had given her back. The two of them were obviously acquainted.

"Khun Mali asked me," she said. "She couldn't take the dog with her."

"You *jai dee mak, na?*"

"I don't understand."

"You are a kind heart."

"No, no, I'm just doing her a favor."

He leaned in a little and she could smell the car polish on his hands. "Khun Mali, you are sure?"

Taken aback, Sarah reacted too sharply: "What do you mean?"

"I think her dog is a little sick."

"She is?"

"Sure she is."

Sarah looked down at the perfectly healthy puppy and remembered how earlier in the day she had thought that she was unloved.

"*Mai suk-ka paap dii,*" Pop went on.

Sarah shook her head.

"I'm afraid I don't—"

"I think she has a cold. A sniff."

He knelt down and took the animal's head in both hands and rocked it back and forth as he murmured to it. It looked as if he had done this many times before, that the two of them knew each other by scent.

So, Sarah thought, Mali comes down here every day with her dog. Either she or the Japanese man.

Perhaps it was Ryo, then, Mali's boyfriend, whom Pop associated with the dog.

But Pop himself was the great observer of the Kingdom, and it was he who came there every day to work on the building's plants and who lingered there till late at night, employed for a few extra baht to turn off the swimming pool lights at ten P.M. and patrol the endless series of glass doors. It was he who made sure they were all closed and that no outsiders remained within the premises. It was true that he had seen the little dog many times before in the gardens, running about in the flower beds.

Yet it was not Khun Mali who walked her without a leash, but an older Thai woman with whom he sometimes shared a cigarette when they were out of sight of the surveillance cameras. And she, in turn, had never mentioned anyone by the name of Mali. It was just that Mali had once showed up with the dog and he had been taken by her memorable beauty. Her name, therefore, had been easy to remember. It was, as he knew, like this with many comings and goings inside the Kingdom. The tenants ignored him because of his low class but he saw exactly how they lived; his head was filled with thousands of immaterial notes about their behaviors. Years before, a dog had been abandoned by its owners when they fled the Kingdom to evade their creditors. It wandered the public areas all night unnoticed by anyone but Pop, until he let it out into the street, where it disappeared into the gangs of feral dogs who patrolled the neighborhood. Perhaps the others had killed and eaten it. It was the law of life. Perhaps it had found a new owner who had taken pity on it.

He stood up and looked into the bloodless *farang* eyes with their intimations of quiet hysteria and their contrary self-control. This one was a double-edged sword.

"You should feed her more. More pineapple—"

And he reached into his pocket, taking out a plastic packet of pineapple slices. Opening it, he gave the foreigner his best smile. Mr. Pop, always prepared and at your service.

Later that evening, feeling the edge of boredom upon her neck, Sarah sent Ximena a message asking if she could bring the dog to Eiffel and sit with her in the garden. The reply: Of course, the old society dames do it all the time. Putting the poodle inside a gym bag, Sarah set off on foot. The restaurant lay a ten-minute walk away next to a colonial-style hotel called the Eugenia, where Bollywood parties were often held on the weekend. One was now in full swing as she passed the hotel, and the Indian stars were outside being photographed by paparazzi among the company Bentleys. There were pools of champagne overflow around the tires. As she went through the front court of the Eiffel, she saw a glass-walled outdoor kitchen with four Thai men in toques turning spits. At the door she gave her name, and the puppy, cowering in its bag, was inspected before Sarah was whisked through to the garden. On the way through the dining room, she understood at once why Ximena felt such scorn for her place of employment. Piped Puccini and cases of Louis XIII brandy with shelves of snifters; lithographs of the Place des Vosges, and a gilt-frame screen that showed a never-ending series of pastiche scenes of European high taste: the amphitheater of Arles, glassblowers of Murano, La Scala opera house. But the garden was better. There were old mango trees and the tables were simple. She was placed in a corner and told that she could put the puppy next to her. A few minutes later Ximena came out.

"So *that's* Mali's dog. She bought it at Chatuchak Market, didn't she?"

Sarah thought back to what Mali had said, but she couldn't recall anything about a market.

"She told me her boyfriend bought it for her."

"She did?"

And there was a moment's stand-off: two different tales, then. Ximena searched her face for a clue, then relented. Sarah already understood that Mali told different things to different people for reasons she couldn't guess at. Regardless, Ximena sat with her for a while since the restaurant was still relatively empty. Sarah went on, as if it needed to be explained, "He's Japanese. They went to Koh Samui for the weekend."

"She's never mentioned that to me. You two must be getting close."

Sarah was secretly flattered that she might be an insider. How had that happened? Mali must have taken a liking to her beyond what she felt for the others. It was a small triumph of sorts. She had always been more comfortable around older people—as she was with April Laverty—but not so much with those her own age. It was something new, something that gave her pride.

"Why do you say that?"

"She gave you her dog to look after," Ximena said dryly. "I'd say that was pretty close."

"I'm not sure—I can't tell what's in and what's out with her."

But Sarah had a contrary intuition. Mali wasn't entirely inside her society at all; she was, like Sarah, voluntarily to one side of it, an actor who has quietly stepped offstage between acts.

"I'm not even going to guess. My philosophy in this country is to just go with the flow."

"How about a drink?" Sarah said then, changing the subject. "I thought maybe I'd have something sparkling. Not water."

"You can have anything you want."

A glass of champagne was brought over, and Sarah sat there for an hour with the dog curled beneath her and the sound of the Bollywood party somersaulting over the garden walls. The bridesmaids were singing in Hindi. As the hour wore on, Thai high-society dames did indeed show up with their own canines, some of them wearing silk jackets. The dogs had their own china plates and chomped on their own filets mignon. The women looked over at Sarah with curiosity, a cool racial distance between them. Enclosed, heavily self-aware, it occurred to Sarah that this was Mali's world, or her family's world—she had suddenly discovered it. It was not a world away from that of the gated rich in California. The Eiffel could have existed in Rancho Santa Fe, sheltered behind stucco walls with security alarms. The people in both places were in any case interchangeable and knew one another. The women were inspecting her not because she was an outsider but because they might have run into her in Rancho Santa Fe. But as servant or equal, they were not sure.

The staff looked on from the windows in their bow ties and watered silk waistcoats, beautiful in their willful paralysis, occasionally admiring their hair in the Second Empire mirrors.

"They all go clubbing together after hours," Ximena said later as Sarah was paying the bill. "But I stopped going with them. I should take you instead."

"Clubs aren't really my thing."

"Come on, you might enjoy it. When is Mali back?"

"Tomorrow night."

"She's an elusive one, that Mali. You know, I've never seen her outside of the Kingdom . . ."

Ximena raised her eyebrows and put out her cigarette. Politicians had arrived in the garden—three old men dressed up for the night—and she would have to return to the kitchen. Maybe they could have a drink together sometime? The parting glance was dry and questioning, and when she had gone Sarah mulled over the oddity of that last phrase. There was a slight contempt in the way Ximena talked about Mali. She seemed to think Mali was an operator when it came to men. But that was a common accusation, rarely fully true. Either way, Sarah didn't agree with it.

She walked back to the Kingdom in a calmer mood. At the top of the small alley, where it branched off from Soi 31, she took Whiskey out of her bag and let her discover the wonders of a street for herself. When they came to the gates, the guards bent down to greet the dog. Sarah picked her up and walked more briskly through the parking lot. A whole weekend, she was already thinking, and so much dead time to burn. The rod lights on the ceiling buzzed as she passed under them and by the lobby the turtles in the rock pool had all clambered onto the sole rock as if something in the water had expelled them.

The staff often said the turtles were barometers not only of storms but of human crises. She went up to the apartment with the puppy in her arms and laid her down gently inside the door. The dog, however, disobeyed and scampered off onto the landing. Mali indulgently let her play there when she felt too lazy to take her down to the gardens.

So Sarah stepped back outside and let the door close behind her as she went to look for Whiskey. The dog was instinctively padding back toward what she knew as home. Venturing out onto the bridge, Sarah was soon in front of Mali's windows, where she saw that the blinds had been drawn up and there was a single nightlight in what must have been the bedroom. A corner of the bed was plainly in view, and she could see that it rested on an expensive carpet with fringes, with shadows from the outside projected across it.

She walked across the bridge, taking in all the other windows, glimpsing an old woman sitting alone at a kitchen table peeling a mango with a knife, two children sitting in front of a television in the dark. At the far end of the bridge lay the emergency-exit stairs that connected all twenty-four floors, and she went down them one flight. Here she was level with Mali's windows and could see into them better. Sure enough, the dog was waiting outside Mali's door. Sarah scooped Whiskey into her arms and calmed her with a stroke. She stepped around to the elevator landing of the apartment and found that the landing door was open. This was Mali's private entrance and, unusual for the Kingdom, it was laid out differently from her own.

It was elegantly spare, with only an umbrella rack and a cupboard for shoes, a single light set into the ceiling. The apartment door was painted a pale lime green and there was a long bench laid against the landing wall, though it seemed a strange place for anyone to sit unless the elevator was delayed. Mali had painted the walls of her landing, meanwhile, a tropical yellow. Mali's world, so near to her own but so different, with its psychedelic color scheme and bourgeois neatness, was a lovely one to step into, even for a short while alone. Sarah listened to moths batting against the lamps in the corridors outside. They were so large that they could be heard from inside the landings.

She could imagine Mali painting the walls herself, laboring to create a delicate effect. Yet she felt uneasy stepping into this alternative world without, as it were, asking permission or being invited as a guest. There was none of the soft tumult that Mali possessed in person. But just as she was about to leave, she noticed a gecko on the yellow wall clinging to the plaster and staring down at her. Sensing her, too, it turned and the two animals examined each other for a while as the sweat dried on Sarah's face and her heart slowed. The gecko tensed, frozen in fear. Were they not a symbol of loving-kindness here, of the Buddhist virtue known as *metta*?

For the rest of the night she sat in front of her laptop following the historic price of gold and platinum and wondering if she should ask Mali for advice about buying from the Chinatown gold markets. She had been thinking of it for some time. The weekend passed in other such ruminative ways. She took Whiskey down to the first floor at night and waited to come across Pop or the other inhabitants with their dogs, but no encounters came to pass. Out beyond the street and the walls that enclosed it, meanwhile, the university gave rise to bouts of drumming and singing, yet another student festival of some kind, sounds that entered the Kingdom as if over vast distances and from a parallel world, as if the air itself were wired for sound. After ten, when Pop had shut down all the lights and the pool was returned to shadows, those sounds felt louder and more singular than they did earlier in the evenings. They had also changed in character. They felt less festive, more hard-edged. There she sat in the swings, while the dog jumped around the flower beds, rocking back and forth in bare feet and listening to the drums. The motion made her mind spin back to her lost life in New York, whose disappearance from view felt increasingly strange and unnatural. It was a mystery, for example, how she could have grown so close to another woman and then both betrayed her and left her in the dust. But it was now an open question whether the past mattered as much as she had thought it did. Inside the Kingdom, no one's past ever seemed to come into play.

FIVE

When Mali returned from the airport, she came straight to Sarah's apartment to collect her dog. She was dressed exactly as she had been when she left, in the same heels, even, but her skin was a touch darker, and there looked like the beginnings of a large bruise on her left shoulder.

"That?" she said when Sarah pointed it out. "I fell on the deck of our suite when I'd drunk too much rum. It doesn't hurt."

She picked up Whiskey and thanked Sarah for being so obliging. The dog had eaten all her prepared meals faithfully, and she seemed as attached to Sarah now as she had been to Pop the day before.

"She's such a flirt," Mali said, shaking Whiskey up and down and then tucking the dog under her arm. "All small dogs are. They have to be to survive. If they're not flirts they get eaten."

Would Sarah come down later for a drink on her balcony? She could meet Ryo, who was still there.

"Sure, I'd love to meet him."

"Shall we say in an hour?"

Sarah found herself yet again in front of the lime-green door with a box of Royce Japanese chocolates she had bought earlier in the week from the Emporium mall. Once she had bought them, she lost all desire to eat them, and they had sat in her fridge until tonight. The door to Mali's apartment was already open—inviting her to enter—and there was the sound of jazz coming from the open-plan kitchen at one end of a long main room that ended with high windows that faced west. Here, Mali stood at a chopping board slicing up a cucumber with a Japanese knife.

She was now in sweatpants and gym T-shirt and her hair was tied back out of her face as she worked. The dog swirled around her legs, and Mali looked up unsurprised. There was a glass of red wine already poured for Sarah, and Mali invited her to take a seat in the living room. Mali came over with her own glass and the dog at her heels. There was nothing in the room but an L-shaped sofa and the table; no pictures or art on the walls, no chairs or rugs or lamps.

"Ryo's asleep," she said, sitting down beside Sarah and touching her arm for a moment. "I was just making him something. You're not hungry, are you?"

"No."

"Let's drink cabernet then."

"*Chaiyo.*"

Sarah asked how her weekend had been.

"We went out on a boat and it wasn't raining. Unlike here. I got a little sunburned—"

The bruise on her shoulder now looked darker and more pronounced. Almost the shape of someone's hand, Sarah thought.

"Ryo's out cold. Let me go check on him." Mali gave her a sly smile. *I know, it's exactly what you're thinking,* it said.

She got up and walked over to the bedroom door, then peered in to check that he was still asleep. Then she closed the door behind her and came back to Sarah.

"I'm sorry, I know it's very rude of him, but he's exhausted. We got up early. Maybe we should keep our voices down."

They talked for an hour, devouring all the chocolates and eventually forgetting him entirely. The room was dark; there was only the light from the kitchen and the steady glare from the city. The murmur of jazz and air-con. Soon a strange thought came into Sarah's mind: They were actually alone and no one else was there. There was no proof for the existence of Ryo at all. She hadn't looked into the bedroom herself and she hadn't heard a sound from him. For a moment she felt like charging to the bedroom door and pulling it open. Instead, they drank two more glasses. Sarah's head loosened. Then, out of nowhere, there was a dull thud from the outside world, a sound like that of a whole wall collapsing in an instant, and they froze with their glasses suspended. It might have been the construction site, but Sarah knew that it wasn't. They went onto the balcony, from where part of the site could be seen.

The arc lamps were on and men in hard hats swarmed around the pits. They strained to see what was happening, but there didn't appear to be anything out of the ordinary. Along the freeways came the flashing lights of police cars, but without sirens, and soon even they had melted away again. But something had happened. In the gaps between the buildings they could see groups of people standing aimlessly at street corners. From those same corners came the echoes of car horns, and around them other people stood on their balconies looking down on the same things. It was a bomb, Sarah thought, and she knew that Mali had thought it as well. She turned to glance at her and she saw that Mali had begun to smile. *It was a bomb and she knew it all along.*

"It sounded like a pipe bomb," Sarah whispered.

Mali reached up slowly and touched the lobe of her ear as if it were time to dislodge the earring and turn in to sleep.

"It might not be what you think," she said.

And, with artful timing, a plume of thin smoke had appeared, rising like the trail of a bonfire.

"What if it was?" Mali said. "Do you know what it means?"

But Sarah was thinking more quickly. The stable tourist metropolis she had assumed would conceal and nourish her had now revealed a fault line, and the secret haven she had chosen for herself was perhaps not as secure as she had imagined it to be. The thought must have risen visibly into her face because Mali seemed to read it there and react accordingly. Sarah was afraid—it was easy to see—because she didn't understand the context of the place in which she was living. Even the name of the building was perhaps obscure to her. She knew that the original developer, Mr. Lim, had been all his life a most fervent patriot and devotee of the revered monarchy. His naming of the building therefore had been no accident. He and his wife, from whom he had inherited most of his money, had intended to make a patriotic gesture and to have it understood as such. At the time of its construction by himself and his father-in-law, the Yoon patriarch, it was one of the most technologically advanced and dazzlingly luxurious residential complexes in the city. Its fame spread far and wide, and TV actors and celebrities, models, and playboys all lined up to put down payments on the hundreds of newly constructed units. Government ministers vied for the garden penthouses, where society scandals were perpetrated almost monthly.

The Jacuzzis and steam rooms that equipped some of these apartments were unheard of at the time, and for six years until the financial crash of 1997 the Kingdom was a zircon in the city's rickety diadem, an address so desirable that the children of millionaires put themselves on its agonizingly selective waiting lists. Yet Mr. Lim was not distracted from his patriotic emotions by this frivolous commotion. He had intended to make a building as beautiful and forward-looking as the country he loved, and in the eyes of both the nation and himself he had succeeded. He often claimed that he had been inspired by Walt Disney's notebooks in which the master had sketched the medieval skyline of Dijon. The marble had come from Carrara—naturally—and the striking blue tiles had been fired in a special factory in Taiwan. He had himself designed the soaring atrium and the public gardens, which had come to him one night in a dream. This included the peacocks, who often came to him in nightmares. He had envisioned a city within a city, but also a scale model of order and interpersonal serenity. His children told him that he had succeeded, and he believed them. In those early days he could often be seen walking through the gardens with his butler behind him wheeling a service cart filled with his morning coffee. Never for a moment had he foreseen the crash that eventually wiped out most of his holdings, along with the fortunes of many of his most prestigious tenants. As a youth Lim had believed in the nation in the way that men believe in their marriages, knowing that Thailand was a kingdom neighbored by Communist states, its pomp and golden throne exalted by the CIA during the Vietnam War. He had grown up in the ethnic Chinese financial aristocracy rooted in tax collection and textiles, tobacco and medicinal drugs—all of which had formed his formidable and autocratic personality. The shock of the crash was immense, though in the end his stoicism had served him well. The Kingdom was shaken, but when the economy recovered he made yet more money with figurine factories in Wuhai and a buffalo mozzarella business in Chiang Rai. He had cunningly foreseen the boom in Bangkok's Italian restaurants. His tenants, on the other hand, had not been so fortunate.

As the crash destroyed their real estate investments many of them were forced to live on inside the Kingdom as ghosts of their former selves. Their cash had dissolved but they still had seven-room apartments with state-of-the-art kitchens, and this faded glamour became their new medium. Many were still there, growing old and marooned, as if stunned by their misfortune. But the country returned to a boom, the elites who had been shaken soon stirred themselves back to vitality, the tourists flowed into the city in record numbers, China tripled its GDP, and Bangkok became a great money-laundering machine for her footloose capital. The old tenants safe inside the Kingdom weathered this new storm, as well as the military coups in 2006 and 2014, while the army, the monarchy, and the urban middle classes and elites faced off with insurrectionary "Reds" orchestrated by the exiled billionaire Thaksin Shinawatra. Now there was a new king and the game had changed. The military, in power for years, had tightened its grip while the new king, who resided most of the year in a villa in Germany and was often seen cycling through the Bavarian countryside dressed in a strange bikini, asserted ever greater control over the real kingdom. The Lims, like the Yoons, were his devoted supporters. They admired his ruthless sangfroid. However, like many of their class they kept themselves withdrawn from the unpredictable vagaries of politics. They had no need of unwelcome attention and they didn't seek it. Enthroned in their lush penthouse surrounded by tropical vegetation they busied themselves with their family dramas and their portfolios while Mr. Lim himself pursued a vigorous interest in amateur astronomy. Everything, in sum, could have continued as it had been in both kingdoms had not the economic downturn altered the equation yet again.

The second crash, though milder and more protracted, had brought the latest real estate boom to a halt, as one could see in the construction sites around the Kingdom that were gradually losing steam. The workers were being laid off bit by bit; the huge machines were less active than they had once been. Companies owned by the great and arrogant families were once again faltering. The dictatorship responded with fiscal packages, media campaigns, and subsidies, but this time the sweeteners had failed to sweeten. Over the winter the air had become so polluted that its indices were worse than Beijing and Delhi. Days of smog so toxic that schools had been closed for a week. But now, since the economy had stalled, the discontents of earlier years had resurfaced in a novel way. A younger generation of students had found their insurrectionary voice, inspired by the protests in Hong Kong. At first it was just small demonstrations inside malls where tourists would notice them, isolated acts of civil disobedience on the trains, but when these were greeted with brutal counteractions by the police the protests had quickly escalated as they had in Hong Kong.

From the balcony, Mali pointed to a line of framed photographs arranged on one of the empty bookshelves in her apartment. They were incongruous in such a bare space but they appeared to contain images of an elegantly dressed Thai woman, undoubtedly her mother. Mali went on smoothly: "My mother holds to one value, what we call *siwilai*. Good breeding, manners, order, modern things. Back in those days it also probably referred to air-conditioning and cleanliness. Civilized. *Siwilai*. What it really means is endless evasion and halls of mirrors held in place by a large army."

In the streets below, the police had arrived and there was an upswell of male shouting, of officials reasserting order. Mali took out her earring and let it roll in her palm while she looked at it, as if the scene were of less consequence than a jade stud. She added something else: that the tenants were largely behind the army in these dangerous days but that the ground staff of the Kingdom, the doormen, the gardeners, the receptionists, the odd-job men, were not at all on the same page. Quietly, and fearing being fired if they ever dared to give voice to their sympathies, they supported the protests rippling across the city and sometimes joined them after work without their employers noticing. It was a comedy, this dance of pro and con, but such was the strict internal order of the Kingdom that it could go on for months without either side confronting the other openly. Nor was such confrontation even necessary. The tensions were always held in reserve, papered over by an innate discretion and dislike of conflict. Held just beneath the surface, those tensions simmered with a quiet permanence and they could be felt only by a mind attuned to its rhythms. To an outsider everything would appear calm, right up until the moment when the system broke down and ancient hatreds returned. It could happen within a single day. If she was unlucky Sarah might see it for herself, but the odds were rather against it.

"I wouldn't worry about it too much," Mali said, enjoying the trace of terror on Sarah's face. "It's still *siwilai*."

Medics had now appeared, pickups with plainclothesmen who dispersed into the shadows. Mali took Sarah's arm and steered her back inside. They walked together out onto the landing and Mali told her again not to worry. There was a coup every ten years here, sometimes every five years, and nothing would ever penetrate the Kingdom. They were protected by high social connections. Even if things got out of hand they could probably watch from their balconies, drink in hand. Her manner had not ceased to be supremely confident and knowing. It was quietly mocking of Sarah's evident alarm. *What did you expect?* she seemed to say with her eyes, and getting no reply Mali assumed the authority to reassure the naïve foreigner. She took out her remaining earring and held it in her palm in the same way as she had the other one, as someone does when they are preparing for bed or a bath. It was curious how easily they had forgotten about Ryo, supposedly asleep in the apartment. He had not come up even as a subject of conversation.

Sarah felt there was a ripple of energy between them, something fiercer than sympathy, as they walked to the gold doors of the elevator and the musty atmosphere of the atrium fell upon them with its floating dust and scent of moldering houseplants.

Mali said, "By the way, I assume you keep all your cash under the bed. You should if you don't. That's the only precaution you need to take."

"I do," Sarah blurted out, and immediately regretted it.

But Mali was no threat to her secrets; she was, after all, merely suggesting that it was normal practice.

"That's wise, Sarah. I do that too. So does my mother."

"Does everyone in this building do that? Just in case?"

"Yes, exactly. Just in case."

The next day Sarah took her swim early and read *The New York Times* until the middle of the afternoon, when the rains began. She sank into an inertia of Winter Palace tea and napped until she was woken by something her unconscious mind must have noticed and continued to watch. High up among the rows of windows a face had appeared, a young girl of about school age as far as she could see, her hair ribboned in the style of the 1930s. At first Sarah assumed that it must be a daughter of one of the tenants on her way to a costume party—they were held frequently at the Kingdom for the benefit of the resident children. Then she counted her way up the windows to determine which floor the girl was on, and found that it was the sixteenth, the one above hers. In her hair were pale pink ribbons, obviously made of silk, because they shone intensely. Sarah half waved, then desisted, seeing no reaction on the girl's part. And yet she had clearly been observing Sarah for some time, patiently gazing downward through the filthy glass. And it might not have been the first time. It then occurred to Sarah that if she was being observed it might not be by the figures conjured by her imagination.

There was no escaping the gaze of an innocent child. You couldn't complain about it to anyone, for example. You had to endure it, work around it as best you could. In many ways, a child was the perfect surrogate agent.

She was about to wave a second time when the face withdrew from the outer light and melted into the darkness of the landing. Sarah decided to go up to the exact place where the girl must have been standing and look down at the spot where she had been lounging a few minutes earlier. It was indeed a perfect vantage point. She looked around, into the landing and the atrium corridors. There was no trace of the girl, no evidence of disturbance.

To escape the claustrophobia of her thoughts, in the late afternoon Sarah went out into the streets. She walked alone up Soi 31 past the Holey Bakery until she was at the corner with Soi 39, where a shisha pipe place stood across from the Gion karaoke bar. There she sat for a while with a mint tea and a pipe watching the Gion girls line up under the lanterns to greet the salarymen and executives arriving in their limos. A teasing hue and cry, a collective bow amid explosively opening umbrellas. *Irasshaimase!* Dusk was the only glamorous hour. Quicksilver clouds emerged and dissolved over the streets and the tangled cables that swung alongside them like demented vines as she pondered at her own pace, between puffs of apple-flavored smoke, the things that Mali had said to her the night before and the unexpected jolt that the sight of the spying girl had had upon her. She had begun to realize that she had misunderstood every single thing up till then. Looking at the geishas at the entrance to the Gion, in their scarlet kimonos one night, dark green the next, Thai girls remade as Japanese, everything in their welcome contrived to make an effect on customers who spoke not a single word of the language. Neither side understood the other, and the men sat in the dark and belted out Nana Mizuki songs while the Thai girls used their eight words of Japanese over and over to

make the financial wheels turn. It was a theater built around de-
sires that could be acted out. She had taken this world too literally. Its face value was not the value according to itself, and below
its surface there flowed cross-currents she could feel but whose
force she could not yet gauge.

The following morning, the maid sent by Nat finally appeared at her door, waiting patiently for her on her landing. Goi,
as Sarah knew she was called, wore a shabby pink dress and carried a shopping bag, which looked as if it might contain a change
of clothes. Sarah had forgotten about her, and was therefore un-
prepared. Since her surprise was written brightly on her face the
maid stepped into the breach. "Is it all right?" she said at once, in
her employer-affected English. "Miss Natalie said I should come
on Tuesday at this time. Is it wrong?"

"I think it was Wednesday."

"Wednesday cannot. Tuesday."

"Well, since you are here—it's all right with me."

Sarah looked at her watch, but it was more to show her annoyance than for any real reason. She was sure that she had
agreed to Wednesday. Yet she forced herself to behave as non-
chalantly as possible, opening the door wider by way of invitation, her privacy finally invaded. The maid kicked off her sandals
and came, half-bowing deferentially, into the hallway. She set
down her bag and Sarah showed her around the apartment with
a breezy rapidity. Since all the units at the Kingdom bore a ge-
neric similarity to one another, the maid already knew where
everything was and how it worked. She could do the washing
and ironing in the outdoor area and maid's room behind the
kitchen, and she could leave anything she needed to leave at the
apartment there as well. But that day, Sarah said, she didn't need

to stay the whole four hours. She could do two hours and then leave early; she could make up for that time the following week, if she didn't mind. "*Ka*," Goi agreed, and Sarah gave her the standard 500-baht fee.

"You can do the ironing next week as well, since there's hardly any to do."

"*Ka*."

When it was agreed, Sarah left her in the kitchen and went to the spare room to lock the suitcase stored in the cupboard. There was no way she could conceal it entirely. She had to hope that the maid wouldn't be too nosy and try to open it herself. Should Sarah make a point of it openly by asking her not to, that would only bring attention to the suitcase. In any case, there was nothing she could do about it now. She let Goi do as she pleased and sat mutely at the bar in the kitchen reading magazines, making sure that the new maid didn't look too closely through her things. Soon, meanwhile, she recalled that the maids at the Kingdom had their own passkeys, and that they let themselves into the apartments while their clients were at work during the day. This raised the question of whether Goi had a key for her unit and could come and go as she liked—it was obviously an honor system that everyone obeyed. She wondered if she should ask Goi directly. But when the time was up and Goi was preparing to leave, she decided not to ask after all. It felt like an etiquette she didn't quite grasp but that she shouldn't question too much. Khun Goi was merry and innocent, and she even offered to make dinner next time, though Sarah declined. She bowed to Sarah and told her that she would be back at the same time the following week.

There was no harm in her that one could see, and when she

had gone Sarah felt ashamed of being so uncharitable toward her. She could see that Goi was kindly and bustling by nature, and since she worked for, and had been referred by, the haughty couple on the twenty-first floor she would be eager to make a good impression and do so as unobtrusively as possible. She wanted to get in and get out as efficiently as possible in return for the 500 baht. All the same, Sarah made a mental note to be at home at the same time next Tuesday. She preferred to have as little interaction with the staff as she could, because she had the feeling that they were inveterate gossips. Did that include Goi? Of course it did. No one gossiped more than maids. They were ambulatory grapevines seething with malice, even if outside the play of gossip they were the sweetest people imaginable, or made themselves seem as much. The persona presented for public display was rarely the intuitive personality that hovered beneath it, as was true in any culture. But then, the same was true of her, was it not? Her inside and her exterior were incompatible realities much of the time, little different from the world inside the Kingdom and the one outside it.

SIX

On the twenty-first floor later that evening Natalie and Roland sat in their penthouse dining room with the air-conditioning piously turned off, the temperature unpleasantly warm. He had insisted that it was better for their lungs. Since she was eating with the girls later she had asked their maid to make dinner for one, and Roland was eating it now while she watched him with a glass of chilled orange wine—a new craze in the city—as he told her, at great length, about his day at work. It was *som tam* with a plate of grilled chicken and a tamarind dip with sticky rice, and he ate it with a deliberate lack of manners because he was annoyed. The maid had made it spicy, and he couldn't take the heat of Thai food. He paused from time to time and waved a theatrically cooling hand in front of his mouth as if fanning an obstinate fire.

That afternoon he had had to take a client to the Zuma restaurant at the St. Regis to discuss a family legal dispute with a high-society or "hi-so" Thai client. They had spent most of the afternoon together—having adjourned across the road from the St. Regis to the Royal Bangkok Sports Club, where the client was a member—and then played squash together and retired to the sauna. Roland was now exhausted and irritable, and his skin was flushed pink from the day's intense discussions and pointless sport. His white shirt was slightly crumpled and a lock of hair fell from his magnificent mane onto his right eyebrow, making him look slightly criminal. Forty-two and lean, but unable to relax in a city he didn't always like. Handsome but off-kilter, tense from top to bottom. But, Natalie remembered, it had been he who was so keen, three years earlier, to make the move from Singapore to Bangkok. She had protested—though the defiance had made no difference. In Singapore, and before that in Brussels, she had had satisfying jobs in cities that made her feel comfortable. "First World cities," if one accepted the appalling terminology of an earlier age, cities with proper sidewalks and uncorrupted tax regimes. Cities with no military government.

She had had to be wrenched out of them by the sheer force of Roland's personality, which in turn was driven by a need to follow the best opportunities his own career offered him. A classic marital impasse. Her own career inside the Hilton group was going as she had intended and she saw no reason to disrupt it. One could have argued that postings at Hiltons around the world were little different from assignments in a colonial empire a hundred years ago, but it was to her taste. The Marriott brand, in any case, was a notch above the other Hiltons, and within it she had carved out an identity of her own. She had fashioned for herself a highly efficient and organized personality in order to compete with him—in order, she sometimes thought, to surpass him. She took care of her appearance, her clothes. She had her business suits tailored at WW Chan in Hong Kong and bought her jewelry in the shops she knew in Paris. She spent time on the façade, which was important to her job, though it sapped her internal energy as time went on.

In order to convince her to move to Bangkok, even from as close by as Singapore, Roland had had to plead with her in excessive terms, to extoll the virtues of a city he had never even visited. He had sung the joys of swimming pools, outdoor breakfasts, and street food. And what about the seedy nightlife? Oh, he protested, somewhat unconvincingly, he'd have nothing to do with that. Lulled by a few exaggerations, she had given way— a mental inch at first and then the whole nine yards. It was true that he had landed a plush job at one of the top firms in the region, with significant opportunities for rapid advancement. The money was superb, and those dollars went further in Bangkok than they ever would in Singapore. Plus, he moaned, Singapore was a drag and you always had to eat out in a bloody mall. From the Thai capital, they could fly in an hour to the world's best beaches. They could take up diving, and indeed when they first moved they had gone to Phuket and Koh Lanta and a few other places to dive and party with some of his colleagues at the firm. Insufferable bores to the last man and woman. It was the tropical equivalent of the skiing scene in Europe. Roland had even acquired a certificate. But the hobby had soon fizzled out. The underwater world terrified Natalie and she found it hard to admit this to him when he was on his macho diving roll, and the après-dive parties in the five-star hotels had grown pallid within a few months. They went back to spending their weekends in Bangkok, and slowly the boredom accrued.

Watching her husband pick over the last of the sticky rice, Natalie was no longer sure what she felt about him. He had changed over the last year. The easy affection, the once-upon-a-time lust, had melted away as if in the heat. He was still her husband, but the terms had shifted. He was still her husband, she might have added, but he was no longer her lover. She had always dreaded the time when that would happen, but it had, and she wanted to know why. It was natural to blame the city itself. In Brussels, the city worked, so to speak, in her favor; in Singapore less so, since the people were more attractive than in Brussels and the nightlife more sexually open. But in Bangkok the balance had swung dramatically against her. They made jokes about it but she had had the feeling—it had begun to grip her the previous year—that Roland was finding his pleasures elsewhere in the vast honeycomb at his disposal. He never went missing at night, but of course he did not need to. The normal laws of adultery were completely suspended, and even the concept of "adultery" here was mildly ridiculous. It was the quaint preserve of white people. A girl at work had asked her a curious question a few weeks back: was her husband a *pii suua*? It was said in a knowing tone but she didn't know the word and had to ask its meaning. It was "butterfly." But it also referred commonly to a ladies' man. The term literally meant "ghost shirt," the perfect image for both the airborne insect and a man who is never in one place for long. And she had been forced to think.

If he had been one all along, then he had suddenly found his natural habitat. An instinct told her that he was no longer entirely hers, and she was not as enraged as she had thought she would be, but if it was true her reasons for staying on in the city were seriously diminished. Everything had turned to quicksand and madness.

The first stirrings of hatred arrived, but it was not an active and needy hatred. It was more like an impatient disappointment and a regret that she had, hitherto, neglected her female friendships when she should have tended them. The paradox was that at this very moment she sensed that he was becoming more suspicious of *her*. Was it projection or guilt? It had to be both. But then, as she now remembered, when they had been students together in London—they had met at the LSE—he had been the jealous and insecure one, the one more likely to call her late into the night and pester her with questions. Their shared love of business technicalities and economics, it turned out, had not been enough to bridge the divide between them once suspicions arose, but for the last four or five years it had been serene sailing. Now this. His face had a hint of low cunning as he ate, and she watched it with a cold fascination.

"Do you have to go downstairs?" he was saying as he drank glass after glass of the orange wine that stood at the center of the table. "I don't even know *why* you have to have a girls' night. What do you talk about? Men and your finances?"

"We smoke weed, mostly. It's not exactly dramatic."

"I should tell reception. They'll come up and beat you with their shoes."

"We'll just give them some weed and they'll love us."

"Corruption," he sighed. "It's everywhere. But I don't believe you anyway. Maybe you have some boys over."

"Come to think of it, that's a good idea. I should suggest it."

He grimaced and opened his mouth wide, fanning the invisible flames again, the chilies burning his tender European throat.

"Fucking hell, why does Goi make the dipping sauce so hot? It's food as torture. To think they designed this as a national cuisine—"

She glanced at her watch. She had to leave in half an hour.

"Don't eat it, then. Get Goi to go to Quince for you and pick up a gourmet burger."

He emptied his glass and looked away, out into the horizon of sparkling reflections, the towers' red warning lights flashing with a steady nightlong beat. He was quite glad to be alone for an evening, and he was thinking even then of a walk down to a bar near Soi Cowboy. A couple of Dalwhinnies at the bar and a pretty girl, a bout of nothingness. No one would be the wiser. Natalie, for her part, finally got up and called in Goi from the kitchen. She knew what he was thinking and didn't much care either way.

Standing in the darkness of the kitchen, Goi had in fact been listening to them for some time. Their voices perpetually rising and falling, driven by anger and restlessness, were like a mysterious field of signs inside which she could detect here and there meaningful illuminations. Since she had been living in the maid's room of their apartment for six months now she knew the nature of Nat's unhappiness, her slow-burn frustrations, the wandering eye of the husband and the scents he was covered with when he returned from his jaunts. It was she, after all, who washed and ironed his shirts, on the collars of which she often found telltale dabs of lipstick. A man has no secrets from his maid, and neither does a woman. As she lay at night in her tiny cubicle behind the laundry area, which the scrupulous Roland would not permit to be air-conditioned, saying she was "used to it," she sometimes calculated how she would blackmail Roland if she ever needed some extra money. It could be done subtly and so that he would not deny her a favor or two. When she washed his trousers or steam-ironed his jackets she was obliged to go through his pockets. Since he never gave a moment's consideration as to what Goi thought, he was careless and consequently his pockets were treasure troves of his indiscretions. Calling cards, numbers hastily scribbled on paper napkins in well-known bars, blister packs of Kamagra.

His secret life could be read easily in a few forgotten scraps, and many of these she diligently kept under her mattress on the floor in her room, along with two handkerchiefs similarly tainted with lipstick, which she had once found after one of his drunken nights out. So many useful proofs. She sometimes peered into his phone, which he left out in the master bedroom when he was in the bath and Natalie was at work, and saw there numbers, names, little icon pictures of prostitutes with names like Gwang (deer) and Smile Smile and Annlove Likemiss. When he and she were alone in the apartment for his evening meal, some wailing *farang* music called Ry Cooder on the sound system and a bottle of wine, which he had taught her how to open, standing it on the table, she watched him from behind as he ate alone, hunched over his stocks. The foreigners were haughty and scatterbrained, perpetually distracted by their obsessions, and her job was to quietly amend the mistakes they continually made. She felt a little sorry for them. They couldn't speak properly, they knew nothing about real food, and were always unhappy in petty and enigmatic ways. What could one do with such monstrous children? They had to be shepherded without them knowing it. This was what she did, and she expected no gratitude from them. But down the line, if she played her cards well, she might get more from them than they had intended. It was always a delicious possibility. Until then she had merely to watch her steps and steal small things here and there without them noticing.

Now she appeared at the door to the kitchen with her customary half-smile and inquiring glance, eternally watchful as Natalie had noticed, but adept and obedient in equal measure.

"Khun Goi, did you go to see Khun Sarah in Unit Eighty-Six? She was expecting you today."

"*Pai laew.*"

"All right, good. And don't forget to go on the same day every week from now on. She's counting on you."

The maid bowed her acceptance, and Natalie gave Roland a kiss on the cheek.

"Don't be so miserable," Natalie said to him. "Go to a bar, have a couple of shots and talk to a pretty girl. You'll feel better."

"I'll probably watch the boxing."

She went to the grand entrance of the penthouse flanked by two carved wooden *apsara*, and Goi came with her to close the door after her. There Nat said to her, trying to be a little humorous: "Make sure Khun Roland doesn't drink too much. If he goes out, make sure he takes his phone."

"*Chai ka.*"

Natalie went to the elevator doors after purloining a bottle of brandy from their drinks cabinet. The landing was sunk in shadow, and a few feet above her head the great stained-glass window that covered the entire atrium echoed with rain. Its gloomily elegant peacocks, which had stepped out of Mr. Lim's dreams, maintained their luminescence within the obscurity. On the far side of the same landing the even more grandiose door of the Lim family apartment remained locked in somber aloofness. She hadn't seen any of the family since the old man killed himself, not even the vivacious and friendly daughter. Late at night, when she was working at the dinner table and Roland was asleep, she heard a faint sobbing coming from their apartment. But lately she never saw the wife, the resplendent Mrs. Lim, and she wondered if the old lady was abroad somewhere to recover from her tragedy. With their billions she could go wherever she wanted.

Natalie had never seen the inside of their palatial residence in the Kingdom but it was rumored to have been designed by the old man himself and had a 360-degree view on the roof from a glass dome where he had liked to fiddle with a German telescope. By virtue of her job she was always filled with sly curiosity about people whose lives were only partially visible to her. People in rooms, ephemeral as they checked in and out. The tenants of the Kingdom were in this respect not unlike the guests at the Marriott, people she saw at breakfast or at cocktail hour but rarely otherwise, phantoms whose lives were veiled by institutional respectability and convention. And yet she found herself thinking about them all the time. At the hotel a guest might check in while she was present at the front desk and she would be struck by a small detail—a fur collar or an unusual piece of luggage—and she would later look up their personal information so that she could learn something about them. It was a form of casual voyeurism. Not unlike that of a maid. She had seen small love affairs form at the bar on the second floor, proud and noble-looking men with firm handshakes return in the middle of the night with drunken ladyboys on their arms. Hotels brought out the worst in people—or maybe just the truth.

She went down to the sixteenth floor and rang Ximena's bell. It played a half bar from *William Tell*.

"You're on time," Sarah said when she opened the door. The American was dressed for a summer garden party and the clothes seemed too bright for her.

"Brandy?" Natalie asked, flashing the bottle.

"I always feel like a brandy."

The table outside was set for dinner, and it was cool now after an hour of rain. Ximena lit the dinner candles and they shared a glass of Nat's brandy. They uttered the first "*Chaiyo!*" and a joint was rolled for a gentle hit. It was the same *gan-chaa* as before. And as before, Sarah went along with it. Natalie asked where Mali was—had she called to say she'd be late?

"Not yet," Ximena said. "She's not that late yet."

"She's never late."

This was true. Ximena cocked her head. "Shall I call her?"

"No, leave it. She'll be here soon, I'm sure."

Still, Natalie went on, it was unusual for her to be late.

"So you know her quite well, then?" Sarah said.

"Not really, now that you ask."

"Ximena?"

Ximena shook her head and her long turquoise-studded earrings captured the candlelight for a second.

"I met her for the first time a month or two ago," Natalie said. "It hasn't been as long as it seems. I wonder why it feels so much longer . . . I felt protective toward her for some reason, even from the first moment."

"I met her at the restaurant, actually," Ximena chimed. "She called me out from the kitchen to thank me for the meal. She asked me where I lived and we had a laugh about it."

"Quite the coincidence."

"Sure. But not such a surprising one. Lots of people in the building eat there."

"Even so."

Natalie reached for the bottle and poured herself a second glass.

"I met her at a building meeting. The owners like to throw these sangria parties by the pool once a month, and Mali was there. I thought she was the nicest of them right away. She came up to Roland and told him he had a noble face. She actually used the word *noble*."

The three women laughed at this, picturing the scene. For Sarah, it only accentuated Mali's conspicuous absence.

"You know," Sarah said, "I think I'll go down and see where she is. Is that a good idea?"

"Sure, go."

Nat then asked her not to disturb Mali if she was busy with her man. It was the one excuse they'd have to swallow.

Sarah got up, saying she would be right back. When she returned to the atrium her palms were moist and she felt giddy not only from the drink but from a desire to know exactly what Mali was doing. Accordingly she went down to the fourteenth floor and from there onto the bridge that ran past Mali's apartment. Here she could see into the unit through its two large windows. Their blinds were now rolled up and she could see directly into two rooms, the bedroom and a study, though now all the lights in those rooms were off. The bedroom was therefore submerged in darkness and yet there was a faint glow emanating from the living room beyond it. Even with so little light, it was possible to see the contours of the room, the chairs, the bed, a cabinet with two metal candlesticks placed close to the window. She was sure they had not been there before. A pair of high-heeled shoes lay on their sides next to the bed, cast off without thought.

In some way she knew what she was about to see, because before every storm there is a shiver in the nerves that corresponds to an outer disturbance. At first it was voices she heard, the man and the woman shouting at each other, bursts of insults and sarcastic laughter. They tilted at each other out of sight, speaking in English and then hissing recriminations whose details could not be heard. Then the human-shaped shadows appeared, the couple tussling in the half-light as they waltzed antagonistically toward the bedroom pulled by the man, as far as Sarah could see. She lowered her head instinctively so that neither of them would see her and watched with her eyes just above the wall. The man, in a corporate white shirt and black tie, now askew, had raised his hand above Mali's head. He was shouting and yet the sound was now curiously muted. His other hand had seized her hair and had squeezed a clump of it into an upright tail. With one blow he brought his hand down on her face and then raised it again, ready for a second blow. Mali made no sound, covering her face, but little threads of blood and saliva fell between her fingers and onto her dress.

The man was breathing heavily, almost in exhaustion, and the second blow took a while to come, thudding down onto her shoulder. It twisted her around onto her side and threw her to the carpet with one arm thrown up to defend her face. For a moment he paused and turned, as if sensing someone outside the scene looking in. He stared right out of the room and into the landing bridge and the atrium, where it was so dark that very little could be seen from inside the apartment. Yet Sarah ducked and cowered under the wall, covering her mouth with her hand. She crouched there for a few seconds not daring to move, not even to crawl away hidden by the wall, but she then heard the front door of Mali's apartment snap open. It was obvious that he was stepping out to see who he had glimpsed observing him. Forced to move, she slithered along the bridge as silently as she could and reached the far landing, where she rolled onto her knees and waited again. He had come onto the bridge, she could sense it, and was throwing a long look down the length of it. He was wearing only socks, as silent as herself, and there was no way of knowing how far along the bridge he had advanced toward her. Shortly thereafter a beam of light from a flashlight shot down the bridge and lit up the emergency doors in front of her but missed Sarah as she pressed herself behind the bend in the wall. For a few seconds it scoured the doors and then was turned off. Ryo, then, had probably turned away and given up his search. As she slowly crawled to the door of the next unit, hoping that it was open, she sensed that he had departed in a different direction. She called the elevator. Almost simultaneously the bell rang and she darted into it, stabbing at the button for the twenty-first floor. It was only as she was moving upward that her mind made note of what she had seen on that landing: rows of shoes neatly lined up, a half-dead potted plant coated in dust, and a general look of disrepair.

She went up to the penthouse floor before returning to the poker night, knowing that once she was there, she would be safe.

She calmed herself and ventured to peer over the wall and down at the bridge she had come from. There was no one there. But at the same time she could feel eyes looking for her, searching out her whereabouts. She was certain that Ryo was still on the bridge trying to ascertain who she was and what she might have seen. But gradually, as the silence of the penthouse floor stilled her and her heart rate decelerated, she prepared herself to reenter Ximena's apartment. She had quickly resolved to keep what she had seen to herself, gripped by a fear that if she told anyone—even the other women—it would get back to Ryo and he would then know who she was. It would be an added complication to her secretive exile. So decided, she went back down to the sixteenth floor using the elevator next to Natalie and Roland's apartment and entered Ximena's landing directly without having to endure the bridge and Ryo's presence there.

Ximena and Natalie were now eating cheesecake with the brandy, and she heard their laughter before she opened the door. It was as if they had forgotten all about Mali and Sarah as they grew tipsier. But their curiosity soon returned. While Ximena went to get a fresh brandy glass for Sarah, Natalie asked her if Mali was home.

"I rang her bell," Sarah lied, "but no one answered. Maybe she's asleep."

"Were the lights on?"

Ximena came to the table and poured her a glass.

"No," Sarah said. "I don't think she's home."

Natalie looked more squarely at Sarah.

"So when you rang the bell nothing happened?"

"Silence."

"Well," Natalie said, "it's annoying she didn't even call to cancel. If she's having a tryst at home—"

The ganja was brought out once again, they sipped at yadong, and for a while they listened to the wind whipping around the cornices of the tower. It seemed to be filled with little particles that hissed against the cement, creating a constant pitter-patter against the glass. A wind filled with cinders, powdered rubbish, and soot.

Ximena thought aloud: "You know, I remember something curious from last week when we were here. I was in the kitchen making lasagna and Mali was in the toilet. I heard her talking on her phone. She was speaking Japanese."

Natalie put down her joint and her eyes were suddenly unseeing. "What?"

"Is it surprising?" Ximena went on. "I don't know. Maybe she needs it for her job. She's a personal assistant, so it makes sense. Many Thais speak it for work."

"Or," Natalie put in, "because they have Japanese boyfriends."

"You mean he's not the first Japanese she's been with?"

"I don't know. It's none of my business. But I asked my sources at the front desk. Don't worry, I did it discreetly. I wasn't being nosy, just curious."

"And?"

"They said she'd had two or three others before this one. Black suits, limos, older than her—the whole deal. It seems to be her taste."

"What do you know about her taste?"

Sarah felt herself losing her grip as the smoke poured out of her nose, though it was also a relief, this slipping of self-control.

Something tapped like a hammer at her temples and she was aware that her heart rate was not in fact as normal as she had thought a few minutes earlier. It was a test of her self-mastery. She was like a singer powdered and wigged for a performance, tensed for the action, half-terrified under unforgiving lights. It was best to not speak, just to listen. And Ximena was still talking.

"Is it true that Thai girls are drawn to Japanese guys? I can see it. They dress better than the others. They're not stingy. They're polite and they have good manners—the sort of manners that go down well here. What do you think?"

"That must be it," Natalie said.

Nat shot Sarah a mocking look, and Sarah understood from it that she was less stoned than herself. But did she not think what she'd said was true?

"Or it's money and a kind of freedom," Ximena said. "They know the Japanese guys won't marry them. So they can cut loose and have some fun. They get spoiled and treated nicely and they walk away from it whenever they want. There's no society or family pressure."

"It doesn't mean they love them," Natalie said.

"Who, the men?"

"No, the girls. It doesn't mean they love those men."

"Who said anything about love?"

Ximena's tone had hardened a little.

"Even if it's not about love," she drawled. "You just get what you need, don't you?"

Natalie emptied her brandy glass.

"I'm not judging her at all. There are plenty of times I wish I wasn't married. You can't live with marriage or without it. Maybe she's got it right. You should find one of those too, Ximena."

"I'm not into the salaryman thing. In fact, I'm quite happy alone here."

"I would be too."

It was only shortly thereafter that Sarah gathered up the nerve to make her excuses and say that she was going back to her place to sleep. A headache, fatigue from the ganja, and then the disturbing scene she had witnessed—though this last she didn't mention. She should not have drunk the yadong, clearly. She got up a little clumsily and for a telltale moment she swayed and had to catch herself with a hand against the back of her chair. The other two, however, didn't say anything, being far gone themselves and unable to notice much. Natalie, though, asked if she was all right to walk back to her unit.

"I'm upright," Sarah said, "which is half the battle."

She saw herself out, and when she was on Ximena's landing she controlled an urge to vomit. She went down to the fifteenth floor and walked along the bridge, passing once again over Mali's apartment, though now the blinds were down and there was no sign of either of them. As she glanced at the windows she asked herself if she really had seen what she thought she had seen. Three puffs of the weed and a few sips of brandy beforehand had made her susceptible to visions, without question. Perhaps it was not Ryo she had seen on the bridge. A night watchman? she thought as she entered her landing and locked the glass door behind her. On the other side of the corrugated glass, meanwhile, lay the dimness of the landing where Ryo could come and go as he wished if he ever had a reason to visit her. There would, in reality, be nobody to call if he did.

SEVEN

Sarah was already in the water at 7:15 a few mornings later when Mali walked into the shade of the trees in a white swimsuit and flip-flops, her hair tied up on top of her head and a pair of goggles around her neck, relaxed, well rested, her skin almost polished. Sarah had heard nothing from her during those empty days following the poker night, and her arrival was therefore a surprise to the American. She was nonchalant as soon as she saw Sarah, throwing off her towel and plunging her legs into the water up to her knees, giving Sarah a playful splash. There was no healing wound on her face, but she wore heavy sunglasses and she didn't take them off as she entered the pool.

"We missed you the other night," Sarah said.

"I should have called, I'm sorry. I came home so tired I nodded off. I was in a funny mood all day. My mother was nagging me in the afternoon—I couldn't bear it anymore."

"We smoked your weed without you."

"I knew you would. Three's company, isn't it?" She looked at

Sarah intently through the tinted lenses, and even screened in this way the surfaces of her eyes possessed an intimidating brightness. "I hope you enjoyed yourselves without me. My mistake was to take a nap when I came home from work. It always kills me. Too much stress at work—"

"Yeah, I can imagine—"

But, Sarah thought at the same time, you hardly work, do you?

"On the plus side, I slept ten hours and got up early." Mali looked up at a hot blue sky that dialed down the prehistoric cries of the swallows constantly crossing it. "And the rain has cleared. I love the skies here after the rain. Don't you?"

Sarah thought to say that in fact they were a little worried about her, but it felt false since she had said nothing to the others, so she let it go. On the roofs around them other birds had begun to mass, chattering in a different way, as if something alarming were approaching. And yet there was nothing but that petrol-blue sky and the faint hum of the cranes out of sight. An inflatable flamingo floated on the surface of the pool, sadly adrift, and she thought of all the sad pools she had grown up with in California—desert pools with fronds floating in them, a dusting of sand on the deck chairs. How could two blue skies produce such varying emotional responses?

As if reading her expression on the spur of that quiet moment, Mali felt impulsive toward her new friend, able to ask a subtly impertinent question: "Are you all right?"

"Not really."

"You look like a lost child. We all have those moments."

"I don't know about lost," Sarah murmured.

"You know what I mean."

"In fact I was wondering about you, whether you were all right."

Mali took this in her stride, no surprise in her voice: "Me? Why would I not be all right?"

"I just had a feeling."

Mali put a hand to her shades as if she were about to lift them, but did not. She said: "You know what they say—facts don't care about your feelings."

"All the same, I had the feeling."

"That's very comradely of you. But relationship problems are what they are. They're not terminal."

"Is that what it was, a relationship problem?"

"I suppose so."

A half-truth, then, with the weightier half left out. The other half was hiding behind a pair of sunglasses.

"You should have said," Sarah said quietly.

"I should have, but I decided not to. It's not anyone else's burden. Sometimes you need to keep it to yourself. I needed a few days to brood on it."

"Did you?"

"What, brood? Of course I did. What does one ever do but brood on those things? Yet it's all for nothing. When you're dying you won't remember any of it."

We'll see about that, Sarah thought.

After all, it couldn't be proved in the present.

"We have a saying in Thai," Mali went on, without any dark shade in her voice. "*Arb nam ron ma kon*. It means 'I took the hot bath before you.' That is, I experienced life before you did and I know better. I'm the adult. So I'm telling you what to expect when it happens to you."

"It would make a great toast."

Mali's impromptu smile brought the brightness of the sky into their mood, or so Sarah thought, and she felt herself give way to her a little. And yet she had been thinking for days about the violence she had witnessed. It was said that bar girls could knock out harassing clients by delivering a blow to the temple. It must have left damage on her face, but perhaps Ryo's assault had struck her head somewhere else instead and the wound was therefore disguised. Moreover she had had a few days to heal. It was understandable that she would not want to draw attention to such a thing—they were not close friends. Sarah lay back to let her legs enter the zone of sunlight and looked up at the windows above them, fiercely bright with reflected sun. Another matter quickly invaded her mind.

"Mali, have you ever noticed a young girl in one of those windows looking down at you? I saw her the other day and I wondered if I was the only one who does."

"A young girl?"

"She was in the window, about twelve, I'd say. There was something off about her."

Mali also looked up at the windows, shaded her eyes, and appeared to concentrate for a moment.

"I can't say that I have. Do you know her?"

"No, but I thought that she recognized me in some way."

"Why do you say that?"

"I don't know, just a feeling."

Mali added that she had only noticed an old man watching her from the seventh floor: voyeurs like that were the norm.

"There are probably several watching us right now. You can count on it."

"Really?"

They lay there for another hour while Mali needled her with offhand questions about her Bangkok life. Did she go out alone? Did she frequent the bars? She told a tale about her own savings. She had done some "deals" on the side and saved up quite a bit of cash, which she had stored, as eternal advice had it, under her bed. She didn't want to say what deals they had been, but they had not been entirely legal. Some of her friends had done likewise. Her cash had to be laundered afterward but since Bangkok was the money-laundering capital of the world it was not a difficult operation to get away with. There were a thousand outlets through which it could be done. Her associates had put her in touch with cash-based businesses like bars and restaurants and she had rolled her profits through them without a hitch. She had the feeling—and she glanced at Sarah with a deliberate archness—that Sarah, just maybe, might have a similar problem. Perhaps that was why she was anxious about being spied on. Mali dared to say it as if already knowing that Sarah would not react dismissively or with offense, for the simple reason that it was true. And such was the case. Too caught off guard to be offended, Sarah said nothing and received the suggestion without protest. It was an admission of sorts, and she knew it would be taken as such. But she found that it was a relief to share a little part of her secret with someone else. Pent up inside her for weeks, the secret had ratcheted up a permanent tension that had begun to stifle her. At a single stroke, Mali had released the pressure. Just for a moment or two Sarah considered a strenuous denial but just as quickly she decided to let it go and accept the premise.

"I can help you," Mali said very quietly. "I really don't care what you did to get it, any more than you care how I got mine. Am I wrong?"

Sarah looked away reflexively, and her acquiescence was clear to both of them.

"It's nothing to be ashamed of," Mali continued. "Between us and the big bad world it's war and nothing but war. There's no point in losing."

And that's just it, Sarah thought with exhilaration. It *was* war and maybe worse.

Mali leaned in confidentially: "I don't want to ask you any questions. But you can come to me if you want. I'd be happy to do you a favor. I figured from the beginning that you weren't just taking a holiday. You don't mind me saying it, do you?"

"I should, but I don't."

"I was thinking you probably were keeping all of it in your apartment. You can't keep doing that indefinitely. I don't want to know anything about it, but would I be right in saying there might be people coming after you?"

"It's possible."

"Then you should wash it, no question. Or hide it somewhere else. It's a great risk you're taking."

Sarah said she hadn't known what else to do, that she hadn't known how to proceed without any contacts in the city. Perhaps a confidante, she was now thinking, would be a useful thing. And now she had the possibility of making her money disappear without a trace. Mali would want a commission—that much was clear—but Sarah trusted this motive more than the improbably friendly gestures on Mali's part. The girl had glimpsed a way to make a quick buck, and that was rational, believable.

Sensing Sarah's change of mind, Mali pounced with a soft touch. She said she needed to know a few specifics. How much was it exactly?

If Sarah wanted Mali's advice, it would be better not to say a word about it to anyone else while Mali got opinions from some of her contacts in the laundering business. She asked Sarah if that was a good arrangement and, on the turn of a dime, they came to a tacit agreement.

We're two operators, Sarah thought, and now we understand each other at last.

It gave her a solid anchor in this unknown territory, and for the first time in weeks she felt optimistic. Mali understood it, changed the subject, and, as if to lock in the newfound camaraderie between the two, asked Sarah if she would let her take her out into the city, just to have a taste of it? The only way to see a city was with a native.

"There's a pro-government demonstration around the royal palace later tonight. It will be peaceful and probably my mother will be there with her friends. They're having their hair done specially. Do you want to go?"

"Let's. I'm so sick of the Kingdom."

"Then let's leave now and get some lunch on the river. The demonstration will be like a picnic for the people who love the regime. Don't worry about anything."

This was how they left the Kingdom in the glare of midday without any fixed plans, taking the train to Saphan Taksin on the river and riding a boat upriver to the temples, as every tourist does. Mali brought with her two wide-brimmed straw hats, which they wore in the white and blinding afternoon heat on the slopes of Wat Arun looking down at the water as the rice barges plowed their way toward the sea. On the banks of the river, meanwhile, a mindless spell had fallen, the temples were mostly empty, the whitewashed spaces and glittering towers of colored glass abandoned to a primeval sun. It was as if they were the only two people foolish enough to venture outside, to brave the crosscurrents of echoes bellowing from a thousand unseen loudspeakers. From their vantage point, the noise of the city became less audible, and the cacophony of warnings, slogans, and admonitions to stay inside formed an unintelligible wall of sound. Mali could no longer translate them and she made no effort to as they lay among the ceramic flowers of the *prasat* walls. There was a subtle hysteria in the air. It didn't need to be translated verbally. Sarah, for her part, felt a certain unease at being so out in the open. But this was tempered by her longing to escape the claustrophobia of the Kingdom. By the time they had reached the summit of Wat Arun, the sun had rendered her quietly unconscious in some way, mindless and satisfied with an interlude of inertia, like a cat laid out in the sunlight. Even later, as they walked together along the river eating frozen mangoes on sticks, past the small Chinese Hokkien temples from the early nineteenth century, which offered a little shade, she found herself caring less about her secrecy. Even she could sense that the city was slowly being overwhelmed by a larger crisis that would make her insignificant and therefore even more invisible. Finally they came to a deserted joss-house shrine and decided to stop in the coolness.

The Kian Un Keng shrine lay back from the river at the end of a walkway with stone posts, offering a courtyard of pale red tiles. Flowering trees were set around it in cement boxes. They sat under one of them, and behind the swirling dragons on the roofs the first mercurial clouds of the day appeared. Mali took her inside and explained the shrine's importance with a certain relish. Her mother had brought her often when she was a child, and she knew its lore. On the stucco friezes and paintings, patches of blue and emerald still survived, tales from the *Romance of the Three Kingdoms*, the faces of Chinese merchants perhaps drawn from life, raised three-dimensionally from the surface. There was a statue of Guanyin, goddess of luck, mercy, and shipwrecks. The incense sticks were alive but the attendants were probably asleep somewhere. Unusual, Mali said, it was a seated figure of the goddess. Sunk in a reddish gloom, the gold-leaf figure offered a moment of peace. She was worshipped as the female form of the male Bodhisattva Avalokiteśvara, and the Chinese name meant "One who hears the sounds of the world." She was the Chinese Virgin Mary, but she was also the goddess of gamblers in the casinos of Macau. Mali had already picked out two joss sticks and she lit them with her cigarette lighter. She made a prayer, and Sarah thought she should do the same. But her mind was blank. What would she ask Guanyin, goddess of gamblers? A safe passage out of her predicament, another stroke of luck to see her on her way? They went back to the tree. It was now past five o'clock and the intricate carved screens of faded wood had begun to sadden as shadows appeared.

Sarah didn't even know what a Bodhisattva was and yet she understood in some way what Mali meant by offering a private prayer. In her mind, she was sure that obscure signs had appeared to her. A spirit had infected her. In some places spirits remain and you are unconsciously forced to believe in them. It wasn't about your individuality. For two hundred years the Hokkien immigrants had come here to ask their favors of Guanyin and to keep alive the souls of their ancestors. It counted for more than one's little skepticisms. So the moral light and shade inside her shifted positions and she felt a tremendous emotion welling up from nowhere.

Back along the river they took the boat near another temple, Wat Kanlayanamit, over to the other side and the large canal that opened into the river at Atsadang Pier. On the brief crossing this feeling continued to evolve as Sarah gripped the boat's rail. It could have been mistaken for an uncontrollable guilt aligned uncannily with the river seething with knots of water hyacinths. It was touched with a new terror, an understanding that her life up to that point had been utterly meaningless. The lighting of the joss stick to Guanyin had triggered it. She had a venomous thought: that the goddess had come to life and reached inside her with a supernatural hand. She had revealed Sarah as an empty clown, a shadow actor in a drama she had not even created herself. Doomed to an early death, an oblivion that would come more quickly than she had ever imagined. It was obvious that she was nothing, less than nothing.

On their boat were monks from Wat Kanlayanamit, young boys infected with a jittery nervousness, and their presence made her more self-conscious of her worthlessness. As she looked back at Wat Arun she caught a flicker of blue light in the banks of clouds that had massed behind Thonburi. It seemed to smash something fragile in her consciousness. But at the same moment, and as they came into the pier, she heard more loudspeakers booming from the direction of Maha Rat Road a few hundred meters inland, and her inner crisis was pushed aside by larger events. Crowds were already massed in the dying daylight, most of them wearing the bright yellow symbol of the monarchy. Along Maha Rat, an old street that curved around Wat Po, they shuffled from the Grand Palace toward the traffic circle and the canal, and from there up toward Charoen Krung Road and Saranrom Park.

Orderly and quiet, with the mood of a street party, the crowd rolled as a slow wave toward the palace whose god-king they revered. Sarah and Mali merged into it, deafened by wooden clackers and whistles and holding hands to keep themselves from being separated as they passed through the buildings of the Grand Palace. These were now deserted behind their low white walls like giant golden toys. The avenues here were wide, and at the crossroads policemen on motorbikes stood idle and waiting, their helmets discarded, for in the face of so many sympathizers with the regime the government had told them to stand down. A few cries of "Martyrdom!" went up, as inexplicable as anything else. She felt Mali's sweaty hand lock in hers, an act that transmitted to Sarah a spontaneous complicity and security in the midst of so much irrationality. She herself was no longer isolated in her guilt.

At Chitralada Royal Villa the crowds were strung out along the stately moats that surrounded the palace, the mood as unpredictable as it was expectant. Mali, knowing her way, guided Sarah around the moats, on the far side of which light displays in the shape of pineapples and lotuses lit up the walls as if expressly designed to calm the crowds and make them feel even more childish. Along these avenues long plastic marquees had been set up with screens to relay demonstrations elsewhere in the city. In them sat hundreds of farmers bused in from the deep south and given a little wage to reward their support for the government. They sat on tarpaulins eating from tin bowls, merry and bewildered, lost in the big city but visibly excited to be there for the first time in their lives, lost among stalls selling paramilitary equipment, gas masks and military knives, air guns and body armor. The two women picked their way through them, and to Sarah, Mali's explanation was hard to grasp. It was a festival of solidarity with the established order; it was a protest against a shadowy enemy that had hardly shown itself. Farther on lay Amporn Gardens, where the same masses had swept up around the equestrian statue of Rama V and were listening to speeches broadcast from a different part of the city. Had it not been so middle-class in tone, the possibility of a riot would not have been inconceivable. But the large numbers of enraged elderly ladies hurling their energy into blowing whistles and shouting support for army and country made it unlikely.

Mali finally let go of Sarah's hand and said that the one good thing about the evening was that they had not run into her mother. She looked up at Sarah's face and understood how she had received the last two hours. The American was good at keeping her emotions to herself, but the heat and the long walk and the atmosphere of hatred had done its work to unravel her. The quiet, permanent antagonism in Sarah's eyes had been replaced by a blank and obstinate refusal to participate any longer. At the same time the masses around them had begun chanting, "*Arrest the black hands!*" and through the park's somber trees came thin men in masks to assist the mood, lead pipes in their hands swinging back and forth like schoolmasters' switches. There was nobody to beat, but the intention had to be displayed in public for the satisfaction of all. The objects of their derision and loathing would be discovered soon enough, walking like cockroaches in plain daylight, the filthy democrats and libertarians paid by the CIA and determined to lay low the proud centuries of Siam.

As the night's curfew approached they defied it by going to a nightclub on Soi 11, a place that must have come to an arrangement with the police. There was a dwarf elevator attendant dressed in a scarlet uniform with gold rope, and on the dance floor were the children of the rich, the same people they had been with around the statue of Rama V, dancing high on *yaa baa*. Sarah and Mali danced as well, and Sarah's darkness lifted when Mali gave her a hit of the circulating amphetamine. The hours accelerated in that way, unnoticed and free of drag. For Sarah it was the longest and most satisfying day of her life. The night filled with spirits and their music. For a moment, as Mali twisted in front of her lit by a strobe, the flickering form seemed both electrified and ethereal. She felt her pulse race. Had they even met Guanyin and walked to the Chitralada Royal Villa, walked among the zombies with their whistles? If that had been a dream, she had woken up as soon as she had swallowed a red *yaa baa* pill. When they left the club at five thirty the curfew had lifted and they walked home along the back streets. It felt even less real than the revelation in the joss house in Kian un Keng.

When they arrived at the Kingdom the doormen saluted with an appreciably diminished formality, and they each went their separate ways without fuss. Sarah ran a bath and lay in it for a long time before falling asleep for the rest of the day, still sedated with the *yaa baa*. In her dream she was sinking in beautiful blue water whose surface was shadowed by the motionless forms of ice floes. A boat was rowing its way across that same surface, the oars dipping into it and churning the water. She knew who was in the boat but not why they were rowing. And from below there rose the echoes of whales passing far below her and looking up at her in turn.

It was eight in the evening when she woke, ordered in Korean delivery, and watched the news on her computer. An army general was there, talking soothingly but beyond her understanding. She turned the laptop off and went to sit on her balcony with its view of the university. As usual there was a stage with lights and a local band playing for the students. A fierce wind ripped through the warehouses and the sky was all ragged, racing clouds and wandering stars. From a neighboring tower block, soft showers of welding sparks floated down into the dark. The sleep had cleared her system and she felt an unaccustomed relaxation, a calm as large as the sky she was sitting under. Everything felt clearer.

The most important event of the previous twenty-four hours, now that she recollected it in a more rational spirit, had been Mali's offer to launder her money. Seeing that some unspoken pact had taken place between them, it was Mali whom she trusted above everyone else in the Kingdom. If Sarah had to trust her with such a dangerous transaction, so be it; that no longer felt so risky to her. There was just the lingering uncertainty to contend with, dating from the very first moment they had met. She had already tried to make her peace with it, but it had not ceased to irk her. She could not position Mali in the class system of a society she didn't know, or even in the psychological niche to which a person of her background would likely belong. There was only her personal charm to go by. As the lights around the Kingdom began to extinguish themselves, the gardens sinking into a gloom pierced only by the lights of the spirit houses, she waited for midnight, when the curfew siren sounded across the neighborhood and the *soi* dogs caught in the streetlamps' glare stood in silent alarm and raised their snouts toward the higher floors.

EIGHT

At three o'clock in the morning the rain stopped and Sarah rolled slowly onto her back and opened her eyes. As she lay half-conscious, staring up at the nightly gecko that seemed to accompany her sleep like a protector, her phone began to ring. She had left it on her kitchen table and couldn't summon the effort to retrieve it, so she let it ring. After a minute of pealing bells, the phone fell silent again. But a few seconds later it started up again. By the time she got to the kitchen it had fallen silent a second time. She might have called back, but the number was concealed. She dried off her sweat just as she realized that the air-conditioning units were off. She must have forgotten to turn them on before she fell asleep, or else the ancient fuses had blown. A moment later, she realized that the lights were out as well. She groped her way to the air-conditioning switch of the main room and the two light switches next to them and flicked them down. The power was out. It must have failed while she was sleeping. Outside, the nearby towers were also cloaked in darkness but the streetlamps continued to burn away between the vinelike cables.

She put on a robe and waited for the phone to ring again—but it remained quiet. It was Mali, she thought instinctively. But why would the number be hidden? She took the phone and stepped into her maid's room out back behind the kitchen. From here, outside in the elements, she could peer into the landings, including her own, even though only the emergency-exit lights remained alive. She wanted to see if anyone was approaching her door from the public landing. Sure enough, the outer door rattled as if someone was trying to open it and then a hand began to rap frantically on the glass.

Sarah went to the door, opened it quietly, and slipped onto the landing to peer through the corrugated glass to the far side. Mali's face came into view, moving right up to the surface, one side half-lit by the exit light above the door.

"Open up," she whispered urgently but quietly, no longer rattling the handle.

When Sarah opened the door, Mali stepped inside the landing and slammed the door shut behind her. A gust of sour wind came in with her. The landing was so dark—only the red numerals of the elevator were lit—that there was an instant confusion between them, a mutual shudder emanating from the strange circumstance itself. Mali didn't need any expressions of surprise; the energy around her was sinister and unprecedented. She was dressed in a nightgown, and even in the shadows Sarah noticed that there were tiny flecks of blood running down its front until they reappeared on the tops of her bare feet, where they had not yet dried. Her hair was matted and shocked into wildness, and her eyes had no stable centers, as if she had been woken up during a nightmare but had not yet realized that she was no longer inside the dream. Then, a second later, Sarah recalled Ryo's plunging hand and the way Mali had tried to protect her face with a raised arm.

Mali looked up and said, "Can I come inside? I can't be out here." Sarah helped her into the main room, laid her on the sofa, and went back to lock the outside door. He must have beaten her again but this time it was worse, and she therefore waited to be sure that he hadn't followed his victim to her landing, then retreated and locked her own door after her. Now that the power was down he would be bolder.

Mali opened her bloodied fingers to reveal her house keys clasped in one hand. It was an invitation for Sarah to take them. Only then did Sarah notice something more obvious even than the blood. Mali's left eye was swollen and her cheek had clearly been struck as well, a sweeping blow of one hand. Her lip had split. It was not difficult to make the inference.

"He's there?"

Mali nodded and looked away, all her playful energy sucked out of her and vaporized. Sarah sat with her, outraged on Mali's behalf, but simultaneously paralyzed by the absence of any ready plan. What did Mali want her to do? The lights were out, the units plunged in darkness. Surely it was more likely that Ryo had left of his own accord. No one would linger in a suffocating apartment with no power. And for that matter, she needed to know how long Mali had been in this state. A few minutes, an hour? It made a difference. But Mali didn't reply to this question. Listless and confused herself, she rotated onto her side and went fetal. Sarah leaned down to her face and smelled the alcohol on her breath, thick and sweet. She had been drinking bourbon.

"What happened?" Sarah began. She laid a hand on Mali's shivering back drenched with sweat. If the room had been hot when Sarah woke up it was even hotter now. The shivering must have been a nervous reaction. Mali began to talk in bursts. As Sarah had imagined, they had been drinking heavily and fallen into a violent argument. So it often went with them, Sarah was already thinking. It was bad chemistry, which she already knew about, of course. The argument had escalated. The beating had begun, the throwing of heavy objects, the tussles and bites. She had bitten his shoulder in self-defense. He had picked up a spatula—yes, as ridiculous as that was—from the kitchen and used it to rain down blows on her legs. She didn't know how it had happened so quickly, so chaotically. It was the alcohol, for one thing. She had defended herself with a jade ashtray of her mother's.

"What do you mean, 'defended'?"

"I hit him with it."

In a single moment the probable truth crashed in upon Sarah's previous assumptions. Mali had wielded the ashtray, all eight pounds of it, as a hammer with razor-sharp edges. She had split open his head with one blow, crushing the attack and causing him to fall backward onto the bed, knocked out cold. At first she had not even noticed. She had run to the bathroom to see to herself. Lacerations and lesions, her lip bleeding—as Sarah could see. She seemed to be making the case for herself before Sarah had even said anything in response. Then, once she had washed her face and legs, she went back to the bedroom ready to deescalate. The shock of the attack had actually made her more lenient. But Ryo was unconscious and the pillows were soaked with his blood. The split in his temple was three inches long.

The ashtray lay in its own pool of blood on the carpet. She realized at once what it meant but she had waited awhile before
deciding to come to Sarah. She was too drunk to think about
the police. If she called them and they came, the disaster would
envelop her entire family. She had a responsibility to think it
over first. Then the power had gone out—a classic Thai *fai-dup*.
But it was a godsend. It had given her an hour to act by herself.
A Westerner could never understand the intricacies of the social
system, the levels of shame and loss of face, the way scandals
worked in the unquestioned hierarchy here. Sarah had to trust
her on these points. From then on, Mali was going to have to
move fast and she only wanted to know if she could depend on
Sarah.

Mali had now taken off the nightgown and was in her underwear. She got up and went out onto the balcony, staring at the
rain as if stabilizing herself. Meanwhile Sarah's mind churned.
Her first thought was to hide the bloodied nightgown, which
she balled up, then went into the kitchen area and stuffed it beneath the large pile of laundry already in the washing machine.
It also gave her a pause in which she could consider her reply.
Naturally, it was a folly to go along with Mali's desire to not call
even the front desk. There was no way they could not find out
what had happened. She would be an accomplice if together
they tried to conceal the events, but was this not what Mali was
suggesting? A dazzling presumption on her part. Even she, with
the obscure connections she kept hinting at, could not conceal
something as momentous as this. *No,* Sarah kept thinking, looking at the girl in her underwear standing outside in the rain, *you
cannot get involved any further. Call the front desk yourself.* But she
didn't want to do it. Mysteriously rooted, her desire was to do

what Mali wanted. It went against all her own interests—but she still had to weigh the delicate pros and cons here. If she called the front desk she would be front and center of a massive police invasion of the Kingdom. She would be interrogated in immense detail, her apartment would be searched and her background delved into. It was everything that she most feared. Her scheme would be exposed and destroyed, inevitably and swiftly. Her immigration status would be explored and calls would be made to her home country, where she was already (as far as she knew) a person wanted for fraud. Making that call to the front desk would be the most calamitous mistake of her life. Perhaps, in fact, that was why Mali had come to her in the first place. She knew that Sarah wanted to avoid the authorities as much as she did.

Sarah was therefore caught in this paradox and was unable to move beyond it. Slowly, she came to understand that the safest thing was to go along with whatever Mali had in mind. It was her society; she understood the rules and the twilight zones and she alone could steer Sarah away from the prying eyes of the law. It was too late, in any case, to become an upright citizen and call the police.

She went out onto the balcony and for a tense moment put her arm around Mali's now-wet shoulders.

Matter-of-factly, and without any modulation in her tone, Mali said that in her opinion the best course of action was to dispose of the evidence and for her to call her associates, people she knew who had experience of how to handle these things swiftly. It was a brutal thing, but it would be less brutal for them if they did it this way.

"I know you don't want the police here," she said to Sarah. "So let's do it my way, OK? I'm sorry to get you involved, though."

"What associates?"

"People I know. They're not friends exactly. But they have their uses."

"You mean underworld people?" Sarah found that her unconscious mind was moving much faster than her conscious one.

Mali scoffed. "That's a big word."

"But it's what you mean."

"You'd rather I asked a couple of janitors?" Mali hissed.

"No, I didn't mean that."

"I think you'd also like to keep it quiet. We'd *both* like that, no?"

Sarah retreated, and her moment's confusion couldn't be hidden from Mali, who seemed to know more than she was admitting. Her paranoia lit up her responses and she quietly went along with Mali's suggestions.

For her part, as if to reassure Sarah, Mali insisted that it hadn't been premeditated. She had lashed out in a moment of blind rage and then the void had come upon her.

"It happened in a few moments—I lost my mind. I had no one else to turn to."

"What about your family?" Sarah said, stating the obvious. "Can they help?"

"My family?"

For Mali and her family the only problem was that Ryo was a foreigner. Not only that, he was Japanese. The Japanese were a privileged caste within the country. No harm could be done to them with impunity. Any event that affected them brought with it complications. Her mother might not want to get involved with something so dangerous. If her daughter threw herself on her mercy, of course, she'd have little choice. But she might try to persuade Mali that the best course of action would be to go to the police, confess, and claim self-defense. They would accept it, surely. With the bribe inserted at that juncture she would, in all likelihood, avoid jail time. It was a common eventuality there: the rich rarely saw the insides of prisons. But all the same, involving her family carried with it risks and complications of a different kind. Far better to avoid all that. Moreover, it was well nigh impossible to keep secrets inside the porous labyrinth of the Kingdom. The corridors themselves were conduits of lightning-fast gossip. As in the wider society, where everything was concealed, it ran on gossip in the way that a car runs on gas.

"Do you know that Ryo really works for a Japanese company?" Sarah asked.

Mali appeared to have a ready answer: "He said that, but maybe it's not true. I don't even know if he works for a company at all."

"Is it possible he doesn't?"

"I've never checked up on him. He just said he worked for one but I never thought about it."

"What kind of company?"

"I think it was insurance."

"You *think* or you know?"

"We didn't talk shop much—obviously."

"Do you know where he lives?"

"He said he was living in a serviced apartment on Soi Twenty-Six. I never went there, though. I mean, he never invited me back."

"Where is he from?"

"Hokkaido."

"So he's just a tourist, a long-term visitor?"

"In a way. I met him in a bar. A wine bar in Thong Lor."

"And he never said he was working in Bangkok?"

"He never said anything about himself. He only talked about his house in Hokkaido."

"Wife?"

Mali shook her head. Never married, no offspring.

Sarah brought her back inside and closed the sliding windows, her mind turning relentlessly inside its own confusions. It was becoming clearer: the lonely man escaped from his sexually pedestrian life back home, a minor job with a moderately significant company, and a taste for the ladies that he could not indulge to the same degree in a developed country. Sarah already knew that he was a petty sadist. Seated side by side in the dark, she and Mali talked more as Sarah pressed to find out what she could before she did anything. She established that Ryo had come without baggage or attachments, and that his death would not be noticed by a large number of people. He had been a loner with fantasies of being a playboy in a city far from his own society. He must have dated other women, but would any depend on his continued appearance in their lives? Like the vast multitude of foreign single men in Bangkok, he was a floating piece of jetsam carried north, south, east, and west by invisible tides that swept them along from day to day, year to year. When they died here, as they often did, nobody noticed or remembered them. Many were suicides, disappeared for their own reasons. Their vanishings, in any case, were rarely headline news. Thais took it to be the natural order of the world and they let such things pass quietly once the outward formalities were observed. This was all in their favor. What they needed in the present moment, Mali said, was a little time, a few hours, the continuation of the black-out. They needed also to hold their nerve, their cold-bloodedness.

It was then, just as Sarah's resolve formed in response, that they heard—distant and very faint, as if emanating from the bottom of a well—a distinct barking arising from the atrium. Mali tensed and they both knew that it was the dog, the toy poodle, who, of course, had been abandoned inside the apartment with a cadaver which it could smell.

"I have to go get him," Mali said.

"No, you shouldn't go back there. I'll go. It's better if I go. Stay here."

Instinctively, Sarah knew that this was what Mali wanted. She insisted a second time and then got up to act upon her offer. As she did so Mali reached for her phone; she said she was going to make the call to her associates and that they would come within an hour. She pointed out that the front desk had seen Ryo come in at nine the previous evening but that the shift changed at midnight and the night staff usually slept on the job. They noticed nothing after one A.M. and didn't care much one way or the other. It all depended on who came looking for Ryo, who needed and loved him enough to notice his absence. To whom was he vital? Sarah thought that they would probably find out by the end of the following day. With that, she went to the kitchen to find a small flashlight that was included in an emergency kit strapped to the inside of the fuse box. She un-clipped it, checked that the batteries were operational, and slipped out onto the landing by the light of its beam. By now the landings were stifling and filled with moths, which had settled along the walls and around the exit lights. The absence of the main lights had stilled them. She opened the outer door to the atrium and quietly passed into the landing with its smell of baked dust and its lofty sound of rain tapping against the roof glass. The emergency stairs were the only way down to the fourteenth floor. There was a smell of burned rubber and gasoline, and the walls oozed with a curious dampness. On the fourteenth floor she shot the beam down the landing bridge, just as Ryo had done himself in pursuit of her a few nights earlier, and something scuttled away from it immediately, a rat probably, or a mouse. She turned the flashlight upon her hand, now carrying the keys. The blood on them had now transferred to her own fingers.

She entered the landing and used the keys to admit herself into the apartment. The first thing she noticed was a heavy odor of men's cologne. The main windows in the front room were open and the cacophonous rain had swept into the room, showering the floors and the sofas. There were tissues scattered all over. She picked her way through them until she was at the windows, the wet wind blowing through them. There were bourbon bottles on the table and a dozen dirty glasses. As she looked them over she heard the soft whine of the little dog, who was cowering under the sofa. She kneeled down and enticed her out into the open. Recognizing Sarah's smell, she licked her face for a moment and then Sarah put her gently back on the floor, where she retreated back under the sofa. Sarah went into the kitchen. The utensil drawers were not open and there was no disorder except for a large mortar filled with crushed herbs and with two spoons inserted into it. Sarah went to the door of the master bedroom and looked in. On the bed, the man lay as if asleep, but she saw in the same instant that his entire form was wrapped in blankets. Little drops of blood were spattered over their surface and next to him on the floor lay the ashtray. A small chunk of bloodied flesh clung to one of its pointed corners.

She waited for her heartbeat to slow after the first shock and then looked quickly around the room. The blinds were drawn, and through the narrow gaps she could just make out the bridge. No one could have seen Mali wrapping up the body, or anything else. She parted two slats with her fingers to get a better view of the whole bridge. The forbidding wall of units was a lifeless blank. Half a dozen of them had a decent view of Mali's windows but none showed any signs of life at that hour, not even an oil lamp brought out to deal with the power outage. It was safe. She closed the blinds again and crept back to the main room. There was no sign of a struggle, just a drunken late-night drinking session. She saw a cell phone on the coffee table and assumed that it was Ryo's; it was worth pocketing. Likewise a pair of calf-leather drivers, which she noticed were lying in the middle of the room, cast off a few hours before. Otherwise she could not see anything else of his. Sarah went back to the bedroom and felt a malevolent urge to see the face at least once before it disappeared forever. She would be the last person to see it before it was burned to ash.

With her breath caught in her throat, she reached down and pulled apart the folds of the blanket, yet refrained from shining the flashlight upon the smashed and battered face inside. The whole left side of it had been reduced to a liquid pulp that had not yet started to stiffen and congeal. She stepped back, throttled with disgust, and her hand rose to her mouth to prevent the upswell of bile that might have broken through her clenched teeth and flowed down her chin. Her stomach contracted and she staggered backward out of the room toward the sofa, where the dog cowered, her senses quivering. The clock on the mantelpiece read three thirty-seven, and a few flies had already drifted in from the outside world, attracted by the prospect of a vast meal.

NINE

An hour later, the power had still not returned and the rain had grown more lavishly intense. The gardens around the Kingdom suffered the onslaught without resistance, the ornamental pools overflowing, the fan palms shuddering on their long stalks. On a neighboring balcony a long bed of rare imported skeleton flowers had turned from milky white to a lustrous transparence in the rain. Sarah had left the doors to Mali's apartment open and there was nothing more for them to do but wait for the men Mali had called to arrive and do their work. The minutes passed as if dragging their heels. Sarah used the time to open the first-aid kit that had come with the unit and dress Mali's wounds as best she could. While she did this Mali was stoic. She told Sarah that they should stay inside and on no account should they go outside in case any of the staff were wandering the landings trying to restore the power. If Mali or Sarah were seen there it would be a serious problem for them later.

Meanwhile, as they passed the time reassuring each other,

Sarah made them tea and the dog curled up on the sofa and fell asleep. Eventually they heard a whirring in the silence beyond the rain. It must have been the elevator going down to the rear of the building, unseen from the lobby. The elevators all ran on an emergency backup generator that by law was never allowed to fail. At the entrance to this elevator, trucks could park while shipments were loaded, and indeed this was how furniture was usually delivered to all the units. Of course: this must be what was happening now—a delivery in reverse. The machinery continued to tick over for some time, and then just as suddenly it fell silent again, and that was as much as either of them would witness of Ryo's removal from the Kingdom.

Down at the base of the tower, she imagined, where the black canal ran under the banana trees, the van would be stationed with its lights off, and there Ryo would be whisked away under the cover provided by a failed electricity system. The whole thing would have taken less than six minutes. It was no different from the discreet removal of the body of Mr. Lim. The Kingdom had its own method for these disposals. The service elevator served a double purpose, then—it could import furniture or export cadavers. The building by its very nature facilitated such discretions. The staff all participated in these rituals, discreet to the last man and woman, perpetuating as a group without written instructions the laws of secrecy that maintained the building's harmony. This harmony, Sarah now understood, would help her to survive.

Though Mali slept on the sofa, exhausted and wounded, Sarah stayed awake waiting for the electricity to return. It finally did so at seven. The fans in her apartment stirred to life and the coolers returned to their duties. The temperature began rapidly to fall once again and the sweat dried on their skin. Mali awoke shortly afterward, and in the instant of regaining consciousness her eyes were black with fear. Then, shaken into self-awareness, she got ahold of herself. She announced her intention to go back to her unit and make it exactly as it had been before Ryo's visit. She would clean everything meticulously, wipe away every trace. It was then that she noticed the calfskin drivers that Sarah had placed on a sideboard cupboard in the main room. So Sarah had been mindful of removing them. It was good that Sarah had taken them, but now she would have to get rid of them herself as discreetly as she was able. It would be best to burn them, but if that was not feasible she could bury them at the bottom of a bag of trash and take it to the same service elevators where the trash was also collected and removed.

"I'm going to go," she said wearily. "I think we shouldn't talk on the phone for a little while. Just stay here and wait."

"I think that's best too."

"Let everything calm down. Like nothing happened."

"Yes."

Yet a cold panic had begun to surface in Sarah. She felt her mouth grow parched and the normal ease of her body contracted.

"When will I hear from you, then?"

"A few days from now. Can you do it?"

"You mean go about my business as usual? Of course I can do it."

"I might go away for a few days myself."

"Understood."

It was a small shock to Sarah. She would be left alone with the aftermath, if any came. Yet she saw the logic of this course of action. She stepped toward Mali and reflexively took her hand for a moment, squeezed it by way of commitment. The girl's eyes were hollow. It was as if she had passed into a different dimension of life, one where she could not be followed. In the next few days Sarah would wonder incessantly about this dimension and why it was so impenetrable. It was not a deliberate coldness or hostility, merely a distance. She reasoned that it must have been shock.

When Mali had finally departed, taking the dog with her, Sarah put the shoes into a garbage bag and left it inconspicuously among all the others at the collection point on the landing. She then looked through Ryo's curiously unlocked phone, whose screen displayed his last three calls to car services and nothing more. No relative from Japan had called, and no one from his office, as far as she could tell. She took out the battery and made up a second garbage bag into which she slipped the phone. She took this out as well, proud of her steady calmness of mind, and then decided to return to her regular life as Mali had suggested. It was wise. Thus the erasure of Ryo, as far as she was concerned, had been complete.

As she returned from the landing after having disposed of the second bag, she heard the elevator bell ring and a form stepped out of the car into her landing just before she did so herself. It was an old Thai lady about to extend a finger to Sarah's bell. Sarah didn't recognize her. The lady had come from the seventeenth floor, she explained, because a small dog had come running up to their floor and she had heard—the staff had suggested to her—that it was Sarah's. Her husband had seen the animal running from floor to floor and had called reception to ask for their advice. If the dog was Sarah's, had she lost control of it?

"It's not mine," Sarah said hurriedly. "Who said it was?"

"I can't remember. I think my husband said it was Pop the caretaker. Is he wrong, then?"

The woman was in slippers and gym pants, her hair hennaed and drawn up into a bob. Sarah had never seen her before, not even in the elevator. *Khun Kaewmak?*

"My husband says dogs go mad if you leave them alone too long. If it's yours, you really shouldn't let it run wild on the landings. It's against the regulations. You do know the regulations, don't you?"

"As I said, it isn't mine."

"Are you sure? Then it's very odd that they say it's yours."

The lady lingered annoyingly, scrutinizing the *farang*.

"I'm sorry," Sarah muttered. "But it isn't mine. It's a mistake on the part of the staff. I don't know why—"

The woman peered over her into the apartment, as if afflicted by neighborly paranoia.

"So you have permission to own a pet," she said. "Who's your landlady?"

Since the woman was obviously senile, Sarah went along with it: "Mrs. Lim."

The woman pedantically explained that the actual Thai-style name was Srilimratanakul, but now shortened to the more obviously Chinese Lim.

"Ah," she concluded. "I thought the Lims had a no-pet policy."

"I'm sorry you were disturbed by someone else's dog," Sarah said again, with an air of finality. "Please tell your husband that the dog won't be going mad. She was probably just bored."

"It's quite all right."

Sarah had to close the door almost in the woman's face. Once barricaded inside, though, she waited for the elevator bell to sound a second time and then let her relief overwhelm her. The Kingdom had settled into its usual torpid inertia. Accordingly, she slept for the rest of the day.

By sundown, mist had curled around the tops of the towers and flashes of lightning took the form of immense trees with dozens of branches that reached down and momentarily touched the earth. A great stillness had descended upon the construction sites and the warehouses where the tree frogs sang. The fading light turned the patchwork of gardens and villas and apartment buildings into a white-and-emerald panorama before twilight finally descended. Outside, in this penumbral moment, the company leaf blowers droned along the canal and little puffs of white vapor rose past the window—the mosquito-extermination service had resumed its work. A few cases of dengue fever had been reported in recent weeks and the insect exterminators were busy.

Refreshed after her long sleep, Sarah went down to the mezzanine-floor gardens to sit in the shade by the empty pool and watch the sun's image burning in the windowpanes above her. By the pool, under the shade of the frangipani, two older *farang* men lay on loungers reading their papers. Sarah was relieved to find that the world had returned to humdrum normality, and that her place in it was as small as it had been before. An immense crane turned slowly above the shacks built insolently right against the Kingdom's upper-class wall, seemingly in defiance of the site's shutdown. The panic of the previous night had subsided and she felt serene in a surprising way. She had performed a considerable favor which she was sure would be repaid handsomely. This had been thrust upon her, it was true, but in this new life Sarah had constructed for herself she had to roll with its unpredictability. There was just the thought of Pop misinforming the tenants about her ownership of Mali's dog. She couldn't think of any reason why he would have done this. It felt like malice, but to what end?

As the gardens fell into gloom, the crane ceased its operation for the day and in the air above her a few fireflies appeared, drifting on the breeze as they wandered among the pillars and the flower beds, their luminescence turning off and on so that as a group they sparkled. It was, she knew, the hour when Pop would come up from the ground floor and survey the garden floor, which was under his nocturnal jurisdiction. She felt his presence, announced by the fireflies, and she stirred herself from the pool, threw on her shirt, and wandered after the glowing lightning bugs.

Within the galleries of columns she now heard a dog's barking, just as Mrs. Kaewmak must have heard it earlier. It echoed from far off, and after a while she understood that it was descending slowly from the upper floors toward the gardens as if being walked on a leash. Sarah withdrew a little into the gardens so she could see who was walking the dog: it was a woman she had never seen before, another old lady from the upper floors, this one dressed in a housecoat with rubber boots and holding a retractable leash at the end of which Mali's dog frisked as it was dragged along. Mali must have paid her to look after Whiskey while she was away, and the woman must have let the dog out earlier by mistake, causing it to run free through the building, disturbing the tenants. Now she walked through the gardens with a limp while the dog leaped uselessly at uncatchable fireflies, before eventually sitting on one of the garden swings to eat a bar of chocolate morosely, kicking herself into motion and letting the dog wander into the miniature palm grove. So, Sarah thought, a little wounded, Mali had not told her everything about her life after all. Unsurprisingly, there was more to the intricate social relations inside the Kingdom than she had suspected, relations that did not involve ignorant foreigners at all. Impelled by a resentful curiosity, she approached the woman, enticing the dog to come and greet her. A few meters from the swing Whiskey and Sarah tussled affectionately and the old woman raised her nose toward the interloper. It was as if she could smell something alien, a different skin, a particular brand of soap. Sarah was about to say something to her but at the last moment she held back. Then the woman herself addressed the dog, asking it who it was who had arrived—*phen krai?*—and in that moment Sarah realized that she couldn't see. Yet her nostrils had flared, and Sarah knew that she was detected by the other senses. She moved backward, very quietly, and made her way to the side of the pool, alerted to the slow realization that what the old woman could sense, with acute precision, was her fear.

TEN

At the end of that same week, Ximena sent her an invitation to meet for dinner at a nearby restaurant. The invitation was offered casually in a note slipped under Sarah's door with an old-fashioned touch of subterfuge, handwritten, but there was no indication that it had been extended to Mali. It was to be at a Japanese place called Ten Sui, which Sarah had never heard of. To Sarah's eye the note seemed offhand and this implied that the other two had no inkling of what had happened between Mali and Sarah. If this was so, it was important that she show up at Ten Sui and pretend that she expected Mali to be there as well. If Mali didn't show up, she would have to affect an effortless surprise. Aside from this she was pleased to be able to go out again. She had spent that week completely alone, seeing no one and not leaving the Kingdom. The burden of that solitude had begun to crush her hour by hour. On the Tuesday night, therefore, she dressed up as haughtily as she could. She wanted the men in their peaked caps at the gate to notice her self-flaunting.

Natalie and Ximena were already there when Sarah found Ten Sui on Soi 16, only a few hundred yards from Sukhumvit Road, and stepped across the stones of a rustic path that led through a raked Zen garden lit by lines of red paper lanterns. These moved in a temperamental wind as shadows were flung around the stone lanterns. They had a table by the outer windows that looked over this same garden, where the rocks and pools were lit at ground level. It was a place for Toyota executives and their visiting mothers from Tokyo, for men entertaining formidable superiors. Ximena was dressed in extravagant black evening wear, merry and already a little tipsy—self-pushed over the edge, Sarah thought. There was no sign of Mali.

Ximena asked her about it immediately: "I sent her a message like I did with you, but she didn't reply. I just assumed she'd come."

But after half an hour she was still not there. As a result, a slight awkwardness descended upon them until they ordered and the plates began to come one by one. Nabe soup in paper cups heated from beneath by burners and natto in black lacquer dishes. The three of them raised a sake toast and Natalie asked Sarah at once if their maid, Goi, had come to see her yet.

"She came, yes."

"Finally! She forgets sometimes. Do you like her?"

"I do."

"We've had her for three years. You're in good hands," Natalie went on, to make the conversation flow. "And Roland says she's the best maid we've ever had."

"I second that," Ximena said. "She's discreet too."

About what? Sarah thought.

"Roland says she's the most trustworthy person in the country."

Sarah asked if Goi had a passkey for all the units. She hadn't wanted to ask her. The answer was that she did, all the maids did.

"Maybe she would know if Mali is still here," Ximena said.

"I can ask her." Natalie turned to Sarah. "You didn't see her yourself, I suppose? Mali, I mean."

"No."

"I have a feeling she isn't here. She comes and goes, as we know."

They kept their voices low now. The political events of the past few weeks had begun to wear on private exchanges in public spaces, as if privacy itself had shrunk as a consequence. Natalie mentioned a strike in the hotel business and an unpleasant scene one morning in the dining room: a government official eating there with his wife had a boiled egg thrown at him by a student. She pointed out that the protests were spreading and morphing. In restaurants, she had noticed, people looked over their shoulders before talking about the situation, afraid of being overheard, reported by an eavesdropping ear.

"I'm surprised they're so busy," Ximena observed, looking around. "Eiffel is nearly empty these days. People are staying at home. They say everyone's moving their money abroad because something's about to happen."

Natalie observed that the hotel had been running at half occupancy for a month now. The high rollers had passed on; the Arab families had gone to Beirut instead.

"I prefer it like this," Ximena said. "I love cities that are half-empty. If I had my way—I would plant bombs myself to create a crisis."

"If it turns bad I'll just lock the door and live on canned tuna," Sarah said. "I have about a hundred cans in my cupboard."

"Spoken like a true American!" Ximena cackled.

"I would just come here every night," Natalie said.

It was Ximena who sensed that there was a slightly different energy in the group that evening. Something had happened, and it occurred to her that it might explain Mali's absence. It was Sarah who betrayed the shift. She was as overdressed as Ximena herself, but it seemed to her that Sarah was advertising herself in a manner that was not in keeping with how she normally behaved. When Mali's name came up she flinched, and a visible effort crept into her face, drawing the muscles tighter. Did they have a row, a falling-out? Her invitation to Mali had gone unanswered, as she had said, but the silence on Mali's part had seemed more total than that. A few nights after pushing the invite under Mali's door she had gone down to ring her bell and ask her directly, and had noticed that the slip of paper was still there. So she was not at home at all. Her instinct had been to ask Goi if she knew either way, but a sense of discretion had persuaded her not to do that. Now, as they swilled their sake boldly, she looked to Sarah for clues. The American girl had a strange air about her that night. Her hair looked unnaturally brassy, as if all its color had been sprayed on. Ximena hadn't noticed that before, but now that she did, it seemed extraordinary. She's a contrivance, Ximena thought, and spent some time observing her hands, the garish color of her face—too much makeup— and the sheer bizarreness of her dyed hair. Sarah was also talking too excitedly, as if making up for lost and misspent time cooped up inside the Kingdom. But apart from anything else, Ximena now realized that the American wasn't as naïve as she had first seemed. There was something pugnacious about her ever-moving gaze, the way the eyes moved quickly when alerted. Bolder, less introverted, she was putting on a performance, which was surely unnecessary. As they drank on, her face grew redder and more greasily luminous. Sarah evidently wasn't used to drinking with such intensity, but she had taken to it. It was possible that she was just biding her time until she could summon up the courage to step out onto the stage of her own little life.

"I suppose in ten years' time we'll all be somewhere else," Sarah was now saying breezily. "I don't know how Western exiles live here—don't they go crazy day by day?"

"Well, some of us have jobs," Natalie observed calmly.

"Do you know what frightens me the most? That the future will be just utterly boring. Forever and forever. Nothing new or exciting is ever going to happen ever again. It's all been done." From out of the past a phrase drifted into Sarah's inebriated consciousness, though she didn't utter it. *The suburb of the soul.* It must have been Laverty who had spoken it to her in a previous life.

"As for the Westerners staying sane," Ximena had begun replying, "it's simple for me. They think history is over and no longer affects them. They don't think of it as involving themselves anymore. Protests, riots, coups—zero interest. It doesn't concern them now."

"I'm like that too, I suppose. I can't help it."

"But it's not entirely true," Natalie said. "It does affect you. You just don't have a theory about it."

"No, I'm not political," Sarah admitted. "I feel like it has nothing to do with me. And maybe it doesn't."

"But it does. Eventually, it does."

"Eventually, yes—but only if you stick around. I won't stick around."

"Because you don't need to."

That's your privilege, Ximena was about to add, but she knew how tacky and modish the phrase sounded now.

"My guess is we'll all be alone in our different ways," Natalie continued. "Our generation is going to be the loneliest. Our middle age is going to be uniquely horrible. We'll be alone with our cats and our books. No one wants to admit it, but that's where it ends up. Solitude plus cats."

For herself, that would be a relatively rosy future. "Well," Sarah sighed as an afterthought, "no one gets out of here alive anyway."

"That's the silver lining," Ximena said. "I mean, that's the one thing that should give us hope—"

Sarah raised her glass, a toast—to nothingness.

"*Chaiyo.*"

Nothingness was in any case suggested by the raked Zen garden that lay on the far side of their window. Around it the tropical trees, slightly out of place, transmitted a more animist energy that reached into the dining room. They felt swayed by it, made fatalistic and inclined to quietism. The pools shook with raindrops. Before long, however, the subject of Mali arose once more and they idly tossed their competing theories about her across the table at one another. Natalie asked Sarah again if she had seen her recently. She sensed that Sarah would lie but she wanted to see how she did it. Sure enough, Sarah lied because she felt she had to.

"It's been a while," she said.

"Did you two never go out alone by yourselves, then?"

"Why do you say that?"

"I just had the feeling. Maybe it was something you said a while back."

"Did I say something?"

Natalie saw the girl raise a hand to the edge of her hair as it met her neck and she sensed, like Ximena, that something was not quite right. She reached forward and tapped her little shot glass against Sarah's and said, "Forget it, I didn't mean anything by it."

"I think," Ximena said then, "that Mali has left the country to be with her family in France. It's like the way dogs know when a tsunami is about to hit. Only the dumb humans stay on."

"That's us," Natalie agreed.

By the time they left Ten Sui, Sarah seemed unsteady on her feet and Ximena took her arm for a moment and asked her quietly, close to her ear, if she was all right. Sarah had gone a bit overboard. Nevertheless they all walked home together, stopping in for a nightcap at an *izakaya* called Juban around the corner from Ximena's restaurant. It was another Japanese den at the end of an alley, whose opening housed a karaoke bar that lay opposite a famous testosterone clinic. Inside, the bar was cool and refined. There were ladders laid against walls of rare sake. They drank another bottle of sake. Half an hour before curfew the lights began to go out and the sushi chefs wrapped up their knives. Still, they were allowed to stay on. They talked about their lives but not their future plans, before heading back to the Kingdom, which alone offered them refuge and privacy.

The Thai girls in kimonos opened the door for them. The lights went down and in the street the karaoke bar on the corner of the alley was going through the same metamorphosis. Escaped from their flowing satin gowns—in which they sat all evening on the porch playing games on their phones—some of these hostesses were already sitting in front of the testosterone clinic across the street waiting for their *motocy*. On the lonely lane leading to the Kingdom, Sarah was the first to break off and go by herself into the lobby, and she was thankful for the gloom of her landing and the seclusion of her apartment after three hours of talk. It was only gradually that she realized that the apartment was very orderly and that Goi must have come by while she was out.

She had completely forgotten that it was the day she had agreed to come, because in fact she had not arrived during the morning as she said she would. Goi must have come later, using her own key to enter. With a start, Sarah remembered Mali's bloodied nightgown. She had stupidly forgotten it in the drum of the machine all week. It was an astounding omission and there was no explanation for it—she had simply been distracted with so many tensions. In the laundry room, Sarah found everything was ironed and folded but the nightgown was missing. Cursing herself, she realized that the maid must have washed it and recognized it as Mali's, then returned it to Mali. It would have been a curious thing to do, but it was possible that in Goi's mind it was entirely reasonable. The blood could have been from a nosebleed, a period, or a small cut. Either way, it was done, and Sarah thought it would be better not to bring it up later. It would have to be left unsaid, something held in silence between them, and she would have to hope that Goi had not spun a little theory of her own, putting two and two together. She was capable of that, but it didn't mean she would do it. The blunder had set her back somewhat, put her at a further disadvantage, but there was little she could do about it now. Goi might be a gossip, but there was a chance she might also be unsuspicious by nature. Either way, Sarah had to roll her dice in a gamble. They had to be rolled a little blindly perhaps, but she had no choice but to roll them.

ELEVEN

Earlier that evening, doing exactly as Sarah had assumed she had done, Goi had let herself into the apartment and cleaned the bathroom with her customary diligence. She did not know what to make of the nervous and frail-looking American girl, who didn't seem to have a job or a man, and who didn't seem to do much with herself except pore over her laptop. Yet she could read foreigners well by now, or so she thought. She could differentiate between the normal families whose fathers or mothers had normal jobs—at the Australian International School next door, say, or else the various embassies or hotel groups—and the loners who were living in the Kingdom for private reasons that were more enigmatic. But even among the latter Sarah was an eccentric. Her apartment was far too large for a single woman. Her passport did not carry the name she used. Stranger still was the suitcase of plastic-wrapped American dollars in her spare room closet. Even more than most *farangs*, she wore her secrets a little obviously.

Two of the rooms in the apartment were virtually empty and unused. Sarah had no companions, and Goi was bound to ask who would choose to live in such a lonely and wasteful way. In her bathroom, there were bottles of sedatives and sleeping pills, as Goi surmised, and an electric toothbrush that sat in its own polished holder. The American shaved her legs with what looked like a man's razor. She kept prune juice in her fridge. On her shelves there were paperback books that she never seemed to take down and, as with most *farangs*, her hygiene was questionable, or at least mysterious. Goi lightly rifled through her affairs out of curiosity and she noted the expensive underwear in the drawers and the single pair of French shoes that Sarah hardly ever wore. She was not a tourist, but not a long-term resident either. She was an in-between person who was not settled down in her life. She cut her own nails with a pair of special scissors but left the clippings on the floor. Was it because she couldn't be bothered to pick them up?

Needless to say, Mali had paid handsomely for these pieces of information and it was none of her business what her fellow Thai did with them. Loyalty was to a Thai before a foreigner, and she didn't feel bad about selling her information. It was understood that a maid ought to know such things and would be able to relay them for a price. There was nothing furtive about it. Doing the laundry with the radio on—she liked a bit of *mor lam* when she was ironing—she had opened the washing machine and pulled out the musty towels. It was there she had found the nightgown spattered with dried blood. She recognized it as Mali's at once, since she had ironed it dozens of times before. But the blood she could only guess at. She laid it out on the ironing board in order to get a better look at it. Mali hadn't said anything to her about the blood, and it struck her as anomalous that she'd neglected to mention it. Yet she hadn't seen the girl herself in quite some time, and her apartment looked as if Mali had gone on holiday. Whatever it was, cleaning up bloodied clothes was a little out of the ordinary for a new maid. In fact, she balked at it for a while and tried to guess what had caused such an outflow of human blood. It didn't look like blood from an injury, which she guessed would have been more copious. Nor could it have been menstrual blood. Blood was a very particular thing, a stain unlike any other kind. Superstitiously, Goi regarded bloodstains as bad luck, symbolic of coming events. She invoked Lord Buddha as she passed her hands over these ones. Then she thought about what she could sell on the open marketplace of gossip. The best thing to do would be to take a few pictures of the nightgown on her phone. This she did, but she also began to calculate the advantages to herself of keeping the original article in her possession. Mali, she knew, was not in residence for the moment and so there was no need to take it back to her unit; and since it didn't belong to Sarah, either, and was in a suspicious condition, she doubted that Sarah would bring it up with her directly. And if she did, Goi would apologize and say that she had mislaid it among her own things and taken it back to her room without realizing it. Neither of them would be able to say much, and they would be forced to accept her excuse whether they liked it or not. She folded the gown into her bag just before she left the unit.

Afterward she went up to the twenty-first floor and cleaned up the Retzinger kitchen while waiting for Mr. Roland to come home. He was nearly always home before his wife.

That night he came back just after eight. He said hello to her in the kitchen and then went for his evening shower. When he came out, he went to the balcony and asked Goi to make him his usual drink—a highball made with Yamazaki. There he sat talking on the phone with one of his colleagues. When he was finally free of connection to the outside world, she caught his attention and signaled with her hand that there was something she wanted to raise with him.

"Yes, Goi, what is it?" Roland sighed, rolling the ice around his empty glass.

"I was in the American woman's apartment this afternoon," Goi began with a coy look. "I saw something that might interest you."

Lately Roland had wanted to know if Goi knew anything about the card parties that his wife went to with the other *farang* women in the building. He often paid for this information too. Goi knew that Roland disliked his wife's poker group and harbored suspicions about what they most likely got up to. He had not been in a position to actually disallow it—Natalie could do what she wanted, of course—but she usually came back from those nights drunk and a little belligerent. It wasn't clear to Goi why he wanted to know, or whether he was just a voyeur, a man who liked to control his family arrangements, but either way his desire for underhand information was certainly useful for her.

He reached then into his pocket for a tip, laid out 2,000 baht on the table, and stepped closer to assert possession of it. But she was not content with the amount. She said he might pay more if she were to tell him what she really knew.

"Oh?" he said, and smiled.

Goi cleared her throat and said that 6,000 might be more

adequate an exchange for a description of what she had found inside the washing machine.

"Six thousand?"

He was at first dismissive, but then his curiosity got the better of him, as she knew it would.

"All right, but from now on this is between you and me. Understood?"

"Yes, sir."

He paid her and she went to get the nightgown from her bag.

"What the hell is this?" was his first reaction.

"I don't have any idea. But it was in her washing machine and it belongs to the girl called Mali, the half-Thai girl."

He spread it out over the table and ran his fingers over the silk.

"This is quite remarkable. And you took it?"

"Yes, sir."

"She's bound to notice that you made off with it. How are you going to explain it if I keep it?"

Goi, with a slightly amended plan, now had to think quickly in order to keep her newly won 6,000 baht.

"I say that I threw it away because I couldn't get the stains out. I say I thought it was useless now and assumed that Sarah no longer wanted it. She won't want to tell me that it was Mali's."

"No." Roland smiled again. "She certainly won't press the matter."

They had been up to something strange, one could tell.

"And what about that other girl, Mali?"

"She's no longer here. I clean her unit but there's no one sleeping there. Something about the apartment is not quite right. But I don't know what. She's a wild girl."

"Wild?"

"She has many boyfriends from the clubs."

"Is that right?"

"I don't think your wife knows about it."

"Does she work in the clubs?"

"It's not necessary that she works in them. She can be looking for extra money."

"Or love," he mused.

"I don't think love."

"It's funny, I thought she already had money. Is she not a rich girl, then?"

Goi was not sure, she had to venture a guess.

"I think she's not rich, sir. Not like the others. I don't think she owns the apartment. I think someone else rents it."

"And who would that be?"

"I think it's a man that rents it. But I never saw a man there."

"Not even a razor in the bathroom?"

"No. Just a pair of leather drivers."

Roland leaned back and thought it over. Naturally, Mali's life didn't concern him directly in the slightest. Not only was it none of his business, it didn't seem relevant to him. And yet the more he thought about what Goi was saying, the more he wondered how much his wife might be involved in something that had produced a bloodied silk nightgown in a washing machine. It was a puzzle his inquiring mind was keen to solve. Making a decision on the spur of the moment, he told Goi to keep the gown in her room even though he had paid for it; he wanted to mull it over for a while and would let her know when he needed it. Then he asked about Sarah. Cleaning her apartment, Goi must know a fair amount about her as well.

"She has an American passport but there's nothing in it—nothing at all. She has a pile of dollars in one of her rooms, all wrapped in plastic."

"She does? How much is there?"

"I can't count it, sir. Thousands, maybe."

"Hundreds of thousands?"

"*Ka.*"

Roland sipped his highball and considered this newfound fact. Hundreds of thousands in cash stored in a spare room of the Kingdom?

"That seems eccentric," he said quietly. "What does she do?"

"That's just it, sir. She doesn't do anything. She seems to be waiting for someone."

"She has a partner? A boyfriend?"

"No. I think she's waiting for someone to collect the money. It's what I think."

"Why would she be doing that? Maybe she inherited it."

"In cash, sir?"

"Ah, yes. Silly me. Cash."

He laughed under his breath and asked Goi from then on to report solely to him about these matters. It was imperative that she say nothing to his wife, or anyone else. Natalie by her very nature wasn't devious enough to think ahead and keep her mouth shut about two such momentous facts. Goi promised, and he knew that she would do exactly as he asked because she always did. It served her purposes and lined her pockets. After she had gone to her room he had two more highballs and nursed these new revelations for an hour while still alone. His mind turned slowly but efficiently, grinding up the elements of a problem until they were turned into a fine, manageable dust. But the

finer he ground the enigma of the nightgown, the less he was
able to sift it. His wife probably knew something about it. She
had therefore hidden it from him, while sharing it with the other
three women. That, at the very least, was an outrage. It could be
overcome, but it was a breach of trust. He ground his molars
together now as well. As his anger rose he gave himself some
time to allow it to abate, since it was always possible that Natalie
had some explanation that might go halfway to squaring this
circle. But if she didn't, he would have to investigate a little further, and he would do it by himself, without letting her in on it.
It was a nuisance, but confirmed his earlier suspicions anyway.
Besides, there was always a small pleasure in having such things
confirmed. But even this didn't suggest any concrete reason for
so much blood on a nightgown. Then again, it was also possible
that his wife knew nothing about it at all. If Sarah had ever said
anything about a hoard of dollars in her possession, Natalie
would surely have let it slip by now. It was more possible that
now only he knew about it. It was between himself, Goi, and
Sarah—and if one looked at it coolly it was quite an opportunity, though he had no idea how to exploit it. The pawn at his
disposal, clearly, was Goi.

Roland and Natalie lay side by side that night with the window
open to a cooler air, which rushed in with the rain around the
Kingdom's upper floors. Mutually numbed by alcohol, they
stared up at the white ceiling, where the reflections from the water cascading down the windows formed a hypnotic inducement
to sleep, yet that desirable unconsciousness never came. Far out
in the darkness, there was a single *pop* of a rifle shot and afterward the silence felt much deeper and therefore harder to ignore.

Natalie turned her head, even though there was nothing to see, and the same thought came to them simultaneously: *It's beginning.* On Asoke, on the far side of the university campus, the traffic had melted away and yet they could hear people milling along the roads in incoherent groups, defying the curfew. Natalie felt the first intimation of fear. The only question was whether it was a fear that would last and deepen, or whether it would be bearable. She was beginning to think that she could bear a lot, but inevitably moments of doubt came over her and she thought about escape: to resign from her job and quickly arrange a flight to Europe. Previously she might have assumed that Roland would also jump at a chance to return, but now she was not so sure. He seemed to be settled into his comfortable tropical existence and showed no desire to run away from it. Would she go alone, then? It was not unthinkable. But then she thought more carefully about herself. She, too, had grown used to the Kingdom and its cozy and slightly decaying ways. There was a seductive quality to the building, she could not deny it. They needed less money there, life was easier, more fluid. European cities were prettier but they were also duller. The creaky, small apartments, the shutdown at eleven P.M. They had their own informal curfews. At the Kingdom she enjoyed her friendship with the other three women just as she relished the kitsch of the swimming pool and the staff in their quasi-military uniforms—she liked going down to the swings by herself after work and listening to the rainy-season cicadas. But here life was in limbo. Things never evolved or progressed. It was a paradise of enforced mental idleness. They, Roland and herself, the other women, the whites and the Japanese, were the water-boatman insects skimming across the surface of a pool whose extent and nature they would never understand. Beneath that surface, looking up at them, were the real inhabitants, who could rise up from the depths and prey on them at any moment. They were perpetually vulnerable. It was this, in fact, that she relished, though it made little sense when considered rationally. But she was sure that it made her feel more alive in some way. Every day there was a slight feeling of risk, of impermanence. The Kingdom protected them and gave them status, but also made it clear that they were ultimately worthless in the social dimension. It was a refuge, a prison, a fantasy, and a luxury living machine all at once.

Roland had rolled onto his side, fully awake after the gunshot, and he reached out to stroke her shoulder with the back of his hand.

"I've been thinking," he said.

"About?"

"A lot of things. Should we move on, with all this trouble?"

"I've been thinking that too."

Roland kissed her shoulder in a rare act of tenderness. "It's a shame to leave without having made as much money as I thought we would. It was the whole point of coming here."

"Couldn't the company relocate you?"

"But to where—Angola? Better to save that million we were hoping to save and make our own move."

Yes, she had to concede that. They had been talking about it for years.

"How much do we need?" she said.

"We have a fair amount already. We just need a bit more. I mean, if we really want to move to New Zealand and start our own company there."

In reality she had forgotten all about New Zealand, but now

that he revived the idea she remembered how attractive it had once been to her: move to Auckland and start a "wild source" food business. But she had lost track of how much capital they would need and how much they had saved up thus far. It appeared that Roland knew exactly how much on both fronts. He was about to suggest something but as he stroked her arm he said instead, "What are the others going to do? The women you play cards with? Isn't there one called Sarah who lives on the fifteenth floor?"

"What about her?"

"Well, I was just wondering. Is she American?"

"So she says."

"What do you think of her?"

It was a question she had expected from him for quite a while, and yet it was unusual enough to make her more alert.

"Why do you ask?"

"I'm just curious. Does she seem suspicious to you in any way?"

She tried to laugh it off: "What on earth—"

"Does she have a job?"

And she was forced to admit that she didn't really know. His questions coincided with her own doubts and so she was stumped.

"I didn't find that out, I admit. It's none of my business, really." Natalie hitched herself up on her elbows. "Are you interested in her for some reason?"

"Me? No, I'm just thinking. Seems to me all sorts of weirdos wash up in the Kingdom. I was just wondering when they'd decide to move on."

"Did you hear something about her?"

"Maybe a little. I don't know if any of it is true, mind."

She sat up a little and brushed away his hand.

"What gossip?"

"Nothing you need to worry about. But I hear she's quite friendly with the girl called Mali who's one of your group. I hear they had a falling-out."

"They did?"

"It's what people in the building say."

"Who would say that?"

He did his best to disarm: "I just heard it, I'm not saying from where."

Goi, she thought instantly.

"Do you think she's capable of being violent in any way?" he went on.

"Sarah? I don't think so."

"Are you sure? But we never really know people. Let's face it, she's a stranger to you."

"You mean—she was violent toward Mali? That's a wild theory."

"Yes, it is. I rather like wild theories."

He resumed caressing her arm and this time she let his hand be.

"I'm merely thinking of you, Nat. I wouldn't want you to get involved in something you don't understand."

"I don't think I'm in that position, frankly."

He leaned over and kissed the spot on her upper arm that his hand had already warmed.

"I'm just thinking aloud, sweetheart. But maybe you should pay attention to Sarah a bit more—the little things. They might be revealing."

"I'm not going to spy on her—I have enough of that at work. I think she's just eccentric in her way. That's not a crime last time I looked."

But already she was thinking once more about the absence of Mali and Sarah's stiff reactions to the mention of her name. From the outside it was a Gordian knot she couldn't slice through, this friendship apart from the others. There was nothing sexual between them, of that she was sure. But it was possible that Sarah was so lonely that she had sought out a friendship, a real one. Nothing was more normal. Roland, of course, had heard more than he was divulging, and the maid had probably passed on a rumor that had persuaded him. She wanted to ask him more, but she knew already that he wouldn't give in to her and reveal what he knew, or thought he knew. All Natalie knew herself was that he suspected Sarah of violence against Mali. When she thought about that with less skepticism, she found that she didn't find it quite as outlandish as she had at first. What kind of violence, then? There might have been a terrible scene that no one knew anything about. An attack, an assault, a drunken argument that had gotten out of control. She was astonished all the same. Yet such was the mental synchronicity between herself and Roland when they were in bed together—though not at other times—that before long, as they lay there in the dark listening to sirens, she felt exactly the same intimation that Sarah had maybe harmed Mali and even consigned her to a local hospital. The two girls had hushed it up, then. Or else Mali was dead and the situation was far worse than either of them could imagine. But about the money Roland said not a word.

TWELVE

The long monsoon had by now settled into its rhythm, alternating violence and periods of silence. Around the Kingdom ghostly laburnum flowers appeared in the empty lots one day as if summoned into existence, a slow-motion blossoming that carried a sinister beauty into the cloudy evenings. In the interior gardens the winds came and went with bewildering speed, blowing the fading moths here and there, and over the neighboring towers a moon with a vast smoky halo appeared, calling the daydreaming mind back to past centuries. The air turned to moisture on the skin in seconds and the starlike white flowers of the Chinese box trees gave off with renewed vigor their curious scent of almonds. On the swings the old lady in flower-colored rubber boots sat with her pots of rice pudding, holding Whiskey on her retractable leash, eating her pudding with a plastic spoon. She wore dark sunglasses even at night, as if the rod lights were too bright for her sensitive eyes. On his rounds patrolling the grounds just after nightfall, Pop often saw her from afar, singing softly to herself as she dipped up and down, the dog running with the motion of the swing as if it were a game she enjoyed. He had seen her many times over the years but had never known who she was. He had once seen her in the company of a middle-aged Japanese man who practiced his golf swings, but he had not seen this gentleman in some time. The old lady made him remember this. But about her, Pop had no theories. Once, in fact, he had quietly followed her to the elevators and noticed that she pressed the button for the nineteenth floor in the northeast tower, the same tower that Mali occupied. Later in the evening, when the Kingdom had settled into its nocturnal patterns, an ambience of sleep and withdrawal, he had followed her path up to the nineteenth floor, where he had found a small landing filled with figurines of bodhisattvas and animist spirits, with a door painted with cheap gold and set with panes of red glass. Having worked at the Kingdom for more than ten years he was familiar with most if not all of the apartments, but this one he had not previously come across. Nor had he ever gleaned the old woman's name, because nobody he asked seemed to know it. Indeed, nobody else seemed to have noticed her at all. He wondered if she lived alone or with an equally ancient husband, and why she had taken possession of the dog he had hitherto seen in the company of Khun Mali and then Khun Sarah. But of course, it could have been the other way around. The dog could just as well have belonged to her. Or else it had been abandoned and the old lady had taken it in.

There was a dustless stillness on that landing that afterward he could not forget. And then he began to understand why that might be. One evening, a little later, he had approached the woman with his flashlight so as not to alarm her, and introduced himself as the groundsman who was employed to ensure nighttime security for the gardens and the pool. She was wearing her dark glasses again and within a moment he realized that she was blind. Yet she never carried a white stick. Stone blind and she must have been living there for years by herself, unnoticed and forgotten, a living ghost. It was quite a find on his part. He politely asked her name, but all that came back at him was a smile filled with long-ago gold. He nevertheless gave her his and said if there was anything he could do for her that she shouldn't hesitate to ask. The dog, meanwhile, had seated herself and gazed up at him passively, her eyes soft. The swing still moved and creaked and he felt increasingly ill at ease, though the woman was mentally sharp and already seemed to know who he was. Trying to be friendly, he asked her about her dog. It was a poodle, wasn't it, and weren't purebreds quite expensive in Thailand? He was curious where she had gotten it.

"I didn't get her; she got me. She came calling one night."

"You mean she came to your door?"

"That's exactly it."

He reached down and ruffled the dog's ears.

"It's a clever dog, then," he said.

"I think Lord Buddha led her to me."

"Is that so? Does Lord Buddha do that?"

"Of course he does. He sees everything, so why could he not guide a lost dog?"

"So she was lost?"

"There are lost animals everywhere. Don't you see them?"

It was then that he sensed that she was referring to something that had happened long ago. For as long as he had been working at the Kingdom, then, the dog had actually been hers.

He reached up to the talismans chained around his neck, fingering them for reassurance as the blind lady lifted her face to sense him better. She then commented that he was wearing a fine pair of shoes. He glanced down at them, surprised. How had she "seen" them? That night he was wearing a pair of Italian leather drivers, which he had sifted out of the trash a few nights earlier. It was among his duties to organize the trash bags assembled at the end of each day on the landings and to load them into the service elevator floor by floor. It was a task that took him two strenuous hours. But one of its perks was that he was free to lift whatever he wanted from the bags. Since most of the tenants were on the wealthy side, the pickings from their leftovers were often surprisingly valuable, and it was from the fifteenth-floor landing that he had retrieved this handsome pair of casual shoes, which, as luck would have it, fit him perfectly.

"They're a dead man's shoes, aren't they?" she said, grinning at him.

"A dead man?"

"Why else would you have them?"

He knew in that moment that she was clairvoyant and that it would be better in future to avoid her if he could. It had never occurred to him that the drivers might have belonged to a dead man, though he was certain that it was not the case. Perhaps he should try to figure out to whom the shoes had originally belonged. The only tenants on the fifteenth floor were the American girl and the fat Thai man who lived opposite her, whose cast-off sandals he had already tried and which did not fit him. These shoes were elegant and slim and could not have belonged to either of them. How had the shoes found their way to the fifteenth floor? The blind woman seemed to know more about the Kingdom and what happened inside it than he did. And he was sure it was because her ears were hypersensitive, so finely tuned that she could hear the tiniest event in the way that radar will pick up the movement even of a seagull. If someone had died, it was possible that she had heard the event and knew exactly where it had happened. When he himself patrolled the landings in the small hours with his flashlight, passing at a slow and inquisitive pace the endless rows of windows—grimy and tragic in their own way—he heard small incidents, little sobs and stifling cries, an occasional laugh, a television purring on its own, watched by a person close in time to death, and he knew that if his ears had been only slightly better he would have been able to understand much more about the hundreds of lives going on within a few hundred yards of his patrol.

He was proud of his arcane knowledge of the Kingdom too. He knew by sight or name almost every occupant. Accordingly, he was rarely averse to stopping before a window and watching these ephemeral ghosts in the flickering lights of their bedrooms or in their remodeled kitchens stuffing their faces with midnight snacks. He despised them precisely because he knew their habits. However, he could never figure out where any of them kept their money, even though it was certain that many of the older tenants stashed it under their beds and had done so for years. He sometimes calculated that there must be billions of baht secreted away in these warrens of apartments, unused and hoarded by these worthless upper-class misers. If ever there were a crisis, and he prayed that it would come soon, he might be able to capitalize, to comb through the hundreds of rooms and make a quick fortune for himself by scooping out all the cash from under the beds. Then he could retire in style to Cha-Am and build himself a bungalow like the ones he had seen in magazines, with a private shooting range out back and a hundred meters of his own beach. Lord Buddha would not begrudge him such a moment of luck. A lifetime of poverty, odd jobs, and three failed marriages had left him thirsty for vindication and a spectacular reward dropped from the heavens.

On the higher floors, where the wealthier tenants lived according to the social hierarchy of condominium height, he noticed here and there a secretive traffic in people, subtle visitations that seemed to be going on in the larger units between the nineteenth and twenty-first floors. The blind lady resided in one of these, which suggested that long ago she had been a person of considerable means but had now most likely fallen on hard times. Sometimes people went up to the Lim penthouse and appeared to enter its hallowed and majestic doors. On one occasion at least he had seen the Mali girl from the fourteenth floor do just this—a past-midnight visit for chamomile tea and gossip with the matriarch? There must have been acquaintances of hers up there, the old Thai couples who had once been magnates and were now broke, the Yoons and the Chins, Thai-Chinese clans related to the Lims but inferior to them in social station now that their money had run out. They still had their properties, of course, as proof of their former magnificence. It was certain that Mali knew them from her own family and was paying them social calls. These society families seemed to all know one another informally, but without advertising the fact, and you never knew who knew whose aunt or uncle or cousin or grandfather's bastard son. But in the middle of the night, and walking barefoot to make no sound?

He had, up until then, not been unduly curious about either

Mrs. Lim or Mali but he had sometimes seen the latter returning late with sundry men, usually foreigners, and he had occasionally seen her silhouette thrown alluringly against her
darkened blinds. She was a girl far out of his reach and he disliked her for that.

The foreigners in general—and Mali was a half-foreigner—
perplexed him as much as they amused him. The newest of
them, the American girl, was sometimes to be found wandering
her floor, talking to herself as if she were not quite right in the
head, and it was in this condition that he noticed her one night
standing alone on the fifteenth floor while he was doing his patrol on the seventeenth. He saw her staring into the windows of
the half-Thai girl on the floor below and thought to go down
and see what she was up to—or whether she needed something.
He therefore descended by the emergency stairs and came out
onto her landing just as she seemed about to return to her room.
Startled, it took her a moment or two to recognize him fully and
when she had done so she made a visible effort to appear normal.
He turned off the flashlight and asked her politely if she was all
right. He had seen that she was obviously spying on the Thai girl
but he felt that it was better to say nothing and just cajole her a
little. With a fine instinct he sensed that she represented an opportunity of some kind for himself. The maid from the penthouse, Goi, had told him that she was a "queer bird." But what
kind of queer bird she had not said. He felt that she was a run-
away, but it was agreed among all the staff members who manned
the outer gates of the Kingdom that she never passed by them in
the morning, which indicated that she didn't have a job of any
kind. Now she had gone pale and she fumbled for words of self-
explanation.

"I was worried about Khun Mali," she said.

"Khun Mali? She's not home."

"I didn't know if she was or not. I thought—have you heard anything about her, then?"

He tried to calm her down with a smile. "Not really, but everyone says she's gone off somewhere."

"Gone off?"

"She didn't tell you?"

"No. It must have been a sudden decision."

He could detect the palpitations in her facial muscles. They walked together across the landing toward the emergency stairs. It was then that she glanced down at his shoes and it seemed to him that she was struck by an enormous surprise. He was sure of it. He looked down at them as well and had an inkling of something strange: she had recognized the drivers. How and why, he couldn't say, but she had recognized them. She had looked up then and said to him that she was all right, there was no need for him to worry about her.

"But I'm not worried about you," he said. "I just wanted to tell you that Khun Mali is not here."

"Right. Thank you for that, then," she stammered.

When she had closed her landing door behind her and receded into her own domain, he went by the stairs back down to the gardens and the small concrete room he used there when he slept over at the Kingdom. His own room was far away in Lat Phrao, and most nights he camped out in the garden cell, where he kept a small television and a mattress with expensive goose-feather pillows that he had purloined from the garbage long ago. There he lay with his cheap cigars and his bottle of Sang Som rum, listening to his portable radio on which he could pick up broadcasts of *muay thai* fights. As he did so that night he let his mind wander over the novel landscapes opened up by recent developments. He recalled the accidental meeting he'd had with Goi in the gardens a few nights earlier, flirtatious and coy, and her comment about the queer bird. She had added that the *farang* was not a respectable person and that her apartment was "not empty." Pressed, she had clammed up immediately, but he had understood at once that Goi meant that Sarah had valuables locked up there that were not legal. So much was certain. He was glad, then, that he had gone out of his way to put Sarah at her ease, though not entirely successfully. The next time he saw her he would be more ingratiating. He would be *pak-wan*—he would flatter her. Perhaps he might even be able to score an invitation to her apartment. He already had secret access to all the master keys through his friendships with the security staff, though never in decades of residence in the building had he ever used them to make any money for himself. It was not, after all, something that one would do lightly, for fear of being fired. Pop had long ago understood that the Kingdom was his golden-egg goose, his one opportunity to save himself from poverty. But one had to wait patiently for the eggs to be laid, and theft in itself was a delicate matter about which one had to think without frivolity.

THIRTEEN

Sarah went down to the lobby mailboxes two days later to collect her mail. There the receptionists now gave her smirking sidelong glances that were not intended to wound but rattled her all the same. Over time they had become perceptibly less respectful, more knowing, and the deference they had shown when she first moved in was little more than a memory. She sensed that it was not just personal. The increasing volatility beyond the Kingdom had crept in at long last and disturbed its dusty certainties. The respect for foreigners, for one thing, seemed to have diminished. It sent a cold and unfamiliar emotion through her.

She scooped out all the bills and flyers from the box and then noticed something left behind, something metallic and unusual. It was a small memory stick. The mailboxes were generally unlocked unless a tenant specifically requested a lock, and she had never bothered to do so. She removed the drive and turned it in her palm, wondering if she had left it there by mistake a while back. But she knew it wasn't hers. It had been laid there for her attention. The female receptionist that day still watched her through the glass doors, and it was possible that she knew who had placed it there. A resident of the Kingdom or an outsider—it could be either.

She kept herself under control as she went back up in the elevator. But in a way she already knew what it was. She put the drive into her computer and found that it contained a single folder called "The Kingdom." She opened it to find a row of photographs. They were views of the internal corridors of the building taken from different angles, and as she looked through them she realized that they were views of the landing of the fifteenth floor and of Mali's windows, taken most probably from the floor above it. And in one of these was a young woman leaning against the wall with her back to the camera, looking down at the windows of the fourteenth floor.

The image was dark but she recognized herself at once. In another she was shown walking across the bridge and lingering—as it appeared—by the entrance to the emergency stairs. Another image showed the moving of a bundled mass to the door of the service elevator—a sight Sarah recognized as Ryo's body. Two men and a woman carried it, made visible by the landing's dim exit lights. It was enough to empty her mouth of saliva in an instant. The vantage point of the sixteenth floor was significant too, she thought. For some time now she had imagined that the piano she occasionally heard there was being played by a girl of about the same age as the one she had seen observing her from the windows of the same floor.

She had no evidence for this, but the idea had formed in her unconscious. The two girls must be the same, she thought. If she was watching Sarah while she took her swim, why should she not be watching her at other times? Any child could operate a phone camera. She might have started doing it just for fun, but one night she had stumbled upon something that she was not supposed to witness. Now she had decided to play a game with Sarah. But as yet there was no ulterior motive for that game. It was just a game being played for its own sake. The girl was letting her know that the game was on, that was all.

Momentarily, Sarah was struck dumb by the immensity of the misfortune, but she didn't at first connect it to the small fortune in her possession. For the moment she had convinced herself that it was a child's sadistic prank and nothing more. But at one blow her relationship to the Kingdom was changed.

She was now afraid to keep an eye on Mali's apartment and accordingly gave it up; likewise her morning swims. It was better to avoid public places altogether and to stay in her apartment. If she had to cross the lobby on her way out, she did so quickly, avoiding eye contact and pretending not to notice Pop, who was often propped up in an armchair or reading a pro-military newspaper. Yet even that was not necessary when she discovered that all groceries could be ordered online through the Honest Bee website and that she no longer needed to go to the stores. She could stay behind locked doors and wait, and such patience was exactly what was called for. Though she had not seen the other women in the building, nor they her, she imagined they had begun to talk about her, but there was nothing she could do to prevent it.

Instead she passed her time on her computer, monitoring events around April Laverty in New York. Since that day in Hong Kong when she had collected her fortune, she had scoured the news for signs that the chaotic estate had discovered the fraud and launched an investigation of the erstwhile assistant who had unexpectedly vanished. But curiously there was no mention of it. She did discover that all Laverty's readings and public appearances had been canceled without further notice. But others running her estate might have been following up on recent transactions and might have been in contact with Chan in Hong Kong for any number of reasons. Her sleight of hand would have come out at once. Nevertheless, there was no mention of Sarah at all.

It might have come down to the discretion of Chan. But now, unnerved by the pictures that had been sent to her so slyly, she began to connect the various points of her unease. Chan himself could have followed her, or his minions could have done so. If it was not the girl on the floor above who had taken the pictures, then it could have been any employee of the Kingdom whom he might have paid off handsomely. Her money must be the source of the cruelty being directed at her.

At midnight during one of these nights spent at the computer a siren rang out over the neighborhood from the direction of the university. It lasted for about a minute before fading away. Sitting outside, she saw the lights going out all over the campus, and then along the streets until the whole city seemed to have fallen into darkness so suddenly that the stars were visible, as they rarely were, and a sense of cosmic space made itself felt.

Even the spirit houses fell into darkness as the power was cut. On cue, the lights in the apartment blocks around them went out as well. Within seconds the Kingdom's towers were the only ones whose balconies had light. Then, after a comic interval—

with a faint *boom* as if from a blown generator—those, too, were extinguished and she was plunged into the same darkness as the other ten million people. The air-conditioning units fell silent and their collective insectlike drone was withdrawn from the chorus of tree frogs and cicadas. Down in the waste lot where the *tagraew* net stood, an oil lamp was lit almost immediately and a group of half-dressed men gathered around it. Here and there, out in the night, a few candles began to appear in other apartments and then lanterns, some red, some pale lemon. People turned small flashlights down toward the generators. When the coolers were turned off, the heat inside the cement apartments rose about ten degrees in a minute and soon people were coming out onto the balconies in their nightshirts, grumbling and fumbling with matches. Sarah did the same in order to light up the table. The moon shone down on the pool of the villa next door like a spotlight and in the distance there was a glimmer of silent lightning, but this time it suggested a different portent. The building had changed its atmosphere, plunged back into the past, and the absence of Mali was now more of a certainty. She had jumped a sinking ship, as Sarah was now convinced, leaving the other rats on board to await their fate.

As she found when she ventured outside to get some cooler air, most of the tenants had taken to going outside while the power was off. In the lobby the power outlets still worked because of the emergency generator, and there the younger tenants massed with their phones, stretched out on the floor with jugs of lemonade filled with ice. Above them on the garden floor the older residents gathered on the various stone benches to gossip and complain as they sat around their portable oil lamps, as they probably had frequently when they were young in the romantic days of unreliable electricity. They made a picnic out of it and whispered about "interesting times." A little distance away, two black terriers humped each other out of sight. Yet higher up, on the swimming pool floor, there was virtually nobody.

She swam alone in the dark, thrilled by the crisis that she thought gave her cover. It was unexpectedly beautiful to look up at the hundreds of darkened windows where a host of candles burned and to think that a slow-motion revolution was moving in from the outer world. She had feared it before, but now she entertained the possibility that Mali had been wrong in saying that coups came and went and made no difference, and that it would break up her suffocating little existence. Now it might come to life, unarmed but still eager for change.

When the lights went out in their penthouse Roland was doing calisthenic stretches in the middle of the largest Persian carpet, with a Korean soap on the TV with the sound killed. He was in his scarlet silk dressing gown and had already opened the Saint-Estèphe, ready to spend yet another evening alone with his minuscule pleasures. When he cried, "Fuck!" Goi rushed in from the kitchen with an oil lamp already lit, prepared for the blackout even before it happened. Roland had never known that they even had oil lamps in the house. His wife was at work and, once again, master and maid were alone for the evening, a circumstance he was beginning to enjoy. He rather liked the middle-aged crook, as he saw her. Seeing her poised now with the lamp in one hand and a spatula in the other, he felt that such times required a capacity for democratic solidarity and therefore asked her to put the lamp on the floor and come sit with him at the table while he ate the curry she had made. She brought it in with a delicious solemnity.

"Why is there an outage?" he asked her. "Again?"

"The last time, sir, it was the fuse box inside the building. This time it's the quadrant."

"The what?"

"The area where they have the electricity."

"The neighborhood is down?"

"Look outside, sir."

He said he would take her word for it. "That's more serious, then."

"*Ka*. They said until nine tomorrow morning."

"Damn, no air-con then."

He gritted his teeth and leveled a silent insult at the entire Thai nation.

"Not even the fans," he went on mournfully. "Maybe I should go to a hotel."

"It's not hot tonight."

This was true. The rain had cooled the air considerably.

With the oil lamp repositioned on the table, Roland offered Goi a glass of wine, which, as social hierarchy dictated, she courteously refused. "Oh, come on," he insisted, but still she refused.

"We're going to be in darkness all night," he went on, in a strangely improved mood. "We might as well be tipsy."

"*Ka*."

But he drank without her.

"I was wondering, Goi, about Khun Mali. She had a boyfriend, did she not—Japanese?"

"Yes, sir."

"Do you know anything about him?"

"He works at a company."

"Don't they all? But what I mean is: does he live in the building?"

She said she wasn't sure about that because Khun Mali had never told her. The boyfriend did sometimes stay in the apartment for a few days, but he didn't carry any personal effects with him.

"I wouldn't mind checking."

"Yes, sir."

Roland's mind was turning yet again, and in a different direction. Who said that the blood on the nightgown was Mali's?

"And you don't know his name?"

"His name is Ryo."

"Then we could look through the tenant list and maybe find him, see if he kept an apartment here. Or I could look myself, come to think of it."

Every unit had a nameplate—it was a Kingdom regulation.

"I can do it for you," she ventured.

"Yes, that would be better. Can you do it now while the lights are off? Maybe—I was thinking—you could take a quick look inside if no one is there? If someone comes to the door, just make up an excuse."

Goi said that it would only take her half an hour. The elevators were still functional, and using them one could access every single landing. Roland looked at his watch; Natalie wouldn't be home until the early hours and she might even stay the night at the hotel if she chose to retain air-conditioning and hot water for the night. He asked Goi if there was any way she could get hold of keys for a tenant's apartment without the management knowing. Hesitating a little, she said that she knew someone on the staff who could get any key she asked for if she could offer them a tip. Naturally that was not a problem. In the chaos and confusion downstairs it would be easier. He suggested in that case that she do it right away and then report back to him in an hour. He would make it worth her while, needless to say. Not quite believing her luck at making such easy extra money, she brought out the dessert she had made for Roland and then left the apartment to begin her task armed with his flashlight.

Each tower contained about thirty units and it took a minute to inspect the nameplate on each landing. It was a tedious but straightforward mission. Because of the blackout, she guessed, at least half of the units were now temporarily vacated and the landings were like tombs. The names were mostly Thai, with contingents of Japanese, Chinese, Koreans, and *farangs*. There were seventeen units occupied by Japanese, and she wrote down their names in the notepad she had taken with her. As she progressed through the last tower, the one to the south of Mali's, she found seven Japanese names on seven different floors. This wasn't especially unusual. But on the fourteenth floor she found an R. Nimoto. The other names did not contain either a Ryo or an R, although that didn't mean that a Ryo didn't reside in one of them. But the R. Nimoto on the fourteenth floor was the clearest suggestion thus far and the one she was determined to bring to Roland's notice when she returned. It was Unit 77.

The landing there was musty and devoid of objects but for an old dirt bike that looked as if it had been abandoned to its fate leaning against the curved wall. She shone the flashlight onto the scuffed door and noticed that the doormat below it spelled out a Japanese word she couldn't read. In fact, it was *tadaima*, meaning "I'm back!" which husbands would call out to their wives when they got home after work. Lost for a moment inside her own thoughts, Goi tried to recall if she had ever seen the inhabitant of this particular unit during her years of working at the Kingdom. The Japanese kept to themselves and were not the loudest or the most visible tenants. They were a subtly elusive presence by design. She had never been asked to clean their apartments, even though the management was always keen to refer her. The Japanese in the Kingdom never hired her.

She went down to the gardens then, where the tenants were still camped out with their lamps and their picnic blankets. There was a distinct odor of sweating bodies, *khao khua*, and fish sauce, and some had laid out sleeping bags on the marble floors intending to spend the night there. She threaded her way through them until she was in the sheds at the back, where Pop had his little room behind a wall of houseplants and coiled hoses. She knew he would be there, seated on a couple of bricks with his water pipe. He had an oil lamp by him and he was stripped to his waist, his *sak yant* glorious and menacing. When he saw her he beckoned her in and asked her if she wanted some pipe. But she was too rushed. She had a twenty-dollar bill with her and she laid it next to him, saying that she needed the key to Unit 77 for an hour. She knew it could be arranged. She asked him if he could place it in the elevator so that she could call the car up to the fourteenth floor and retrieve it. She would bring it back down later.

"Unit Seventy-Seven? Who is it for?" he asked, pocketing the bill.

"It's for the *farang* in the penthouse. He wants to look at it."

"Oh?"

"He might want to rent it, I think."

But Pop already knew that there was something unusual about Unit 77. He had kept tabs on the occupant, a middle-aged Japanese salaryman by the name of Nimoto, but recently, and indeed over a few weeks, he now realized, he had not seen him. Perhaps he had gone on holiday somewhere. Every salaryman got two weeks to himself for a yearly vacation; that much Pop knew. But in this case he sensed that the disappearance was more permanent. Perhaps Nimoto had moved out without telling anyone, because normally when a tenant moved out everyone knew about it. But no one had talked about Nimoto. He had simply ceased to be visible. Pop no longer saw him leave for work or come back late at night after carousing with his colleagues. He had not thought about it much before, but now that he did he was perplexed. Where was Nimoto, then, and why was Unit 77 so silent?

"Never trust what *farangs* say," he told her, wanting to keep these reflections strictly to himself. "You know he has a different reason. So do I."

Goi had to decide whether to tell him, since she felt that he knew already. He knew everything about the Kingdom, every square inch of it.

"If he does, it's nothing to do with us," she said cautiously. "It's to do with his wife and the white girls."

"I don't believe that either. It's about the American."

He said he knew she wasn't authentic. He gave her a charmer's smile and threw a lazy arm around her plump shoulders. He said that he would get her the key but on one condition: she would tell him how much money the American had in her apartment. Goi squirmed away from the arm, but Pop's tight grip stilled her.

Back on the fourteenth floor she waited inside the landing, peering down through the slanted and half-opened windows at the tea lights that had appeared all over the outdoor walkways, while Pop slouched his way down to the lobby, where the reception desk was in a state of merry abandonment.

The boys there were mostly asleep, since for them the power cut was little more dramatic than an extra holiday. Pop already knew where the backup keys were kept, and the cabinet was not even locked. People were constantly locking themselves out of their own apartments, and it was easier for the staff to keep the cabinet open. He pocketed the keys for Unit 77 undisturbed by any of the other staff, who all knew him anyway, and made his way across the lobby to the glass doors of the southwest tower.

He felt that he had grown in power within the Kingdom now that the system was breaking down, and he felt more confident about doing exactly as he wanted. The maid, he also felt, was using him for her own purposes, but then he, too, would need her if he were to access Sarah's world. He called the elevator to the ground floor, tossed in the keys, and waited to make sure it was called back up only to the fourteenth floor. When it was, he went out into the lobby and looked up at the unlit atrium, where the glimmer of candles placed on the walls made it look like a catacomb. On the fourteenth floor Goi would have picked up the keys and no one in management would know. He was convinced that most of the powerful owners and committee members had already left for their houses at the beach and would not be back for a while. Now, then, was the moment to strike.

When the elevator doors opened Goi snatched the keys from the floor and rang the doorbell of Unit 77. A claustrophobic anxiety came over her as the bell chimed, because she could already smell the stale, heat-driven decay of a place that was no longer occupied. Yet she waited for a while, ringing again and again, for fear of making a blunder. Eventually she was satisfied that Unit 77 was empty and tried the key. The door opened with a little pop of dust.

She closed the door quietly behind her and left the lights off, wandering into a hallway that had been stripped completely bare. She knew at once that the tenant had left for good and that his nameplate was still up only because management had not yet found a replacement tenant. The rooms were empty, only the rented furniture still in place. Using her flashlight she ventured into each of the rooms, sweeping the beam across thinly papered walls, a Chinese screen, and two denuded beds. A wide front room offered a view of the freeway, where the traffic had been stopped in its tracks. It was, essentially, the same view as that from Mali's apartment, which lay in the equivalent place in the opposite tower. She went into the kitchen, which was surprisingly modern and well equipped, with stainless-steel surfaces. There was a large American fridge and wine cooler, a range of slotted knives, and bone china plates that must have belonged to the management. She progressed to the bathroom, where there was a glass-walled rain shower and a tub. Everything personal had been taken out of it, the tenant having been clearly meticulous with his evacuation. She went to the basin and held up a hand to touch the surface of the mirror, now also coated by a film of dust. How quickly apartments in the Kingdom succumbed to the dust. It was almost overnight, decay always waiting in the wings, ready to reinvade and conquer their precious living spaces. As she made a mark in the dust she noticed that the edges of the mirror were crusted with a dark substance that was also present on the taps. She shone the light onto it, and it appeared to have dried out around the spout, forming a brittle rim. She stepped back with a slight unease and threw the beam down to the floor, which she had not noticed as she entered the room.

It, too, was discolored with horizontal streaks of the same black, which reached into the corners and seemed to have accumulated around the doors. So the management cleaners had not yet come to prepare the place for a new tenant. The white bathroom and the adjoining living room, she now saw, were covered with this black film, which extended to the floor of the kitchen as well. It might have been scrubbed many times and resisted all detergents. She went to the fridge and opened it, curious about what the tenant might have left behind. A full or empty fridge, after all, was the surest sign of whether a person was living in an apartment. All that remained inside it was a package of brown paper tied up with string, stark and solitary in the cold light of the empty fridge, suggesting something fancily gourmet. It had been left on the second rack, an oversight in a moment of haste, no doubt. Satisfied that the occupant was unlikely to return, Goi reached down and retrieved the package. She took it to the counter and opened it carefully. Inside the brown paper was a second layer of white wax paper, folded with precision, and inside this was a small block of what looked like high-grade sashimi tuna. Something about its gloss and color seemed expensive, or so the maid, who had never tasted such a thing in her life, assumed. She was stirred by a sudden curiosity. She had heard that even tiny portions of fatty tuna from Japan commanded prices that could not be believed, but she had never imagined that she might one day be able to sample it for herself.

Yet her animal instincts were roused in a contrary direction: the meat, for a moment, repelled her.

Laying the flashlight on the countertop, she took one of the knives and sliced off a thin portion to taste, cutting the sliver first into quarter-inch squares. But with the first taste she realized that it wasn't tuna. She peered down at the block, subtly marbled with fat. It was from a mammal, not a fish. Still chewing the little square of flesh, she began to feel strange, then eventually spat it out into her hand. It was surely pork, but a kind of pork she had never tasted before, a rare Japanese imported pork that connoisseurs would know. Perhaps it was from a special organic farm in Hokkaido; some of the other maids had talked about such things when discussing the contents of their employers' fridges. Then a doubt descended upon her like some silent ash falling from a fire. She put aside the chewed morsel and rewrapped the block, tying the string exactly as it had been before. As she took it back to the fridge she sensed something relayed by her taste buds. It was not pork, and it was not a gourmet treat. It had the distinct taste of an animal's tongue, but she could not place the animal. It must have been unclean, because it made her recoil with revulsion. Returning to the counter, she then wondered if she should take it to Roland and ask him what he thought.

She went to the tap and drank from it until the taste in her mouth had dissipated. Then she sat in the darkness for a few minutes collecting her nerves and wiping her lips with one of the pristine dishcloths. It was a small misadventure that she would not relate to Roland after all. He would not understand it any more than she could, and yet he would certainly order her to come back down and retrieve the package, whereas she had already decided she could never look at or touch it ever again. She could not shake the question: what was it? She therefore turned the flashlight once more upon the blackened floors and tried to think about what had happened there. It was something that the building had not yet discovered. Perhaps the tenant had possibly killed a whole pig by himself and then fed himself with the remains for a week. Finished with his ritual, he had moved on to another apartment to repeat it elsewhere. It was a joke Goi made to herself, but as she returned to the landing she pondered how impossible it really might be.

As she reached the door she noticed a small table in the hallway that bore a heavy stone ashtray in which a card lay, as casually left behind as the sashimi in the fridge. She took it with her onto the landing, locking the door behind her, and shone the flashlight on it. It was from a local bar called Demonia on Soi 33, the next street down from their own. Here, at last, was a scrap of evidence that she could pass on to Roland. She slipped the card into her pocket as she took the elevator up to the penthouse floor, back to her employers. She would return the keys to Unit 77 to Pop later that evening.

Roland by now was seated at the garden table on the balcony, where the breeze was fresh enough to make the scene of gloom and medieval darkness below him enjoyable. All around him other tenants had dragged mattresses onto their own balconies and were sleeping in their underwear. Natalie had already called to say that she would be spending the night at the Marriott, where the generators never failed, and he was in fact quietly happy to be alone with a glass of port, an oil lamp, and a viewing platform from which to survey the breakdown of society. Goi found him there eating a plate of cheese with grapes and batting away clouds of moths with a rolled-up newspaper and cursing in a language she didn't recognize. Even the interior of the spacious penthouse was so hot that the balcony was an oasis of cool battered by the accelerated winds that came before yet another storm. When she came out to see him, he raised his eyes like a guilty dog and then straightened himself and remembered his masterly manners.

"Did you get the keys?"

"Yes, and I went into the unit."

"Is it his, do you think?"

"I can't say. It's empty. Whoever he is, he's left already. Maybe a week ago. I did find this, though."

She gave him the Demonia business card.

"Demonia—is it a bar of some kind?"

"Yes, sir. It's nearby."

"Is it an S and M place?"

"Chocolate, sir?"

"Never mind. Anything else?"

"Nothing, sir."

"I see. Do you still have the keys?"

"I take them down later."

He was about to ask her to hand them over so that he could go down and look over the place for himself. But it would surely be pointless, since she had already verified that the tenant was gone. He quietly thanked Goi and told her that she could go back to her room for the night. She had performed well, and a tip was waiting for her on her bed. She bowed and dissolved away, as she knew how to do, so silently that it would not give Roland a second thought. As she was leaving, nevertheless, he asked her in future to look over Mali's apartment as well in case something of interest showed up. Postcards, unusual letters or bills. He left it vague in the hope that she would exercise a bit of cunning. Naturally, he added, she was not to mention any of this to another soul. Also, if possible, he would like any photographs of Mali that might be in the apartment. If anyone noticed that they were missing, he said that he would deal with it and she was not to worry.

When he was alone again he spun the card between his fingers and ran the bar's name over his tongue: Demonia. There was something quite witty about it. The girls would probably be dressed as satanic underlings with red satin horns and devil tails. It wasn't difficult to imagine on Soi 33. The only odd thing was that he himself had never noticed it on his many jaunts down that same street. He resolved to find it next time he was there. Perhaps they would remember this Ryo.

Later that night, as he slept on his sofa right next to the open windows surrounded by a dozen smoking mosquito coils, he reflected on what a find Goi had been. Yet for months he had the feeling that his wardrobes and drawers were being rifled through with a subtle hand. The maid had a way of observing him that was equal to the way he observed others. This was why she was useful and admirable to him. Despite the trust he felt for her, it was possible that Goi went through his things when he was still at work in the same way she recorded the lives of others. What's more, he had given her the key to do so. He couldn't control her every movement, nor her motives if she had any. Had his wife's suspicions been aroused and had she asked Goi quietly to do this? Or it could have been that Goi had her own reasons. He knew almost nothing about her. Natalie had found her on a bulletin board somewhere and she had arrived out of the blue one day with her lispy, well-learned English and painted nails. Even her name was a little ambiguous. With one tone it could mean "little finger," but with another, it was a vulgar term for the male member.

Goi herself lay on her bed in the sweltering heat and to pass a little time counted the money she had made on tips. Her dream, when she had saved enough, was to take a trip to the islands and spend a few nights in a nice hotel, after paying her grandson's medical bills. The *farangs* didn't deserve to have so much money in the first place. Exhausted but satisfied, she lay very still, listening to the cries and sirens coming from the curfewed streets while still turning over in her mind the images of the taps and floors drenched in dried and darkened pig blood and the lingering taste under her tongue. It was exactly what Roland wanted to know, but the knowledge was far more powerful if retained only for herself. It could be used later, in ways that were not obvious thus far. What the foreigners did among themselves, after all, had nothing to do with her except insofar as she could blackmail them. They were animals in their hearts, untouched by the grace of Lord Buddha and his bodhisattvas, touched instead by something subtly demonic and alien. Even their kindnesses were odd. They existed in a prison of their own making, and she entered that prison only to make a living. For in the end there was no other reason to enter it at all.

FOURTEEN

Throughout the night the power returned in bursts, then died again for long spells. Asleep on her mattress under the scattering geckos, Sarah felt the cooling units shudder on and then restart, the elevators humming along the vertical length of the structure and the lights she had switched off blazing for intervals and then promptly returning her unit to darkness. The source of this irregularity would remain forever enigmatic, since the Kingdom's nervous system was often on life support and no one could understand why, not even the permanent members of the committee that ran its operations. Eventually, however, the coolers became a constant white noise and the new morning offered a renewed normality. Her nightmares, transformed into cobwebs, broke apart and the sound of rain—light and restrained—invaded her mind and restored it to sanity. Beyond the rain, human voices massed into a single space, a chattering like that of grackles assembled in the Anza-Borrego mesquite trees she remembered as a child.

They had gathered in the warehouse enclosure below her balcony, from where she could see a huge mango tree that had been upended and tragically felled. A drilling machine had been set on a movable platform and its point was thudding its way into the outer wall of the warehouses. Around the tree a small crowd had gathered with pink and blue umbrellas, many of them residents of the Kingdom who were either mourning or neutrally observing. The tree had either been toppled by high winds or by the demolition crew that had arrived that morning—it was hard to say which. Equally strange, golden wildflowers had burst into life all around the lot's walls while the fuse boxes tied to the poles in the street had burned out and were being repaired by workers from the electric company before the same onlookers.

She dressed and went down to the lobby with an eye to joining this same crowd, but on the street she found a mild carnival atmosphere: the open-truck fruit sellers were there with piles of dragonfruit and lychees, the local convenience store had *mor lam* on its speakers, and the owner was dancing a shuffle hand in hand with one of the doormen from the Kingdom. A host of students from the university had walked down from the campus to fill the metal tables alongside the canal, and they sat in a kind of gentle torpor in their starched white shirts, their heads dusted with wet petals. It was a semiconscious festivity created by the long power cut. The construction workers flowed through it in their yellow rubber boots, all eating ice cream, and covered with a loose dust the color of icing sugar. Sarah merged into them and found herself at the gates of the waste lots, which were still partially flooded. Just inside the enclosure stood the spirit house of the elder Lims who had died in the tuberculosis epidemic during the Japanese occupation. There were fresh marigolds laid at their feet, and rows of red Fanta bottles. It would seem that the workers from the site next door paid these tributes, perhaps to appease the ghosts for the imminent destruction of their former lands. But there were also other small shrines here, hastily assembled in the shadow of the ruins, where rotting fruit and cakes lay crumbling in the humidity. She walked right up to the warehouses and the rain tree roots flowing through them. It was unknown why the Lims didn't demolish them and replace them with yet another condo block. It must have been from fear of the spirits. As she stood there alone, a little apart from the crowd, superstitious for the first time about the dead who surrounded her, she sensed the gaze of someone behind her, perhaps someone who knew her. It made her turn, feeling the eyes of a watcher, and as she did so she saw a slight movement under the flame trees near to her, and a form materialized out of the rain.

It was a schoolgirl of about twelve or thirteen in a standard navy uniform and ankle boots, her shoulders spattered with raindrops and a satchel slung over one shoulder. The girl's eyes were upon her, and it was obvious that she knew who Sarah was because she had no hesitation in stepping toward the American, her face lit by a silent greeting. She held out an envelope to Sarah and suddenly the two of them felt as if they were alone inside the crowd. The girl *wai'*ed and said that the envelope was for her, someone had given it to her a few moments earlier. But when Sarah asked who, the girl shook her head, smiling even more, indicating a limited knowledge of English. Sarah looked quickly at the gates and the road beyond, but saw nobody, and the schoolgirl was already excusing herself and beginning her retreat. Within a heartbeat she had melted away into the street and Sarah was left holding the envelope. She took it with her to a café called Lily on the ground floor of a condo building oppo-site the Kingdom and, once she was sure she was alone in its small courtyard garden, opened it. Inside was a letter written with indigo ink on watered paper, very formally, and addressed to her personally. The English words were laid out as if by a na-tive hand, with a practiced elegance that must have been learned at a school long ago, she thought at once, with a forger's intu-ition. It was only when she had read four lines of it that she real-ized it was a blackmail letter, certainly from the same person who had deposited the memory stick in her mailbox. In simple terms it asked her to fill a rucksack with $100,000 in hundred-dollar bills and to take it to the night flower market at Chatuchak at nine P.M. on the following Tuesday. She was to leave it by the entrance to the MRT station behind the market, then walk away and not look back. Then, the flourish of a threat: the writer knew that a garment had been found in her apartment and that it could be produced if she was not in agreement with these terms. It was an anticipatory checkmate.

She read the letter over twice, trembling slightly, her mouth dry and acidic, and then thought about the little schoolgirl. The girl on the sixteenth floor who observed her in the swimming pool was about the same age, but surely a child that young could not have written a letter so assured and in such commanding English. Still, the image of the girl was there. There was a simi-larity, glimpsed at a huge distance. But she could not have known about the nightgown. Perhaps Goi had shot her mouth off with the other maids in the course of an idle bout of gossip, or per-haps it was a prank. She had no way of knowing. Barely control-ling her panic, she rushed back to the apartment, momentarily forgetting about the letter and its contents, and opened her own door with her thoughts still racing. She had made a grave mistake and was beginning to understand exactly what it meant.

That night she locked the outer door to her apartment with the dead bolt and turned off her lights, leaving only a small desk lamp on next to her computer. She was sure that it was not her imagination that the building had grown much quieter ever since the power had been restored. One by one, the wealthier tenants were slipping away to their country houses or abroad, much as Mali had probably done, and voices could no longer be heard either from the unit below hers or from the one above. Even the piano she had occasionally heard from above had fallen silent. Rumors were spreading about a coming military crackdown, and she had noticed walking through the parking area that the number of Mercedes cars had diminished. Her blackmailer had chosen the moment well. Confusion and disorder were a perfect cover. Alternatively, it could have been a group of the staff who had combined to defraud her of money they knew she had stashed in her apartment. The *farangs* in Bangkok entertained such theories about Thais all the time. The Thais, for their part, said exactly the same things about the *farangs*. It was a system of mutual recrimination based on racial resentments that were mysterious even to the people harboring them. It all came down to money, as she herself knew all too well. She was not any different. Money made people into natural paranoiacs, and although Sarah knew this consciously, her unconscious was a different matter. She lay awake considering whether to cancel her arrangement with Goi. After all, the maid was the only person who had been inside her apartment apart from Mali.

But there was also Ximena and Natalie. Natalie didn't seem to need the money, but the same could not be said of Ximena. It was a wild theory, she had to admit, but it wasn't impossible. Her easy and comfortable trust of Ximena wavered for a moment as she tossed the idea inside her mind. If the chef seemed trustworthy, it was also true that she would have made a concerted effort to seem that way if she wanted to extort money from Sarah. Goi was, in the end, her maid as well. And there was nothing stopping Goi telling Ximena what was inside Sarah's apartment. What did she really know about the girl from Chile?

She counted down the days until Tuesday, still undecided as to whether she would go through with the payment. One hundred grand was half of what she had skimmed from her scheme. Paying it would potentially free her from an unknown tormentor whose next move she couldn't predict. It still left her with one hundred grand; the blackmailer must have calculated that it was just enough to make her swallow the loss. Any more, and she would have rebelled. He or she knew exactly how much she had in the spare room. She would pay it, then, and could take her time later finding out who had extorted it from her. You could fit that amount of cash in an average-size briefcase—she remembered reading in a book somewhere that even a million dollars in hundred-dollar bills weighed only about ten kilos. So $100,000 would weigh a mere kilo. It was an easy drop-off, and there was no reason it would be a hoax, she told herself. So she thought, anyway, descending deeper into confusion and doubt, and then a familiar guilt about what she had done to acquire the money in the first place. She couldn't help thinking of the helpless old woman back in New York, her mental stability decayed by age and wear and yet somehow aware of the acolyte who had defrauded her so easily. In a Buddhist atmosphere, karma no longer seemed quaint or farfetched. It was, on the contrary, a matter of life and death.

On the Sunday night she walked across the university to a restaurant called the Local on Soi 23 and ate alone on the terrace of the old house. It stood at a crossroads with a Watsons convenience store and, opposite the restaurant itself, a popular Japanese *izakaya* called Matsumori. But that night the Japanese customers who usually frequented the *izakaya* were nowhere to be seen, and the Watsons's white lights shone into an empty crossroads. Down along Soi 23 the massage parlors were subdued and the girls outside catcalled to only an occasional passerby. Their lights were going off day by day. She ordered an *anchan* blue-pea cocktail from the outside bar and a plate of *phu nim* soft-shell crab. It was in such moments of distraction that the sediments that drifted inside her were able to float slowly downward and find a bed. She had concocted so many layers of lies around herself that fact and fiction had begun to merge, and as she labored through each day she had to reground herself in memories stirred by a sip of blue-pea tea and vodka: a house at the edge of the desert where her parents had once lived, the jalopy her father drove to the base and in which he sometimes drove her out into the desert, that sun-warmed land of sandy arroyos and ocotillos bursting into flower.

It was the spirit house in the restaurant's parking lot that stirred up these fragments of the past. The Lords of the Land sat there with their beasts and servants: zebras, elephants, tiny men and dancing girls who served as playthings of the spirits, since immortality has its boredoms. The animals served as transport for the spirits, but there were sometimes also little models of taxis and airplanes because even spirits might prefer more modern options. The fairy lights lulled her. Whenever she walked through the university campus at night she stopped at the larger white *san phra phum* shrine, which contained a blackened gold image of the Hindu angel Phra Chai Mongkol holding a sword and a moneybag. For weeks she had wondered what it signified without finding out, and now as some of the staff came out of the restaurant after their shift they *wai'*ed at the shrine in the parking lot: it was a reflexive gesture toward a folk now past. But Sarah's past was also there, honored by a gesture or two—she, too, made offerings to her parents, who were themselves both long dead. She saw the Hindu angel as if that golden deity had the power to summon her own past: her mother, who had disappeared with another man when she was twelve; her delinquencies from schools; and her bouts of depression controlled by a health-care system with which she had never communicated.

Her father, too, inhabited the same dimension as the Thai spirits, watching her at her shoulder. She felt him urging her to make a decision, pay the blackmail money, and save herself yet again—after that she could move on and fashion yet another identity. No one could catch her if she was nimble enough. Sarah felt her brief spell of passivity and confusion break apart as her plans formed themselves: get out of the Kingdom as soon as possible, head toward another city, another new life, as quietly and agilely as possible and with at least some of her money intact. Paying the ransom would be the first step of her escape.

At the end of her cocktail she walked home through the campus precisely to pass by the shrine with the angel and to let her fear stand before a supernatural being holding a sword. By that

hour the playing field had been abandoned by the student jog-
gers who patrolled its edges at sundown, but in the spaces between the trees around it groups of teenagers sat playing guitars
and harmonicas amid the cacophony of the cicadas. There was a
brooding malevolence, their previous innocence and lightheartedness lifted out of them. It was a mood that matched her own
as she went between them and came out into the walled alley
that led back to Soi Sawatdi. Just as rapidly as it had come over
her, her past dissolved and she returned to the equator.

At the Kingdom she paused by the turtle pools. As she did so a
motorbike drew up to the glass doors and Ximena jumped off
its back. The driver was one of the restaurant staff, whom Sarah
recognized, and Ximena, seeing Sarah, thanked him curtly and
strode toward the turtle pool with a slightly forced smile. It was
an accidental collision that was not entirely welcome for either
of them. They had to make the best of it as they took the same
elevator up to their respective floors.

"We've missed you," Ximena said as they waited on the
ground floor. "The building seems deserted, doesn't it?"

They looked back into the lobby through the security doors,
the coffee tables with their yellow flowers, a color symbolizing the
monarchy and therefore the political sympathies of the owners.

"It does," Sarah agreed. "It's like when elephants sense a coming tsunami."

"Elephants?"

They stepped into the claustrophobic car.

Sarah went on, "Apparently they can. Dogs too."

When the doors closed they saw themselves nightmarishly
reflected in the mirrors that now enclosed them on all four sides.

"What happened to the card games?"

"They fell by the wayside, I guess," Ximena said as she pressed the button to her floor. "Nat's been very busy too."

But the absentee who mattered was Mali, the animating force.

"We were wondering about you," Ximena added, more cautiously. "You're all right, aren't you?"

"I'm fine."

"You can always call me if you're not. Do you want to come up for a drink?"

They reached the fifteenth floor and Sarah's stop.

"Maybe not tonight," Sarah said, but she thanked Ximena for the offer of solidarity while avoiding her eyes. There had always been that subtle trace of mockery in the chef's gaze toward her, but what did she find so funny? Sarah hurried into her landing with a quick "Good night" and waited for the elevator to move before taking out her key. She found, to her surprise, that her hand was shaking and she turned to make sure that the elevator continued to Ximena's floor. The chef no longer inspired confidence, and Sarah could not decide why; her fear of her blackmailer had become generalized.

On the Tuesday night, she took a taxi down to the junction at Asoke and the Skytrain station with a spare suitcase loaded with the money, climbed up to the trains in dense crowds, and rode the Mo Chit line all the way to the end. It was the tail end of rush hour, the office workers pouring back to the outer neighborhoods, the trains packed with exhausted girls in perfect shirts, their eyes slow and drained. She must have been the only person in that city who loved the rush-hour trains, because she was the parasitic alien who had no real need to be on them. As the crush intensified, the individual diminished: it was the erosion of her own self that she so relished. Below, in the dry darkness, the roads were jammed with headlights. She came to the terminal at Mo Chit.

A river of people spilled down the narrow stairways that led to the street, where rusting and windowless buses waited for them with a promise of suffocation. She was carried downward by this river and deposited at the entrance to the underground MRT, which was empty and cool by contrast. It was one stop to Kamphaeng Phet Station. The exit stood by the back entrance to Chatuchak Market, which was closed except for the plant trade. A metal gate had been left ajar for the small number of people arriving from the MRT station, and she waited there for a while as if she knew what she was looking for. And yet she had no idea what to expect. Through the gates the pedestrian path circling the market could be seen, converted for this one night into a forest with ordered groves of jasmine, bamboo, and palms. Despite the curfew at eleven, which was in any case generally disobeyed, the market was crowded—a Thai passeggiata in a simulated forest. And at the far end, elevated trains snaked past in the mist with their brightly lit windows. But by the station itself it was quiet.

It was not a place where people lingered. She found the trash cans the letter had mentioned and set the bag down behind them well out of view of stray passersby. A dull anger tore at her and she almost changed her mind. The thought that it had all been for nothing, or almost, was a difficult pill to swallow. To be ruined by a blackmailer whose face she would never see. But what unsettled her the most was her acquiescence, and how pathetic it was.

Leaving the bag, she went back past the station entrance and stood for a moment by the bus stop on the main road, where the waiting crowds had thinned as the evening wore on. Now only a few people were descending the steps from the Mo Chit BTS station. Without turning, she went back up those same steps and onto the platform for the Hua Lamphong train, where many of the night-market shoppers had gathered with their portable potted flowers and cactus, and there she caught the next train returning to where she had started out. The thought that a stranger might pick up her treasure almost made her turn back, but by then it was far too late to feel any regret about being outwitted. Being on the train again, rejoining a mass of other humans who didn't know her and who had no idea what she had just done, was a welcome liberation. She could take any train she wanted, choosing to step off at any station at random for no reason other than she liked the name. In this way she found herself at Victory Monument, carried along by a vast crowd wearing surgical face masks, borne down into the streets below, where the heat overwhelmed her and carried her to a small restaurant above the canal. There she ate a boat noodle soup with hands shaking with a fine vibration, as if all the nerves running through her body had been set in motion by her own relief.

———

FIFTEEN

Later that week, Roland walked by himself down to Soi 33 to find the bar designated by the business card Goi had found in Unit 77. It was another night when his wife was working late, and it was ten by the time he had arrived. The street was famous for its bars devoted to the theme of dead European artists. He had had a few drinks before at the tilting, as-if-melting bar of the Dalí, and had passed a few dark hours at both the Renoir and the Degas with clients and work friends. Never had the Paris of 1890 seemed so distant. He had always philandered there with others but never as a solitary customer. It was not really his scene, when he considered the matter. There *was* no scene to which he belonged.

They went on occasion to the Monet, where the girls sometimes wore water-lily-themed skirts, but the conceit had never attracted him. Yet the street now was alive with its own animus. After the previous rain, the heat had returned like the stagnant gas from a volcano and the masseuses lay flat on their backs on

the loggias of their parlors, fanning one another with a quietly
repressed exasperation that seemed to him hardened by centuries of indifferent outcomes. For him, cynical as he was, it was
only in rare moments that the city's soul returned. He rarely noticed it himself. He was too rushed normally, too agitated by his
own concerns. But he noticed it now. They washed their hair
squatting in the gutters, throwing buckets of water over one another and their soap-sudded pet dogs. The gossip of the street,
bandied from loggia to loggia in incomprehensible argot, the
small businesses turned into the station of a spontaneous grapevine. Half of the neons had been turned off and many of the
girls had migrated to the curbside tables, where carbide lamps
offered a different light. The trees looming over them were stationary, trapped by the heat: it was only the rain that cleared the
air for an hour and caused them to sway. And on the matted and
long-abandoned cables that looped their way across the surfaces
of the shop-houses a few birds sat morosely, as if waiting for
someone to make a mistake.

Halfway along the *soi*, and buried amid the thickets of bars
and clubs, he found the small golden sign for Demonia and its
dark wooden door framed by two ornamental trees and two
"European-style" wall lamps. There was a girl dressed as Satan
outside, with a red cape and two red horns atop her head, but
cheerful enough to be completely unconvincing. A poster on the
door announced a "Midnight Mistress." He went straight into a
dark interior with token indications that it was intended as a
premonition of hell, but equipped with blended whiskeys and
peanuts. There were a few other solitary drinkers, a few girls, low
music, and a barman himself in glowing horns. He had the feeling that *farangs* here were rarer than Japanese or Koreans. The

other drinkers, all Japanese, looked up for a moment, then it was
oblivion again. The barman now gave off a slight surprise at seeing a *farang* with obvious signs of superior wealth planted at his
bar, but Roland put him at his ease with a few large notes and
ordered himself a highball. He asked what and where the Midnight Mistress was and received only a shrug in reply. The place
was not yet full and it was, therefore, a good moment for Roland
to describe Mali as best he could and then to shyly proffer the
photograph he had just acquired from Goi, pilfered from her
unit. Mali in her young glory, instantly recognizable to another
man, he would have thought. The barman seemed to be thinking
what to say before telling him that she had been there once in
the company of two men. She was *luk-thuung*, so easy to remember. Perhaps, though, it had only been one man. It had been one
of his Japanese customers, but he was not a regular either. The
regulars, as Roland could see, were all around them.

"So she wasn't working here?"

"No, no. But the girls seemed to know her. Are you collecting
a debt?"

It made Roland chuckle before the denial: "No, nothing like
that. I have nothing against her at all. It's a private matter. And
the man she was with?"

"Japanese, like I said."

"Were they *together* together?"

"I can't remember. It was a few months ago. But I do remember her name was Pom."

"And his?"

"There are too many of them, their names—"

"One of the black suits?"

"You know the style. They come and go."

But then the barman remembered more: the man had been in a few times after all. A salaryman of medium build, one would say, his suits a cut above the rest, a standard black car that brought him to the club and picked him up afterward. Before "Pom" came on the scene—the barman said—he would sit alone at the bar and drink vodka tonics and then walk up Soi 33 by himself to drink at the Hailiang whiskey speakeasy at the top of the street. He explained this to the staff at Demonia in great detail. They would ask him if he wanted a girl from Demonia, but he refused. He didn't want a bar girl, not even the more sophisticated ones who worked on Soi 33. No one ever saw him at the other bars, meanwhile, and he never came with work colleagues as most of the Japanese men did. A man rather refined and solitary.

"But you would say he had money?" Roland insisted.

The barman rolled his shoulders. "He had a tab here for a while and it ran into the tens of thousands of baht. But that's not unusual."

"Then what was his last name?"

The implication was that the barman could look it up with a sufficient tip, the tabs all being recorded. But it was against house policies of discretion and privacy. Roland suggested that he could just tell him man to man and no one would know. But the barman was not pliable that night.

"He paid the tab before going back to Japan. I think he went back. He doesn't come in now."

"And what about Pom?"

"Maybe he took her with him."

"She must have fallen for him," Roland muttered.

"It's a way out," the barman said with merry eyes.

"But she wasn't working the street. She had a decent office job."

"She did? Lots of the girls here are engineering students. So what?"

Roland should have known. The shadowy line between the world of respectability and the coterminous world of prostitution was porous, so that it was like stepping from one room in a house to another. Even the doors of these rooms had been taken off their hinges. But if she didn't work here, Roland thought, how did she end up here? He must have brought her for a drink, or the other way around. Gratifyingly, his wife's naïve assumption that she was a society rich girl had proven easy to disassemble and it had taken less than fifteen minutes of agreeable conversation in a single bar. At the same time, the barman appeared to recall more about her paramour than about Mali. It was he, then, who was the habitué of Demonia, in all likelihood going there after work or dinner in much the same way that Roland did. He and the barman had talked about golf, since all Japanese men in Bangkok seemed to share that same sad enthusiasm. But this gentleman had never once discussed his profession; only his love of rare whiskey. Golf and whiskey: the diversions of the Japanese man in Bangkok. Perhaps, the barman suggested, he might want to take a walk up the street to the Japanese whiskey establishment called Hailiang; the owner might remember the man better than he could.

By eleven the clubs on Soi 33 were slowly filling and the immense trees had taken on a baroque grandeur. The street's bedlam of cracked façades and neon signs, of doorways drenched in rose light and ramen palaces filled with white shirts, was so familiar to Roland by now that it was like a braille that he could feel his way along without looking. Outside Monet, the girls with little artist palettes in their hands and a quick *Bai nai?* as he passed. How many Japanese men were there roaming that street after hours? They were there in their thousands but, because they were polite and unassuming, no one noticed them, no one begrudged them their private pleasures.

In that respect they were entirely unlike the whites. It was as much their city as anyone else's and everybody knew it. But because they behaved themselves in both public and private, and because they brought in money from afar, not to mention the vast operations of the Toyota corporation, Thais respected them. What was curious was that the whites and Japanese and Thais rarely interacted in any deep way, and in the case of the whites and the Japanese not at all. The latter could generally not speak either English or Thai, and so formed a society within a society within a society. They didn't interact with anyone outside of their workplaces and the bars they liked, which were mostly reserved for their exclusive use.

This gave room for men like Ryo to move silently through the city's undergrowth. If he ever put a foot wrong he would embarrass not only his hosts but also his employers. He inhabited a hidden world within the larger urban one, a world you could glimpse by opening up one of the glossy entertainment and retail directory broadsheets for the Japanese, which one could find in any Japanese restaurant. Inside were endless adverts for *onsen*, hostess bars, supermarkets, and golf ranges—the golfing-equipment stores in Thaniya Plaza occupied pages all by themselves—and miraculously detailed maps of different neighborhoods with everything marked in kanji and hiragana. It was a world Roland knew little about, but it was everywhere around him, and Thais knew no more about it than he did. These parallel universes did not intersect.

Ximena returned to the Kingdom from the nightclub at three in the morning that night, slightly high and proud that she had evaded the curfew simply by walking in shadows. Work had been abysmally slow that evening, and so they closed early for the night and she had gone clubbing with some of the waiters. Earlier that week, the restaurant had been deliberately attacked for its high-society associations. A group of kids had swung by with golf clubs and thrown them at guests in the garden, then destroyed the kitchen windows with their clubs. It had been so bizarre that the staff had not resisted as they should have done. Now the *ker-fiu* had emptied the streets and the restaurant didn't stand a chance. The French owner, Gregoire, sat at his own bar, depressed and drinking, and waved them off as they left.

Ximena took the elevator up to the sixteenth floor but instead of letting herself into her apartment, she took a walk out onto the landing and laid both hands against the wall. In the dry spells, when the rain no longer tormented the stained-glass roof, the atrium and the vast space below the roof fell into a torpid silence within which the slightest disturbance created a clear echo. A cleaner dropping a mop out of sight, the gears of the service elevator starting into action as the garbage was taken out for the night: they formed sounds that felt close by even when they weren't. Since the staff was not working at that hour, the building was so quiet that she could hear the night porter padding in bare feet across the lobby, swatting mosquitoes with a rolled-up newspaper. There was a strange smell in the air, like gunpowder. The pest-control people had been spraying the ca-

nals around the building for hours to control the outbreaks of
dengue fever that came with the wet-season mosquitoes. She
could see the two landings below her and, of course, at the far
end in the opposite tower, the windows of Mali's long-empty
unit.

She came to that landing on occasion after work to smoke
and unwind. She liked observing the building's insides, with the
rows of windows offering glimpses of people's lives. She enjoyed
the silent dramas. She, too, had noticed a thinning-out of the
occupants. It was the less-well-heeled tenants who had stayed
on. Sometimes she caught the fleeting movement of others, quiet
as cockroaches moving away as soon as she moved her head toward them. On the same floor as herself, on the landing bridge
that connected the four towers, she sometimes saw an old lady in
house slippers making her way toward the fire exit as if she intended to use it. Many of the senior citizens who lived there
were eccentric in their habits; they wandered about as if they
had long ago forgotten where they lived and why. They paused
by the open windows, where the cooling winds were strong, and
gazed out over the city, which had grown unrecognizable within
their own lifetimes. But which unit did the old lady inhabit?
Once, late at night during a storm, Ximena had glanced up and
seen a shadow move away from the light, a person who had been
watching her as she smoked her last cigarette of the night. Who
were these people whom she glimpsed only on these shadowed
landings late at night?

By the time she retreated to her own apartment, she was
chilled by a sense of being watched by someone she didn't yet
know. One of the secretive tenants barricaded in their units, who
could almost physically smell a foreigner intruding into their

world. She lay on her front-room floor and smoked a joint while listening to Silverstein. From far out in the night came the same sound of the rifle shots, which had continued for several nights now, and yet there were no sirens. They seemed to be getting closer, a noose tightening around them. It made her feel that life should be enjoyed even more while it was still possible to enjoy it. The military would crack down soon and they would all be forced to stay at home for weeks. In fact, to her mind it was not unlike the events in Chile that her parents had lived through before she was born. But they and the family had recovered, prosperity had returned, the cadavers in the basements of the military police had not been entirely remembered after all. It would be the same in this country. The wave of violence would roll over it and afterward the grass would grow again, as it always did. The problem was that Eiffel would not survive. She was already wondering which restaurant might take her, or whether she would even have to move to a different country. They didn't have coups in Hong Kong or Singapore—not yet, at least. A stable authoritarian pattern was good for restaurants. The diners soon lost their anxieties about the loss of democracy and returned with relish to their steak tartare and dinner dates. Money remained money, and sex remained sex.

She herself was happy to exploit the nexus, but what she really wanted was the capital to start her own restaurant. You didn't need that much in Bangkok, certainly far less than you'd need in any Western city. Still less than you'd need in other Asian ones. What she needed was a windfall that would enable her to open a small place near Thong Lor specializing in biodynamic wines and tapas. She had it all planned out. For a while she had considered asking Sarah or Mali for a loan, one she thought they could manage comfortably. It had been one reason to join their group and sound them out. She had quickly ascertained that both women had ready access to money that was not transparent. She had become more curious about Sarah in that regard. If she had money, and she was sure she did, it had an unmistakable odor of being newly acquired. It was something she could feel, something subtle but quite obvious.

Ximena slept badly and woke early, against her own intention to sleep late. Instead of showering she threw on a silk dressing gown, made some coffee, and wandered outside onto the landing, which was suffused with warm dust. She stepped over to the half-opened windows that overlooked the pool, as she often did in the morning while sipping her coffee. She gazed down through the dusty panes at the oblong of brilliant water and the frangipanis. A lone swimmer did her laps at the center of this sunlit tranquility, while around the pool the villas looked as if their inhabitants had also moved out for a few days. The curtains drawn, the shutters in place. In the garden area, one level below the pool, a building cleaner in the Kingdom's color-coded yellow T-shirt swept up petals with a dustpan and brush, her head covered with a floppy sun hat. The girl swimming was Sarah, as it so often was. A mediocre swimmer, but still able to do seven or eight laps without pause. Eventually, though, after that eighth lap, she would stop at the shallow end, lift up her goggles, and raise her eyes to the window where Ximena was standing with her coffee.

The two women did not seem to recognize each other, or at least Sarah would never wave to her as if she did. The distance maybe was too great, or the sun was in her eyes. And so Ximena was able to see her as if anew, with a fresh gaze. The American girl had something unusual about her. An unhappiness, a mania that she kept entirely to herself. You could see it in the way she stood there with her goggles raised onto her forehead, her eyes squinting and concentrated into a frown.

Ximena had to ask: who was she, in the end? A New York loner washed up on this tropical island like an English sailor of the eighteenth century shipwrecked on the beaches of Tahiti, only with sacks full of idle money. So much money, in fact, that she wouldn't even notice being relieved of a fair amount of it. Continuing her thoughts of the night before, she recalled that Natalie had told her that Sarah was a millionaire; she herself had heard it through the Kingdom's grapevine, and not just from Goi. Probably the accounting office knew it, or the small clique of wealthy landlords who leased out these units to select foreigners. People always got wind of the *farangs* who were loaded. Men who had found a darkening paradise and had no desire to leave it. But Sarah was different. She and Ximena were of a different generation. They were here for different reasons. They were both quietly desperate in their different ways.

Above the Kingdom, curling and vaporous clouds now threatened the sun and the light dimmed a little as they touched its outer rim, and the pool went from aquamarine to mid-blue. The swimmer hauled herself out of the water and walked over to the trees. A sudden wind swept their branches for a moment, rippling their leaves. Ximena turned and went back to her apartment. She showered, dressed for work, and then made more coffee. That same wind had now picked up and the large mango trees below had begun to writhe. In the largest villa near them, two maids raced across the lawn and swept up a footloose terrier.

The clouds finally captured the sun and a block of shadow fell across the gardens and villas and ramshackle lanes. Ximena shuddered, even in the heat. She suddenly noticed how quiet and empty all the *soi* were. Was it a national holiday, one of the many she could never keep up with? She checked it on her phone and saw that it wasn't. Something else was afoot.

Looking toward Sukhumvit and the dinosaur theme park whose Ferris wheel she could just see, she noticed a faint pall of smoke hanging above the thoroughfare and rising slowly. Then she realized why it seemed so becalmed. The huge, antiquated air-conditioning units stuck to the outer walls of the Kingdom had all gone silent and her own units were among them. In the middle of the day, the electricity had been switched off yet again.

She was going to work at the restaurant that day, but when she reached the elevator she saw at once that it had been turned off as well. She leaned over the landing wall and peered down at the distant lobby. Nobody was making a fuss yet. She went to the emergency stairs and considered the matter: she could walk down from the sixteenth floor, but could she walk back up in the heat?

After waiting a few minutes, she decided to go down and risk it. The staff at reception would be able to inform her about the outage and at what time the current would be turned back on. On her way down the stairs she heard a few cries and the echoes of slamming doors. The inconvenience was beginning to stir annoyance. But she met no one on the stairs.

At the reception desk the two men there claimed that they had no idea what was going on. It was not the building's generators that had failed this time. This might have been a lie to fend off irate complaints, but they said they had called the authorities and been told that the power would come back on in two hours. It was what she wanted to hear.

She walked out into the street and it seemed plunged in a deeper shade than that cast by mere clouds. The men in uniforms were sitting by the canal with homemade fishing rods and didn't notice her passing. What could they have been fishing for in water colored like gunmetal? Along the little *soi* the student restaurants had closed and the convenience store was shuttered; the *motocy* boys had called it a day and the stand was occupied only by two sleeping dogs with their heads resting on their front paws. By the time she reached the junction with Soi 31, a few warm drops of rain were falling into the ragged sugar palms that stood in the waste lot on the opposite corner—the deserted garden of a long-gutted house that was too haunted to restore.

At Eiffel, she found the owner, Gregoire, alone in the kitchen, drinking a glass of brandy and doing an inventory. But where were the others?

"I gave them the day off," he said imperiously.

Then she noticed that the lights inside the restaurant were out and that it was hot and stuffy in the kitchen. *The generator is down,* she thought. And yet the generator never failed. It was more reliable than the grid itself. So it was certain the entire grid was down too.

"The whole sector?" she burst out.

"A few streets around us, yes. The fridges are down too: we'll have to throw a lot of stuff out. Obviously I closed the restaurant for tonight."

"You sure it won't come back on soon?"

"No one knows. I made some iced coffee this morning," he added in resignation. "But it'll be warm in an hour."

They went into the garden to drink it. The parasols kept off the raindrops and the air was cooler than inside the restaurant. They ended up staying there all afternoon, drinking bottles of warming rosé that Gregoire was now resigned to selling off.

"We're probably going to have to close the restaurant," he said as he opened the first bottle. "I don't know what to tell you. It's as you see. If we have to close every night because of the troubles, there's no way it can go on. People will be just too scared to venture out at night. Perhaps *scared* is the wrong word—they're a stoic bunch. More stoic than us. But all the same, they're prudent. They don't want to be sitting in some French restaurant when the rubber bullets start flying. Or the real ones."

They toasted Fate, and it wasn't so grim after all. He went on: "You know how we operate. We're on the high wire all the time. It's the way this business runs. Do you have a backup plan for work?"

"I hadn't really thought that far ahead."

"Any savings you can fall back on?"

"Some," she lied.

"Enough to pay the rent?"

"For a while. How long do you think this will go on?"

"My sources say the military will come down on them and it will be over quickly. Fingers crossed, eh?"

Fingers crossed for bloodshed, a lethal blow to the little people, and a return to a full house every night.

It was dark by the time she set off back to the Kingdom. At the top of Sawatdi a cluster of *soi* dogs began to follow her through the shadows. The lights of all the condo towers were still down and so were the public streetlights. The jungle sounds of the great trees that soared up along the stagnant canal were deafening, as if the insects knew when a moment of invasion and dominance had arrived. Here and there a flashlight broke the darkness on the balconies above the street, or deep inside the construction sites. Peering up the side street that led directly into the Srinakharinwirot campus, Ximena saw a carbide lamp set on the ground by the guard post, and the silhouettes of the spreading trees behind it were submerged in a lovely dusk light made sonorous by the hordes of little birds massed in the canopies. The guards at the Kingdom were playing cards by another carbide lamp set by the canal and they barely acknowledged her as she passed through the portcullis. They had grown more surly. In the parking lot there were more of the carbide lamps, but the overhead neon tubes were extinguished. In the lobby, the heat was tremendous and she sat down for a moment in one of the rattan armchairs. There was no one at the reception desk, and it was only then that she realized that in reality she had been fired.

Inside the atrium, a few of the same small birds—swallows or martins—had managed to enter and were spiraling around with shrill cries right under the roof whose own vitreous creatures seemed to beckon them in. Drops of her sweat splashed down on the floor and she had to wipe them out of her eyes. In half an hour the darkness even here would be almost total if the power didn't come back on. She had already calculated that she had candles at home, bottled water, and a small gas stove for cooking: she would be all right for a night even if the outage lasted until the next day. But first she would have to climb the sixteen floors in ninety-five-degree heat, with no light.

The stairwells were crowded with geckos, as if they had all gathered there by some collective instinct. When she shone her phone's light on them they didn't scatter but stared back at her without fear. Who could say what they hunted now on those slimy walls. When she paused to catch her breath, she heard footfalls high above her, the slow scraping of the elderly, and by the windows the crackle of a bonfire in the waste lot, where the drivers played *tagraew*. The taste of the smoke reached her tongue. By the time she reached the fifteenth floor she thought to drop in and check on Sarah. It was likely the American would be ill equipped to deal with the power outage. Sarah's landing by then was so dark that Ximena had to fumble her way to the bell. The ring was loud and yet no one came to the door. She rang a second time and was patient; sure enough, the peephole came alive with an eye.

"Ximena?"

"I came to see if you were all right," Ximena called out.

The door creaked open and Sarah was there in a tracksuit and bare feet, eating a pot of Bulgarian-brand yogurt, which Ximena also bought at the Villa all-night supermarket. She looked merely timid rather than afraid. She opened the door wider, and by that action invited Ximena in. Behind her there was a merry glow of tea lights.

"You have candles!"

"I do. Once you light them it's not so bad."

They suddenly laughed, overwhelmed by the absurdity of their predicament. The tension between them during their previous encounter in the elevator had eased.

"You want a drink?" Sarah said. "I have some vodka that's still cool in my fridge. Even some ice cubes."

"Yeah, I could use a drink."

But, Ximena thought, I've been drinking all day. She stepped into the apartment, the floors cool and polished. The windows were open, since the outside air was, incredibly, cooler than inside, and tea lights had been set along a spacious table where Sarah worked. Her laptop still had some battery life and there was a portable charger ready to step in when it died. It was a neatly organized space, with two shelves of books arranged inside a cabinet and a small bronze bodhisattva presiding over them. It was the apartment of a woman who spent almost all her time by herself and liked it that way. Ximena had the feeling—surely irrefutable—that hardly anyone had stepped inside this place aside from the maid. Outside on the balcony the breeze cooled their faces and they sat around the glow of the candles in their protective glass shells while the wind blew their hair about. At the horizon, the silent lightning had returned, and the hulking cement tower blocks possessed their own candlelit luminescence, with hundreds of tiny flames set along the windows and balconies all around them. It gave the neighborhood the atmosphere of an open-air catacomb.

"Did you hear the gunshots earlier?" Sarah asked, but without any apparent anxiety.

"I did, but no one knows what they're about. Did you listen to the radio?"

"I did but I couldn't understand it. The Internet TV has gone blank. There's just a government broadcast and military music—but I lost reception this afternoon anyway. I think they're closing everything down."

Ximena tossed back her shot of vodka and winced. "That's what it is. We can't even leave to go to the airport. There are no cars anywhere."

"I tried calling Uber and Grab, but it was a blank."

"But where did you want to go?"

"Oh, I don't know." Sarah shrugged. "I was just seeing if I could take off if I wanted to."

In reality, though she kept it to herself, she had already been looking at flights back to New York. No better moment to leave had presented itself thus far. There were plenty of flights, but no one could say if they could actually leave.

Ximena went on: "I'd leave, too, if I could. I'd take a taxi to the border if I could find one that would go."

"I can't believe how sudden this feels—"

"Not really—it's been building for weeks out there." Ximena gave Sarah a long, cool look as if subjecting her to an entirely new assessment. "Did you notice that most of the cars in the lot have gone? It's like an evacuation."

"Want another shot?"

Ximena hesitated. But ahead of her lay nothing but a hot and uncomfortable night on her balcony, doused in mosquito repellent. She wouldn't sleep a wink. They slugged back another shot each and the heat began to feel less oppressive. Yet the rain refused to arrive in full force.

They could hear men on the ground floor of the building talking excitedly, shadows slipping along the canal with the subtlety of brigands. On the far side of the barbed-wire fence the *tagraew* field was empty except for the dogs who had gathered there in extraordinary numbers. They had formed a mob that had not yet found an anti-human purpose.

"I hate those fucking dogs," Sarah said quietly.

"They're getting bolder. It's not an encouraging sign."

"They can sense that the humans have abandoned the field. I

guess they all have country houses to go to. It's just us *farangs* who get left behind to fend for themselves. I'll bet some of them have gone abroad too."

"Like Mali," Ximena said.

"If she did. We don't know that."

"She seemed to know what was about to happen."

"Did she?" Sarah seemed genuinely surprised.

"Yes," Ximena insisted. "She did."

"Well, yes, perhaps she out of all of us would know what would happen out there."

It was striking that they now used the words *out there* to describe the city. *In here* then was the Kingdom. Ximena raised her tumbler and touched Sarah's.

"Come on. This might be our last night on Earth, for all we know. They might burn down the Kingdom during the night."

"They might," Sarah admitted, thinking of the resentful staff as much as the rioters. "They very well might. If they do, good luck to them."

If they did, she was thinking to herself, she wouldn't mind too much.

The previous night, Sarah had fallen asleep on her sofa with a book, only to be woken by what she thought was the rain. But it hadn't been raining. She heard sounds from the landing like that of something nosing about and then, a little after, a whining exactly like that of a small dog. Her first thought was that one of the tenants had left for the week and their dog had escaped from their unit. Trapped inside the labyrinth of landings and passageways, the animal was confused and looking for signs of human life. She had gone to the door and pulled it open, but there was no dog outside it. And yet, as she was standing there, she heard the whining again, but from farther off, and she thought distractedly of Mali's little pet.

"Was it her dog, then?" Ximena said.

"I never saw it. But later, when I was sitting in the front room, I heard it again at the door. Then I began to feel afraid."

"Maybe she left it with someone and didn't tell you."

"Didn't tell me? I'm the one person she would have trusted to keep that dog while she was away. I'm the *only* person she would have asked."

"So, that means—"

"She left it."

Or she didn't leave, Ximena thought.

"There has to be an explanation."

Ximena now noticed Sarah's hands shaking slightly as they rested on the table. The moths dancing around the candles made her flinch. She looked gaunt and brittle in the half-light, as if a wave of anxiety had broken over her and smashed her normal composure into pieces. Her eyes kept darting toward the ceiling above them and Ximena finally asked her if there was someone still in the apartment overhead. Or had they left with everyone else?

"No, I think they are still there. It's the strangest thing. Sometimes—not very often—I hear someone hit a single note on a piano I think they have in there. Then I hear someone walking. Just for a few moments."

Sarah downed her third shot and reached for the bottle in the middle of the table. At that moment there was an interruption: the loudspeakers had returned, and Ximena understood the words although Sarah didn't. It was an order to clear the streets and return home, the same order that she had already heard many times. The voice whined out in the night, as if frustrated or even outraged that its previous commands had not been obeyed, and then the city fell silent again. The streetlights flickered on again for a moment and then fell back into their own obscurity. In a single moment the rain broke. Ximena looked at her watch. Three hours had passed since she entered the Kingdom and she had no idea how they had passed so quickly.

"Let's finish the bottle at least," Sarah said, and it seemed out of keeping with the way Sarah had always struck her before. She had come unstuck, the glue holding her together had been melted by the drink. But at least she was less hostile than she had been earlier.

"If you say so," Ximena agreed.

Now she, too, wanted to knock herself out.

But Sarah was no less hostile beneath her jittery exterior. She was merely waiting to see how Ximena behaved. Nonetheless they drank together morosely for a while and Sarah watched the other's face for signs that her suspicions had been correct: Ximena was not telling her something; she was playing innocent in a way that Sarah herself recognized all too well. She did it herself, after all. It was cat and mouse, as always with human beings, and often the cat became the mouse and vice versa. And yet she had become the mouse with her blackmailer and it filled her with rage that she had been used, duped. Even the great April Laverty had not been able to use her. The tables had been turned and she had been punked by an upstart. Therefore she had become obsessed with a burning need to discover who it had been. Across from her at her own table, it was possible that the culprit was sitting there drinking her vodka, and the idea was almost thrilling. She had an instinct about Ximena, even though she liked her; the girl was slippery and shifty, a grifter looking for an exit. Rather like herself, in the end. She poured her shots hospitably and as they drifted into drunkenness she wondered if she really minded Ximena taking her money and insolently sitting there enjoying her hospitality—she had to admit that it was amusing in a way. A tremendous joke if it was true. And if it was true, the Chilean was an admirable actor, a true professional. She looked into Ximena's eyes as best she could, but as she did so she suddenly doubted herself. No guile, no treachery, no artifice could be seen there. That was the problem: one could be wrong just as easily as one could be right about another person. From one moment to the next the needle of one's moral compass shifted direction. She wanted to tell Ximena that she appreciated having her as a friend, and thank her for stopping by. It would be a drunken expression, half-false, but the chorus of howling dogs had started up again, packs of the animals roused across the neighborhood, and perhaps across the whole city, sensing their moment of opportunity. Ximena turned to the open windows and her expression was fatalistic.

"Hear that? The dogs are in revolt," Ximena said.

"They'd come and eat us, if they could."

"*Chaiyo*," Ximena said, touching her glass.

Ximena remained standing and looked down at the craters that had now replaced parts of the tobacco warehouses. Throughout the last few days the demolition had continued apace, unnoticed by her until then, and the outer walls of the structures had been breached, the internal concrete staircases reduced to rubble. It was here, in fact, that the dogs had found a place to congregate at night. They swarmed in fluid packs inside the broken walls and newly created pits like soldiers adapting to a bombed-out landscape, keeping quiet and unseen as they manned their positions. Ximena asked Sarah if she had noticed how quickly the warehouses had degraded. In a time of crisis it made no sense.

"Did you see that?" Sarah cried out, pointing a finger to the sky.

As before, giant bats had begun to dip and wheel around the towers of the Kingdom, shrieking and gliding close to the balcony where they were sitting.

"They've only been here two days," Sarah went on. "They're all in the trees around the site."

"Is something drawing them in?"

"That's what I have been wondering. They have a keen sense of smell."

Against the horizon's constant eruptions of lightning they looked more like ravens, large enough to make one recoil as they came close.

"Don't you feel they could be spirits?" Sarah asked.

"Spirits?"

It seemed to Ximena that all the pressure and paranoia that had been building up slowly around Sarah found that moment to surface and become physical. Her appearance bore it first: there was a wildness in her eyes, and the look she wore was more tense and drawn than usual. For the first time, Ximena noticed a shock of dark roots at Sarah's hairline, in stark contrast to her usual blond. She saw, too, a surge of aggression cross her face, a flicker of malice that came and went with the commotion in the air.

"I know you're far too rational to agree with me, Ximena, but

I've been feeling it more and more. There *are* spirits. And we have to keep them at bay."

"I thought the building was purified by monks every year," Ximena said, half-joking.

"But it isn't enough. It clearly isn't working." And now Sarah felt an urge to tell Ximena everything. Only at the last minute, she pulled herself back. "Whenever the power goes off, like now, I can feel them moving in. They're waiting for a vacuum, just as the dogs are. They know that when the electricity is on, when the lights are on, no one believes in them. They have to be believed in order to exist. Do you see what I mean?"

"In a way," Ximena drawled.

But Ximena was now thinking only of getting out of this apartment and away from the dead blackness of the eyes across the table. Yet at the same time she remembered that earlier in the evening she had noticed small shrines that had sprung up all along the corridors, and by implication inside the landings as well. They were filled with marigold garlands and incense sticks and they must have been placed there by the tenants through the action of a collective mood. The atrium was touched by the floral scent of the incense, the shadows cast by the tea-light candles set around them. It wasn't just Sarah. It was the building's atmosphere that had overwhelmed her as well, as if the Kingdom's inhabitants no longer believed that the power failures were entirely natural. When Ximena did eventually get up to say that she was going to bed, Sarah didn't get up with her, and her reaction was sluggishly distant. Her parting shot was to tell the Chilean that the corridors were no longer safe from visitors from the afterlife and everybody in the Kingdom knew it.

SIXTEEN

Sarah woke at two in the afternoon the following day to find that the rain still hadn't stopped and the lights had not come back on. Her room was saturated with a dank and faintly floral humidity. The night before, after Ximena left, she had begun to hear a scratching and whining coming from the landing, but she had been too unsettled to see where the noise might be coming from. She had imagined something waiting on the landing, alive and wet, dripping on the tiles. It could have been a dog or a human, but whatever it had been she had heard water moving around her landing and heavy breathing, panting almost. She bit an Ambien in two, swallowed half, and tried to fall asleep as thunder shook the building. It was her nerves, she decided, as soon as she woke. As she was nearest the edge of her physical limits, her exhaustion made her hallucinate.

When she opened her laptop, she saw that it had fifteen minutes of power left and her phone maybe thirty. It was the moment to quickly look over the one-way ticket to New York she had been considering. She felt a relief knowing that she had at least an exit in hand if she wanted to purchase it. Sweeping into her bedroom, she opened a suitcase and began cramming her clothes into it. She threw her toiletries into the case, snapped it shut, and hauled it out into the main room. Then she returned to the bedroom to pack the money. Two bags would be enough to flee swiftly. At least she would be ready. Calmed a little, she went back to her computer. She planned to walk to the Terminal 21 Mall and use a public outlet when her devices expired, but before she had even taken her cold shower the lights suddenly came back on and the air conditioners stirred into life. The emergency dissipated, and something like normality seemed to reassert itself. She took a hot shower instead, made some coffee, and recharged both of the devices as well as her portable chargers.

With the windows now closed, the apartment gradually cooled and became bearable again. The modem came back on and she connected to the Internet. There was no news on the sites permitted inside the country about what had happened, but various forums were filled with crackling gossip about insurrection during the night and clashes in several places that had escalated in ways that no one could verify. The television stations were still blacked out and the radio had fallen silent. She went out to the landing and checked that the elevator was running again, then locked the door behind her and set up her desk for a few hours of reconnection to the world. She went straight to a search for April Laverty. Though it was almost habit to do so, Sarah had felt it in her sleep, no doubt in a dream she could no longer remember. Some news about her employer awaited her. But even then, nothing could prepare her for the discovery that the great author had passed away the day before at her house in

Sagaponack. With the pain came an immense burden-lifting, rather than the dread she might have expected. It was more a vindication, a confirmation of what she had known was coming. It was also the moment to finally buy her ticket. She did so almost immediately, feeling an assurance that her return would now be unlikely to cause her too much aggravation. She would monitor the situation from afar and change the ticket if need be. But for now she was quietly sure of herself. Every instinct she possessed told her that the danger she had feared there would not materialize. With a hundred grand in cash she could resume her life at the Paris Building and claim to the Laverty estate that she had been trapped in Bangkok by the closure of the airport. It was a credible excuse and only a few weeks had passed, after all. Already she had begun to plan her next move, her search for the next unwitting provider, and it seemed to her that she could resume her life if she was sufficiently cunning, humble, and tactful. It was the Kingdom, in fact, that had taught her how to dissemble better and how to survive. The spirits had not come to devour her after all.

Her real feelings toward Laverty revealed then an ambiguity. Even at the time of her employment the writer had grown irascible, and Sarah had often thought that on balance even her work was overrated. Her ego had bloomed in synchronicity with the decline of her faculties and talent. But at the same time, there were books of hers that Sarah had revered, possessing almost talismanic power when she was a student. How meticulously she had studied Laverty for all those years, and long before she had ever moved to New York. Her plan had never been conscious at the beginning. Respect, affection, contempt, and indifference had been mixed within her all along, and now they returned with all their old force. There was, moreover, no mention in the news of her letters or sales of her manuscripts, and for the first time a magnificent prospect offered itself: that the estate, now in total chaos, had not verified the sale to Chan, and that in the confusion they had not noticed anything untoward at all. Her sleight of hand had gone unregistered. It was true that the disappearance of Laverty's principal assistant—the person closest to her affairs—would have produced a scandal in the people around the writer, but since Laverty had been dying for some time it was just possible that one catastrophe had occluded the other. The con artist's brilliant timing.

As the afternoon drew in, the doorbell rang with an abrupt irritability and she was forced to give up the various threads of her thoughts in order to answer some intrusion from the outside world. But the peephole revealed a surprise. Mrs. Lim, her landlady, was standing there, dressed in a startling emerald silk dress and pearls, her hair immaculate after an hour at the salon that day—no power cuts in other parts of the city, it seemed—and her nails painted with the fieriness of younger days. She announced that she wanted to see how Sarah was coping with the unfortunate circumstances through which they were all obliged to live these days. She looked the American up and down and found that she had deteriorated quite a bit since the last time she had seen her. To her eye, Sarah's skin was haggard and the youth had seeped out of her mouth and eyes. She looked ten years older, and her hair looked awful, the worst dye job she had ever seen.

"The outages are beyond our control," she said, kicking off her sandals and coming into the apartment she owned without invitation. "Have you been all right without A/C? We're used to it, but not you, I suppose."

"I had to put up with it, like everyone else. I'm fine."

Mrs. Lim strode to the center of the main room and looked at the walls: everything seemed in order. Her eye took in smudges and cracks alike, and then the telltale signs of an imminent and hasty departure. A single forgotten sock lay on the teak floor, a glaring oddity she didn't feel prepared to comment on.

"Are you scared to be alone, Sarah? My daughter said to me that since we have a house in Hua Hin you could go down there, if you liked."

"That's very kind of you. Will the power go out again tonight?"

"We can't say. Probably not. The situation will be resolved soon enough. Don't worry. From time to time we have these crises. It's nothing to worry about." *Everyone is brave*, she wanted to say to the American, *until a soldier prepares to blow their head off*.

"I see many people have moved out of the building," Sarah said.

"Only temporarily. Of course, our family isn't moving out—we have to be here. And we *refuse* to move."

Mrs. Lim gave Sarah a splendid smile, bearing all the self-confidence of her class, a smile to still the nerves and inspire the nation.

"When you say 'resolved,'" Sarah said, "you mean the army will get on top of it?"

"Of course the army will get on top of it."

"Is that what they do?"

"That's what armies are for, isn't it? If you're not going to go to

Hua Hin, then I think you should stay. It'll be fine. Just because other people panic doesn't mean we have to. There's something unappealing about people with no nerve." She looked the American up and down. "Is there anything you need meanwhile? The staff have been whispering about ghosts and the like. I hope you don't pay them any attention. They're country people. They're spooked by the outages and are now saying they are seeing them on the landings. Don't pay any attention. If my husband's ghost were walking around because of a power outage I'd be the first to know, believe me. It's just gossip." She smiled radiantly.

But Sarah had heard nothing of the sort. She had, more incredibly, come to her own conclusions on that score.

"By the way," Mrs. Lim went on, growing a little more glacial. "One other thing the staff mentioned is that you were very friendly with the Kaewmak girl across from you on the fourteenth floor."

Since Sarah had not heard that name before, she simply said, "Mali?"

"Is that what she calls herself now? I should have given you a printout about some of our tenants. Of course, they all come from good families, you don't have to worry about that. We're very particular about that here at the Kingdom. But there's always bound to be some eccentrics and misfits. All I can say is we had a problem with her rent last year and she was very difficult. She had an affair with a very well-known man in the building and the tabloids came sniffing around. It wasn't appreciated. Personally, I don't get involved with the lives of tenants, but I do think that one was a little out of the ordinary."

"She left?"

"The lease has come free, yes."

"But she owns the place. I mean, her family does."

"Her family?"

Mrs. Lim, having just mentioned good families, was suddenly put on the spot.

"Her aunt gave her a reference which I accepted, if that's what you mean. But her family doesn't own anything in the Kingdom. Not even a parking space. She was a renting tenant, not an owner. Not that I have anything against renters. You fine people are where the money is." She smiled again, one hand forming a ball and slipping into the other as if hiding the nails. "I have nothing against her either. She doesn't owe me any money, at least. If she owed me money it would be a different story."

In reality, Mrs. Lim recalled her dislike of that tramp. To her, Mali was fake and arrogant. She was not one of them, the *pu yai*, the good people who ran the Kingdom and everything around it as far as the eye could see. She was a half-breed interloper who spoke a tilted-to-the-side Thai that didn't please the ear, and she had a habit of looking you in the eye insolently. Her aunt was probably a fake as well. She didn't even recognize the name as being from among those of decent families. Still, she had come calling a few times and of course they had a few business interests together. Mrs. Lim couldn't help smiling. The foolish American had no idea who she was dealing with, but it would be far worse for all concerned if she did.

"So her apartment is empty?"

"She didn't tell you when she left?"

"She hasn't told me anything."

"Empty and due to be redecorated. It's like she just walked out and forgot to turn off the lights."

"Do you know where she went?"

"Why, yes I do. She wrote to me from London. She said she was seeing her aunt and wouldn't be coming back because of the disturbances. Her aunt is terrified, apparently. You didn't know she was in London?"

Sarah shook her head. Her heart was beating fast.

"Maybe she doesn't want anyone to know she's there," Mrs. Lim said. "She only told me because she wants her deposit back. I always return the deposits, unless someone's dog has ruined the parquet."

"What about Mali's dog?"

"Did she have one? She didn't register it if she did—are you sure she had one?"

"I met him many times, even looked after him for a weekend."

"Really? She never told me. In any case, there's no dog damage in the unit."

So she's in London and she never told me, Sarah thought, trying to make sense of it.

"I think she must have taken the animal with her," Mrs. Lim declared. "And I'm glad she did. Can you imagine if she'd left it?"

Sarah had to gather herself for a moment, her thoughts resuming their frenetic pace at this new information. "Thank you for telling me she's in London. I appreciate it. I'm tempted to follow her. But perhaps I should wait until things calm down."

Sarah was at pains to reassure her landlady that she wasn't about to bolt, which was precisely what she was planning to do. Mrs. Lim pretended not to notice.

"It's an admirable plan," she said. "One should always have one."

But here the older woman's interest ran out and she eyed the door.

"It would be best," Mrs. Lim said as she retraced her steps toward the door, "if you didn't answer anyone knocking on your door. I'm afraid the men at the front gate—I am trying my best to replace them—have been encouraged by the scum on the street and got ideas in their heads which we can't correct. Naturally, we'll fire all of them when we've regained full control, but for the moment we're going to have to put up with their insolence. What that means is that we can't be sure who is coming in off the street during the night. The security has gone to pieces. I don't think it'll have any consequences, but better to be safe. It'll only be for a few days."

"Is it a coup?" Sarah finally asked when they were out on the landing.

"What a tiresomely dramatic word. How could they possibly have a *coup*? It's only a coup if the army mutinies. They're not going to mutiny. So calm down. There's not going to be any such thing."

The old lady's face was perfectly controlled, not a single muscle disturbing the patina of makeup. She was a tough breed.

Sarah believed her, and so in her exhaustion moved on to a different thought: "There's one thing I wanted to ask you. There's someone playing a piano in the unit above mine. It's quite . . . distracting. Is there any way—I mean, could the management ask them to play within certain times? I didn't want to ask, myself."

"Which unit do you mean?" Mrs. Lim's eyes had narrowed.

"The one directly above."

"Above you? It's been empty for months. I've been looking for a tenant, but it's a bad market."

"So no one else has complained about the piano?"

"If the place is empty, how could they? I think you've misheard. What have you been hearing?"

Here Sarah faltered. Now that she reconsidered, it was possible that she had imagined it. Internally she conceded the point and gave way.

"I suppose it's possible—"

The sharp Lim eyes were upon her, now openly skeptical, and she knew what the woman was thinking. Sarah raised a hand reflexively to her hair and realized then that her roots were beginning to betray her drastic dye job, and that the old lady's unerring eye had noticed it. It was in that moment, as Mrs. Lim looked at her with disdain, that Sarah decided to leave the Kingdom and find a hiding place somewhere else. She had already made too many mistakes. Later that day, the power went down again with a soft finality.

When she had closed the door behind her, for her part, Mrs. Lim strode to the elevator and went up to the next floor with her master key in order to let herself into the apartment above Sarah's. The place had been occupied by a nice family of her acquaintance who had departed when the father was posted abroad. She remembered that they had held a sale of their possessions on the mezzanine floor. But there was indeed a piano in the main room—they had been unable to sell it. She went up to it now and opened its dust-encrusted lid. Had it been the little girl who used to practice on it? Mischievously, she hit one of the white keys with her finger and listened to the note reverberate around the room. The American was neurotic, you could see— they all were—but there was no way she could have known that an unused piano still stood in the apartment above her. Mrs. Lim closed the lid and looked around at the pink walls that the mother had painted herself ten years earlier. Momentarily she couldn't remember their name. A small daughter and a slightly older son. For a moment, slightly stunned, she thought she was sure the girl had been called Mali. But then again, it was a popular nickname for girls. Perhaps she was wrong. She went back out and took the elevator up to her penthouse, from where a view of the metropolis lay beneath her dead husband's telescope.

She put a record on her husband's antique record player, the soothing aid to her daily melancholy. It was an old one her parents had loved, a song of Suthep Wongkamhaeng from the early '50s, with a typically lilting brass section and sentimental lyrics. She didn't even know what the song was called, she only knew it by its opening words: *rak khun khao laew.* "Falling in love with you." She had listened to it when she was a small girl living in a large teak house in the lot adjacent to what was now the Kingdom. It had been the house of her grandparents, razed at her brothers' insistence upon the death of their father. Fear of lingering ghosts, greed for better returns: there was the story of the city as it came under the spell of an age that despised its own past. Her grandfather had been an ethnic Chinese tax collector who had branched out into silk, tobacco, and textiles: a millionaire both before and after the war. A glamorous man who got his suits made in Hong Kong at the Chan house, who wore whites and two-tone "spectator" shoes. The patriarch had built that house himself at enormous cost, every board made of teak, which her rapacious brothers had later sold separately after the house's demolition. Teak now was impossible to find.

She lay on her sofa with a pot of Earl Grey listening to records and feeling the bitterness rise inside her. Everything in her world had turned to dust except the Yoon money, which thrived with a life of its own and yet was dwindling by the day. Down in the waste lots by the tobacco warehouses, which she also owned by inheritance and which she was leveling to sell the land, her grandparents and her parents sat as tiny effigies inside their spirit houses, their magical zebras and slices of mango furbished weekly by her staff. But where were they in reality? Wandering in the past, or in the spirit world, and inconsolable. She had always thought that the building of the Kingdom had been a savage betrayal of them. This pile of leaking concrete and vulgarity had nothing to do with their exquisite taste and spiritual tact. But still, wandering as they did around the premises, they could hear the music they had loved so much in life. On the mantelpiece were all her family photographs, including several of her mother as a small girl, as if lost in the balmy summers of the 1930s. There was one of her in extravagant silk ribbons, holding a rabbit on the veranda that had been destroyed long ago and squinting at the camera as if the photographer owed her money. She could still remember those ribbons. Her mother had kept them in a box and took them out to try them on her daughter. She said they had been a gift from a Japanese officer. Their pale pink color had impressed themselves vividly on her memory, and yet she had never thought to ask herself what had become of them. And so, by the same route, her thoughts turned to the American girl and to Mali, who symbolized everything she detested in the present time.

They were an odd friendship. The half-Thai scavenger was

after something; the American was adrift in life. She was sure that Sarah had a nervous tic in one eye, or that some sudden nervousness made her twist her fingers together. And that preposterous hair. But there was also something more violent in her that Mrs. Lim could sense, something held just below the surface. Her husband always used to say that *farangs* were the ghosts they had to endure in order to atone for their own failures. Even now, in the afternoon, she felt his own ghost creeping around in his slippers, watching her from the top of the newel stairs that stood in the middle of the room with the slightly angry stare he had worn all his life. His gilded elephants and kilims were still there. There were pictures of him as a child in French sailor suits still on their mantelpiece. His telescope was still trained on a skyscraper far away, where he had been convinced his business rivals were plotting his downfall. Only he had known the extent of their coming bankruptcy, the fall of the Kingdom caused by their collapsing investment portfolios. She spoke aloud to him while the thunder rolled in the distance. Her insiders told her that the tenants were preparing to flee, the Mercedeses and BMWs were leaving the garage. As she had told Sarah, and as she told him now, the staff were becoming uppity and restless. "But then again," she said to him, sipping her Earl Grey and laying her head against the faded silk of her mother's sofa, "we're bound to have an uprising once in a while. It's nothing to lose sleep over."

Since she remembered several coups since her childhood, plenty of bodies lying in the streets, she was dismissive even to him. The scuttling of those human cockroaches down the side streets around the Kingdom did not faze her. Her grandfather had taught the values needed to control a family, a clan, a building, a business empire. Such things were not won or retained by charm and chatter. It was then, pondering the unstable sky, that she remembered that she had meant to summon Pop to the penthouse to catch up on the latest news from inside her domain, which she could not collect herself. These days he was the only person she trusted. He had worked for her husband for decades. He had seen it all, and known everyone, and that indeed was the purpose for which her husband had hired him, first as a foreman in her grandfather's tobacco warehouses and then as the groundsman for the Kingdom.

She and her husband had gradually come to rely on him for information more than anything else. He could repair generators and pumping systems, but as he had grown older and more eccentric they had let him stay free in his garden room and summoned him once a week to have tea with them and discuss the gossip he had picked up with his incomparable ear. It was a habit that had served her well over the years as she perfected her hold on the Kingdom and its finely meshed inner workings. It enabled her to keep control of the building's social complexion and to monitor the strange ways of the various foreigners, who were potentially subversive—they complained bitterly at committee meetings about the maintenance of the swimming pool and the jurisdiction's far-from-transparent finances—but exquisitely profitable. She liked them because they had no rights and could be kicked out at a moment's notice. In any case, it was the hour for the summons and she went to the electric bell that her husband had had built to connect the penthouse with Pop's miserable cell twenty-one floors below them. After she had pressed it she knew that Pop would appear at her door within five minutes, bringing with him as he always did a smell of flower beds, paraffin, and Butterfly agarwood perfume.

This time he brought some flowers from the gardens and he gave them to her before *wai*-ing and shuffling off his sandals.

"I was wondering about you," she said as she made some roselle tea for them on her gas stove. "What did the Metropolitan Company say about the power?"

"They said it's going on and off all over the city, madam."

"So they've lost control of the situation. How about our generators?"

"They should be working soon, but if at any time the power doesn't come in from the outside—"

"Never mind, we'll live. My husband always said if anyone could fix a generator, you could."

"Thank you, madam."

They sat at the rosewood dining table and he poured her tea.

"Bad weather this week," he said.

"Same as every year. I don't notice any difference, do you? I wish people would stop talking about the weather. I'm more interested in my tenants than the weather."

In that pragmatic spirit she wanted to know about the American girl, the Thai girl she was friends with, and the latter's love life. In their previous meetings Pop had not divulged what he knew concerning these topics, but he did now. The Thai girl, Mali, seemed to know many people inside the Kingdom and, for that matter, he was aware that madam also sometimes had her up for tea. There seemed to be a network that connected many people on the upper floors. Next to her lived a Japanese man by the name of Nimoto. And here was an oddity, Pop told her: re-

cently the Japanese man had not been seen. He appeared to have
vanished, even before the troubles began outside the Kingdom.
Pop had not noticed any movements on his patrols up and down
the fourteenth-floor landing, which passed by the man's windows. His unit was unusually quiet and rather somber outwardly. Of course, he kept Goi's secret visit for the *farangs* on the
twenty-first floor to himself. Even if the tenant were to have left
the Kingdom, Pop might have noticed a company car picking
him up, or his luggage in the lobby, but it occurred to him then
that he hadn't actually seen the man leave the building.

"He's a recent tenant?" Mrs. Lim asked, slightly surprised that
she didn't know this already.

"Yes, madam. He moved in during the winter."

"Is he married?"

"No, and he kept to himself."

"It doesn't seem unusual to me. The Japanese are always the
loneliest tenants."

"Yes, that is true."

Trying to recall details about the man, Pop had to admit
to himself that there was something distinctly nondescript
about the man. The Japanese salarymen all looked the same to
him, and they all played golf. Since they were more elegant than
the *farangs* they were paradoxically less noticeable. But what
struck Pop then was the particularity of his name: R. Nimoto.
He thought back to the middle-aged man practicing his golf
swings in the garden, the man he had assumed was Nimoto from
Unit 77.

"Don't you find it more than coincidental," Mrs. Lim said, as
if sensing the direction in which his thoughts were heading, "that

both Nimoto and Mali—two tenants with adjoining units—left the building at about the same time? Khun Kaewmak paid her rent two months ahead but she hasn't asked to freeze it. What on earth is going on?"

Pop was paid by Mrs. Lim herself directly to patrol the landings between midnight and five in the morning in order to detect anything unusual. She would not tolerate any criminal or suspicious behavior among her tenants, unless of course she was herself involved in the transactions. That was her right, after all. Over the years he had detected clandestine dealings here and there: a secret poker club where players from all over the city gambled considerable sums; two high-class escorts plying their business from suites rented by obscure companies; a boiler room run by three British men back in the days before the dictatorship; a high-society couple dealing drugs to their social peers. Such things came and went quietly and Mrs. Lim, having been informed of them, had discreetly asked for her cut from the operators and left it at that. These had enabled her to amass a small hidden fortune off the books, and she wasn't averse to continuing the practice as long as the criminality wasn't overt or severe.

Pop thought then about the blind woman and the dog he had once thought belonged to Mali. Now it seemed more obvious. The girl had borrowed it from the blind woman just for appearances.

"Maybe," he said tentatively, "it has something to do with the American girl. The two girls were very friendly. I saw them often in the pool together. Lately, the American girl has been behaving erratically—"

"Yes, I noticed that myself."

"Can I ask, does she pay her rent on time?"

"She pays in advance. *Months* in advance. That's not the problem."

What if, Pop ventured to suggest, she were involved in something in the black market that she had not divulged to anyone?

"How would you know that?" Mrs. Lim said.

"The maid says it's probably so."

"Which maid? And why?"

It was then that Pop told her about the money, the way it was stored in a spare room.

"Well, it's none of my business," she said finally. "Most of my tenants keep all their money under their beds."

"Yes, madam."

"Of course, if you could find some way to—"

He leaned forward and refilled her teacup, the sentence not needing to be completed. But Pop, meanwhile, was already thinking forward to his retirement, to a profit he might not have to share with his employer. There were things about Mali that he thought it best not to divulge. The girl's midnight trips to other doors in the Kingdom, her endless influx of boyfriends and dealers, and her long hours spent sitting by her phone completely immobile. It had occurred to him that she was a private dealer of some kind—drugs, sex, the usual things—but lately he had come to a different conclusion. She was laundering things inside the building, supplying a network of people who remained within their twilit privacy. What this trade might consist in he had not discovered.

As he was heading down in the elevator, having received his payment from Mrs. Lim, and having assured her that he had told her everything he knew, he recalled the leather drivers he had found in the trash and Sarah's reaction to them. He tried to remember if he had ever seen them on any of the landings he inspected nightly, and especially whether he had ever seen them on the landing of Unit 77. Or on the feet of any of the Japanese men he had seen so many times walking their dogs in the gardens—or swinging their golf clubs in mime. But now that he thought of it they *all* wore such leather drivers when they were milling around the building. It was part of their off-duty uniform. And yet he had his gut feelings, like Mrs. Lim, and they told him that the shoes, Mr. Nimoto, the American, and the fraudulent Thai girl and her dog were all connected to the sudden vacancy in Unit 77.

As he worked through the storm-cloud afternoons thereafter he heard cries from the streets almost daily and the sound of glass shattering in distant places, car horns wailing and security alarms echoing down the streets around the Kingdom. These eruptions were followed by long periods of silence and calm, rain falling against the windows and the palms and the rotting walls, voices going to and from inside the building. By six the power had faded away yet again and he knew this time that it would probably not return for a long while. He didn't mind. He was self-sufficient. By religious duty he continued to light candles inside the shrines littering the corridors and to make sure that they burned all night long, and that concerned him more than having electricity. Mrs. Lim also paid him to do that, but he would have done it anyway. The sacred order of the building had to be maintained in the face of anarchy. But in the late afternoons, when he drove his ancient motorbike to the supermarket through now-hushed streets, he felt the tension emanating from the knots of soldiers in green standing under the Skytrain and the emboldened camaraderie of the *motocy* drivers whom he knew well, haters of the regime who in normal times kept their peace but who now openly flaunted their opinions. The traffic had thinned and there was something anachronistically peaceful in the pedestrian pace, even in the body language of the soldiers who had nothing to do and in the tired salutes of the men in uniform who opened the doors of the supermarket to shoppers. The gardens were all his in the nocturnal hours, and he used a Bunsen burner to make his tea among the flower beds. If it came down to it, he would be the last person left at the Kingdom if he had any say in the matter. He and the dogs.

SEVENTEEN

On that same night, an hour after the power was cut, Sarah read by candlelight, and by the lowing sound of the frogs she mulled over Mrs. Lim's denial that there was anyone living in the apartment above her. The implication being that Sarah was either lying or aurally hallucinating, while Mrs. Lim's own motive for being so evasive was obvious. Not only did she not want to take responsibility for the annoyance to one of her tenants, she didn't want to bother another tenant, with whom she probably enjoyed a long relationship, with the grumblings of a mere *farang*. Mali had warned her of this sort of mentality and advised her to roll with it without getting too upset. It was an "us and them" society, *siwilai* or not.

Soon, however, she felt claustrophobic in her dark cave where the air was unbreathable and wanted to talk to someone. She considered laboring up the emergency stairs to the penthouse floor and calling on Natalie and Roland. She felt she didn't know Natalie as well as Ximena, but she was sure she'd be welcoming in the circumstances. Yes, and they probably had an ingenious way of keeping their wine cold. Driven by thirst, then, as much as by anything else, she slogged up the dark stairs to the twenty-first floor and walked across the bridge under the pitter-patter on the glass roof. None of the apartment windows were filled with light and the place now felt largely deserted, as Mrs. Lim had said; a mournful laboratory from which all the pampered mice had fled. The power crisis had finally scattered them.

But she was now face-to-face with the Lims' door and she felt a disquiet being so close to the lords of the Kingdom. She rang Nat's bell hoping that they would answer it as quickly as possible. But no one came to the door. Instead, when she pressed her ear to that door, she heard a verbal fracas between husband and wife, the two of them shouting at each other in what was clearly the main room. Obviously they had not even heard the bell. From under the door came a feeble flicker of candlelight. She couldn't make out the words or what they were arguing about, but she sensed that it was connected to the physical breakdown around them. She waited for a while then tried the bell a second time. This time Natalie yanked the door open impatiently and for a moment there was a mutual astonishment between them, as if they had not seen each other in years.

Natalie was dressed up for a grand departure of some kind. She wore heels, a waterproof raincoat, and jewelry. Perhaps they had a car waiting downstairs.

"You?" Natalie said quietly, then remembered to smile and opened the door wider by way of an invitation to enter.

Behind her, amid a confusion of packing boxes, Roland stood lit like a gloomy saint by dozens of candles. He was more imposing than Sarah had imagined him to be, more swarthy.

"This is Sarah, from the fifteenth floor," Natalie said to him by way of introduction, and there was a note of deflating sarcasm in her voice, as if Sarah had been an exaggerated bone of contention between them previously.

"Ah," Roland said, stepping forward with a salesman's outstretched hand. "You finally appeared just as we are leaving!"

"You're leaving?"

"Aren't you?" Natalie said. "They say the power isn't coming back until after the crackdown."

"I didn't hear anything about that—"

A cruel smile came to Roland's mouth. "They didn't come up to inform you? Well that's very unchivalrous of them. Beasts."

"They put notifications under the doors," Natalie said. "You didn't get it?"

"Nothing, I don't think."

"Maybe you missed it in the dark. There's no point staying now. We're going to the Marriott for a few days. Maybe longer. Do you want to come?"

"You really should," Roland said, but without the slightest urgency or conviction.

"I can get you a free room," Natalie went on. "It's not like here. They have *real* generators. Imagine, hot showers and air-con. A restaurant—"

The offer was tempting, but there was an obvious reason that Sarah could not accept on the spot: she had booked a flight to leave in two days' time. The money was still stored in her spare room, a shadow of its former self but still a considerable amount. Checking into a hotel, surely it would be noticed now that they were inspecting all bags at the doors for security reasons. She felt dizzy for a second and made a move to sit down. They did the same, all three of them orchestrated in the same movement by their shared awkwardness. Already, Natalie had felt a silent shock at Sarah's disheveled appearance. It was as if she had gone mad in a very short time, entered a spell of derangement that she might not come out of. She had to wonder if it really was just the cutting of the lights that had sent her over the edge.

"I can't imagine the power will stay off for too long. Mrs. Lim says it will come back on soon."

"Does she?" Roland countered. "She's lying, for obvious reasons. I think you'll find everyone has left by now."

"What about Ximena?" Sarah said to Natalie.

"I believe she is staying with friends for the time being. Sarah, you really can't stay here. The place isn't safe."

"And Goi?"

"It's funny you should mention her," Roland sighed. "We were talking about Goi just before you rang the bell."

"She didn't leave as well?"

"We don't know where she is," Natalie put in irritably. "But she took off with some of our silver cutlery. Normally we'd make a fuss and call the police. But as I'm sure she knows, we can't exactly do that now. It's a free-for-all. Everyone steals whatever they can get their hands on. I don't blame her in a way, but still, I read her wrong. I expected better of her. She emptied out her own room without me even noticing."

"That was deft," her husband added. "She's a smooth one, all right."

"Only the cutlery?" Sarah asked.

"It's worth a fortune. A small fortune, I mean."

"She must have felt—"

"She could get away with it," Roland went on. "In that respect, alas, she was completely correct."

"But surely there will be some people staying on here. They can't all leave."

"Depends how much you need air-con and an electric oven and Internet. Some of these old-timers don't care that much."

"But they won't stay," Natalie insisted. "The streets are getting too dangerous. It's too isolated here."

Sarah said, as lightly as she could, "I can put up with it for a couple of days. After that, maybe I'll join you. Can I?"

"You don't need to ask."

Natalie leaned over to give Sarah's shoulder a reassuring squeeze, but her demeanor suggested an impatience to get out and be gone. She gave her the Marriott card and told her to call when she was ready to pack up and move. When Sarah extended her hand to take it, Nat noticed the rims of dirt under the nails and the scuffs on the knuckles. Her hair looked even stranger than it normally did, the blond disfigured by dark roots, shaggy and unwashed. Natalie felt a stabbing pity for her. Sarah was unraveling, but the process was so slow and unobserved that no one had properly noticed enough to step in. She could tell that Roland was quietly alarmed as well. He had expected someone more groomed, more well kept. Yet her clothes were nice. They came from expensive stores and retained their own elegance. The overall effect was bizarre. A scarecrow, Natalie thought, wearing Gucci mall rags. She glanced at her watch as a signal to Roland that it might be best for them to leave. She felt a relief that she was finally getting out of the Kingdom with little intention of returning. The car, as Sarah had suspected, was waiting for them downstairs. Sensing it, the American got up. She shook Roland's hand and kissed Natalie on the cheek.

"Don't worry about me, I'll be fine. Send over some ice if you feel like it."

"It can be arranged," Roland said.

Sarah left them feeling that it was improbable that they would meet again, and by the wall enclosing the penthouse landing, struck by an obscure regret, she paused to peer down into the atrium. She saw that Roland and Natalie had been correct in claiming that the units were by now mostly evacuated, and small birds had taken possession of the higher floors. A ripple of awareness of her presence ran through them and, nervously coordinated, they tilted their heads to look up at her. She was now the intruder.

On the emergency stairs she picked her way slowly downward, feeling the walls with her hands until she had reached her own floor, her head beaten softly by clouds of moths. The outer world of insects, riots, and disorder was openly penetrating the inner world of elevators, generators, privacy, and locks. Inside her apartment the humidity was so high that the sweat running across her body only grew more insistent. Once the door had been bolted she stripped off and took a cold shower, since at least the water supply had not yet dried up, and then she lit her candles, drank a liter of bottled water, and went out onto the balcony for some air.

Her lungs felt compressed, starved of nutrients. Soon she realized that the air was in fact saturated with cinders and drifting smoke and that from the unlit labyrinths of streets spread out beneath her sparks and glowing points of light were moving on unseen breezes like the fireflies she normally saw around the swimming pool. Yet there was a tremendous quiet about the scene. The bats now circled the ruins from which they had been displaced and flew right past her, their cries occasional and pointed. The clouds of sparks from bonfires she could not see had roused their hatred of humans.

On their way to the Marriott, Roland and Natalie passed along the length of Sukhumvit Road, the Skytrain tracks overhead spilling a continuous curtain of water that hit the windows of the car with a menacing repetitiveness. The lights were off in the tailor shops and the wedding-dress outlets and the tourist restaurants, which, after stiff resistance, had opted for discretion over valor. The Sheraton Grande was fenced by men armed with hip holsters and flashlights which they used officiously to move the few cars along—no stopping in front of a five-star—and beyond it the lights of the Muslim Quarter around Soi 31 had stayed on as a formality. The alleys of Iraqi and Yemeni cafés were deserted. Across from them, their eternal complement, the redder lights of Nana and the bars had also stayed on. But here they saw the girls standing in the rain outside the eponymous hotel as they always did after hours, customerless and obstinate, waiting stoically for their dividends. Those girls, mostly from the rice fields of Issan in the north, were in secret solidarity with the insurgents, who that night had not shown their faces on the main roads.

On the car's radio they heard that someone had been shot under the overpass at Ploenchit along the grassy railway lines that still ran there. A body in the grass for a day and night, an object of pity but also of superstition. It was a boy of about nineteen shot through the ribs and left to die, then to decompose like a cur hit by a van. It then struck Natalie how isolated from those events she had been for weeks, willfully closed off inside her professional world and its fortresses, the Marriott and the Kingdom, and yet it was also clear that there was nothing aberrant about such isolation. All people were like that. The Arabs were still partying at the Grace Hotel on Soi 3 almost within sight of the Marriott on Soi 2, and sometimes she herself went over at midnight to the cabaret on the ground floor and watched the belly dancers shaking to an oud orchestra from Cairo. None of them had any inkling of the society around them, and if they had they would have cared even less than they already did. They were there for medical procedures, plastic surgery, mall shopping, sex, and a moment's escape from the surveillance of Allah's terrestrial enforcers. They came from worse and they noticed nothing. It was likewise with the Chinese, she had noticed. They had flown from one dictatorship to another but at least in this one they could use Facebook and Gmail. On what basis would they feel any disquiet?

At the hotel there was a frenzied scene at the doors, which stood at the top of a small ramp. Among the decorative palms and the doormen in livery, a multinational crowd had gathered to demand access to reception in the hope of finding rooms, but were being kept out by the livery. There was shouting and pushing. The glass doors shuddered as pressure was applied to them and then snapped into shape as the livery pushed back against the crowd. As a manager, however, Natalie was given privileged passage through them. Inside, the lobby was as it usually was: a *ranat* player in silks sat on the main bar platform playing calmly for a few exhausted Gulf millionaires who were sprawled in the armchairs with mint juleps and shopping bags. The bar was carrying on as if nothing was happening outside. They left their bags with the staff and sat there for a strong drink while Natalie talked with her managers. The rooms had run out and the people outside would eventually have to be turned away, they said. At the same time, a wealthy Thai family had taken over the Executive Floor and were holding an all-night party there. No one seemed to know who they were, but they had paid in excess of full price. Roland and Natalie ordered double gin and tonics and tried to shake off the mood they had absorbed in the Kingdom.

"All the same," Roland said, "I feel a bit strange leaving Sarah in the building like that. We should have insisted."

"She wouldn't have agreed."

"What is she so attached to there?"

He knew, of course, but it was important to pretend otherwise.

"I don't know her that well," Natalie said. "We only met a few times and even then—I couldn't get a handle on her. As to what she's attached to, I don't know, perhaps she's locked in some sort of internal struggle with herself."

"Like everyone, then."

He pouted and offered a glib toast to their suddenly quite uncertain future. Secretly he was enraged that they had left the Kingdom so pathetically and that Goi appeared to have gotten the better of him. Not only had she taken their silverware, she had taken the nightgown that might have proven so useful and, he was sure, a few things he didn't yet know about. It made him feel doubly sorry for Sarah. She might have thought that she was clever, but she was clearly no match for a Thai maid. What the next forty-eight hours would bring to her was anyone's dismal guess. Even here the lights were shuddering from time to time, the generators straining. There was an air of sedate panic being kept in control by the armed guards visible from the bar through the lobby's cathedral windows. He crushed the ice cubes between his molars and wondered about the next few days: presumably his office would be closed, though enigmatically they had not said anything about it to him. He might even have to consider relocating. Reaching over for Natalie's hand he made an unusual gesture of affection and told her that in his opinion they should stop worrying about strangers, or near-strangers, and instead concentrate on themselves. Why shouldn't they go join the party upstairs for a half hour before settling into their room?

"Oh, God," she groaned.

"Come on. They're just pricks like everyone else."

Reluctantly, she let him persuade her. The party had indeed taken over the entire Executive Floor and on the outdoor balcony, which was long and cleared of tables, a hundred young guests danced to earsplitting Thai pop, otherwise known as String Music. Natalie even recognized it: Tata Young, music she had played sometimes for social events at the hotel. A DJ in a silver bowler hat swayed as if blind and there was a continuous sound of women screaming and glass breaking. In the heat of bodies and their sweat she danced with her husband and realized as she did so that she hated him more than ever. He had not understood anything. He had not understood her or Sarah or the wayward Mali—it was all a mystery to him. He had not even been able to guess that something darkly obscure had gone wrong and that a storm had come close to them and almost destroyed them. How could a person so intelligent remain so naïvely incurious about the people around him? Yet as they danced, sometimes hand in hand, she was not aware—not even slightly—that he was thinking exactly the same thing about her. It was something that he would not tell her for years to come.

Natalie slept in her own bed that night. She found herself swimming in dark blue water in a snorkeling mask, feeling her way with both hands along a bank of translucent ice. Far from the frozen surface she could hear echoes and lowing coming through the depths, like the calls of whales or walruses, and the deeper she progressed along the bank of ice, the closer these sounds became. For a moment she let herself slip away from the glossy ice and drift downward, her hair spiraling above her, and as she did so she reached a point of equilibrium in which she could look up at the pale light on the surface. A boat was crossing it, a rowboat whose oars smacked into the water and churned it. She heard light laughter from the upper air and was surprised that it reached so far down into the depths where she floated. Slowly, she came to recognize the voices. The other three women were having a boat party without her, no doubt sharing a bottle of wine as they rowed across the ice. From deep within the darker blue below her something stirred and a massive shadow appeared, nosing its way, like her, around the ice shelf. She cried out to warn them, and the sound turned into a rising cloud of bubbles.

EIGHTEEN

———

Later that night Sarah again heard the approach of someone on her landing, the door she had forgotten to bolt creaking open. Roused from half-sleep, still immersed in candlelight, this time she went to the door and looked through the peephole. There she saw the fully fledged form of a man, standing in the landing's obscurity, and he was knocking softly on her door. She wondered if it might be one of the receptionists who had come up to tell her to leave the building altogether. But fifteen floors in the heat? Then, unexpectedly, there was a flash on the landing and it was clear that the visitor had struck a match to cast some light on his surroundings. He had stepped back from the door with the match still burning in his hand and she saw at once that it was Pop. He held up the match and peered around, leaning forward slightly. When the match went out he didn't retreat, however, but remained there breathing against the door, calling out her name very quietly. Something must have caused him to climb all the way up to her apartment, and although she was

loath to open her door to anyone, she felt that it might be wise
to do so now. She knew him and she knew that he was harmless,
more or less. She shifted the bolt and chain and clicked open the
locks, pulled the door open an inch.

"Khun Sarah, you are still here? Everyone has left."

"I'm fine, there's nothing wrong."

"I know, of course. But still, I was worried about you. Mrs.
Lim told me to look out for you and come see if you are all right."

"That's very kind of you."

"*Mai chai*. It's my job to look out for the tenants."

"You shouldn't have come all this way up."

Looking behind him she saw that he had laid his heavy rubber flashlight on the wall underneath the half-opened windows.
Yet he had struck a match to see her door.

"Mrs. Lim moved to her other house in Nonthaburi. She
cannot stay here with no power. There's only you."

"And you."

"Ha, yes, I am staying behind to look after the place while the
power is down. It's my job."

So it's just you and me left, she thought. Strangely, she felt no
unease. He was being remarkably solicitous.

"Well," he went on, "I know it's impossible to get any delivery
now. Would you like to share some curry I made downstairs? In
the garden."

"Curry?"

"Yes. *Gaeng som*. I found some shrimp today."

The idea was attractive to her. The garden would be fresher,
and the vile heat could be alleviated for an hour. She was also
hungry and tired of canned tuna. Something hot, something with
some taste.

They began to descend the emergency stairs with the flashlight leading the way. Halfway down they stopped and Pop told her to use her ears: along the bridges there was a rustling sound, a movement of a pack of dogs racing across from one stairwell to another. It came from the floors above them. A quiet whirlwind of animal energy, shapeless and without direction. Pop whispered that they had taken over the landings the day before and that alone he was powerless to do much about it. They were searching for food on the landings where the garbage was usually stored, but one had to wonder if eventually they would not break into the apartments as well. He avoided them as best he could; before long their ingrained fear would give way to something worse. For the moment he asked her to be as quiet as possible in case they were detected. They crept down as far as the gardens without being molested, but as they exited the stairs and came into the windy, rain-soaked gardens she heard a wave of barks from the higher floors, as if the human scent had finally reached them. But Pop, when she asked him, didn't know where these animals had come from. From the street, now that there was almost no security at the gates, or from the apartments themselves, from which they had been liberated and abandoned by panicked owners. As they wandered through the gardens Pop told her that thus far they had not invaded the public areas because he had his slingshot to drive them off and they were wary of him. It was just as well, because otherwise nowhere would be safe from them. Dogs unlearned their fear in a matter of days. One had to treat them with respect. But as he said, he had his slingshot and the gardens were his domain.

At the shambolic living space he controlled, he had occupied a corner of the flower beds as his own and set up washing lines, cooking equipment, and boxes of tools with which he was tinkering with the electrical system, awaiting the day when the power from the outside would return. The lines of laundry looped across the flower beds and were fixed to poles running along the outer wall. Within them, as if within fabric walls, a stove had been set up and was lit beneath a metal wok filled with orange curry. It was so dark that all she could see was the blue flame and the white glow of laundered sheets hanging on the wires. From the beds came a smell of fertilizer and damp soil, and around them the crenelated walls of the Kingdom gave off the luster of broken glass.

She went up to the pool for the first time in a while to break the fear that had not left her all day. The water was still there, but the surface was now dirtied by leaves and twigs and there was a fine sediment of grit laid along the bottom. A few wet ashes lay also on the surface, deposited by the fires outside. As she looked up at the backlit storm clouds, she thought she heard the man who sold brooms every day on a motorized stall trundling down the alley outside with his loudspeaker crying "Mai kwad!" But after a moment or two, she realized that it wasn't the broom seller but a political announcement. Looking down at the portcullis, she saw that the canal water had risen almost to the level of the street and soon would overflow. The windows were now all darkened and soiled and the trees on the higher balconies had begun to wither. Only the foliage of the Lims continued to be resplendent, since Pop would never desert them. There was a trickle of life within the Kingdom that would never be extinguished until the city itself sank into the waters that were rising an inch every year. Then the generators would give out for the

last time and the Kingdom would become an underwater arti-
fact inhabited by barracudas.

The sky, partitioned between electrified clouds and sparkling
deep space, projected a delicate light down onto the vine-heavy
trellises around the pool, the European-style coach lamps, and
the plaster Germanic milkmaids suspended upon the walls. The
tower above her also reflected at its higher floors a vague light
emanating from the freeways, where barricades had been set up.

Her reverie was interrupted by a movement along the back
wall that separated the pool from the lower garden. A huge
monitor lizard had climbed the wall somehow and catapulted
itself over, then propelled itself reflexively toward the body of
water. It had done so silently and she had noticed it only as a
fast-moving shadow under the surface. Now it raised its slender
head and opened its mouth as it focused on her. They were
everywhere in the city even in normal times, preferring the canal
alongside the Kingdom when it rose during the rains. Now, like
the dogs, they sensed an opportunity.

She had crept back to the steps to the garden below just as it
headed toward her, its tail thrusting it forward, its six feet of
green-and-lemon muscle shooting toward the deep end. There,
diverted by the pale blue wall of the pool, it circled and watched
her until she pulled back without any sudden motion. It took
her ten seconds to regain her composure. It had been attracted
to her smell, her motion. There was a scent of blood about her.
In the garden, Pop was smoking a pipe and had opened a bottle
of yadong with two shot glasses at his feet. There was never anything hurried about him. He took things as they came, and even
the good things in life seemed to weary him.

"There you are," he snorted, obviously pretty high already. "I thought you'd been eaten."

"By what?"

"That lizard. They have a bad bite. You didn't know that?"

"No."

"If they bite you, you decay."

"Are you going to just leave it in the pool?"

"What else? It's his now."

She shuddered and sat by the gas stove, which had been reinforced by a fire in a brazier stacked with coals. The smoke curled up and formed a static layer against the lofty roofs.

"They like to live in cemeteries, where spirits are always near them. They are bad luck. We call them *hiia*. It means 'creep' or 'worthless man'—an insult. It's an evil animal. In Koh Tao—"

As they ate his curry he related the death of a young European woman on the island of Koh Tao not too many years before. Her body had been found in a tree in the forest after she had supposedly hanged herself, half eaten by monitor lizards, though it was known that she had not committed suicide. The locals there knew how to hang *farangs* and feed them to the lizards.

"The *hiia* know everything we do. They are evil spirits, too, and even your way of keeping away would not have worked with them. You know they hear the dead."

He offered her a shot of the yadong, and before she could retort they had clacked glasses and downed the liquor.

She found that she was ravenous and, as he had probably guessed, yearning for a little inebriation. She took a second shot and then a third. The curry was searingly hot, and soon her mouth was numb. For some reason, just before she slipped into tipsiness, she dimly recalled that she had left the door to her unit open without locking it. There hadn't seemed any need, and yet it wasn't the wisest thing to have done. She rolled back a little onto her back with the shot glass still balanced in her hand and her eyes rose to the washing lines as if there were something worthy there of being noticed.

"It's funny," Pop was saying, lighting his pipe again and refilling their glasses. "I always thought you were a blonde. But you look more pretty with your dark hair. The maid always said you dyed your hair but I didn't believe her. It's like that with maids. You can never trust a word they say."

"I didn't know that," Sarah said dryly.

"Oh yes, it's well known."

It hardly mattered what she looked like now—there was no one else to whom he could relay this sensational information. It was a small liberation that made her feel normal again. The charade could be over at least as far as this unknown man was concerned. She had always felt that he knew all about them anyway, watching them come and go like rats in their aerial nests. She reached out with her shot glass and said, "Another?" and he smiled and obliged, since they were alone at the end of the world.

"*Chaiyo*. You know, Khun Sarah, you are a remarkable girl. I've been watching you since you came here. I think you are the only tenant that has realized one important thing about the Kingdom."

"What is that?"

"That it's more haunted than people understand. But you—you felt it right away." Pop paused to rub a hand over his chest. "It is because you are not a bad person, just an unhappy one. An unhappy person can feel it more than a happy person. You came here to hide, but one thing I can tell you is there are no secrets in this world. We even have a saying about that. *'Kwam lub mai mee nai loke.'* I think that's the one thing you forgot."

His eye motioned toward the washing lines and, following the line of his gaze, she saw hanging there the nightgown with its faded stain, not washed but simply displayed for her and for her alone. It hung from two plastic pegs, stirring slightly as the breeze moved around the towers and caused the leaves of the mango trees to whisper. A stabbing shock went through her, but she didn't react outwardly.

"Whose blood do you think that is? I know you have been wondering, and so have I. One thing I know—it's not human, as you were thinking. It's the blood of a dog. How can I tell? I know these things. I grew up in the country, Khun Sarah. You can tell those things straightaway."

"A dog?"

He leaned forward to stir the coals and a handful of sparks whirled up into the great space above them.

"Sure, a dog. That girl you called Mali—that's not her name at all. I watched her for a long time, too, and Mrs. Lim asked me about her many times too. You see, I think she and Mrs. Lim have an arrangement. When I said there are *no* secrets, what I meant was that in the end the secrets come out. They all come out.

"Maybe," he went on, "you remember a man who used to come down to the garden to practice his golf swings? I do."

And after a moment's effort she remembered him too.

She saw him now as a nameless and faceless phantom, a ghost of the Kingdom. In that moment, Sarah understood that Mali had chosen her victim well, with nobody to mourn or miss him should he disappear. The only thing of which Sarah could be sure was that Mali was a mirage. Perhaps, Pop said, she had befriended this R. Nimoto character—which could have stood for Ryo—and had defrauded him in the same way. Thus her Ryo was just a name stolen from a man she had herself caused to disappear and which she had then given to her collaborator, whoever he might be.

"Ryo" was most likely a Thai criminal from her underworld connections, a man adept at posing as a jovial Japanese lover, only to be murdered and his battered corpse left for Sarah to find. Pay the boys at reception on the sly and they turn a blind eye, just as they had with the gambling salons. This man, this "Ryo," she had seen lying in his own gore; but she had not taken a closer look. The scene had been staged, she now understood, and of course the lovers were still alive, prospering with her stolen money, sequestered in all likelihood at that very moment at a beach chalet somewhere in Langkawi. They must be enjoying a quiet satisfaction between themselves. The karma was garish.

She glanced down at the warehouses and waste lots between bursts of jungle where piles of junk sat next to the spirit houses. The great islets of rainwater shone even without the streetlights along the road projecting their light into the enclosure. Under the abandoned tobacco warehouses there must be plenty of boarded-up cellars where a body could be hidden. They could have taken Nimoto there and left him unnoticed. It would be decades before he was discovered, if he was ever discovered at all.

She might have asked Pop a hundred questions about the things she had misunderstood, but something was fading inside her own consciousness the more she drank, and gradually she felt tired and disordered. The yadong itself, she was beginning to understand, was not normal. It was spiked with something un-known, and yet he was apparently drinking from the same bot-tle.

He told her about how he had come to work at the Kingdom all those years before, hired by the cruel and insane father of Mrs. Lim and then by her husband, a good businessman who had had a thousand mistresses strewn all over the city. One couldn't begin to understand such families. And then the King-dom, which he felt they had all built together in their different ways. The tenants who were never profiled or investigated, all kinds of riffraff and con men and socialites and TV actresses who as a matter of policy would be allowed to come and go as they wished, no questions asked. It was a fine black-market business when you thought about it. And it could have gone on forever had it not been for the attempted uprising and the mili-tary crackdown. That was the black-swan event that none of them had been able to anticipate. Yet it was the easiest one of all to predict. He, for example, had indeed prepared for it. One had to be nimble to profit from unforeseen events. It didn't take a genius to realize that sooner or later the whole edifice would begin to crack and fall.

"But Mali," she said, slurring her words uncontrollably, "where did she come from?"

"You never know where these people come from. They blow in with the wind. I thought she was the child of a German emi-grant and a bar girl. There are thousands like her. Who knows where they end up. They change their names every six months. Not respectable, like you!"

From between the grandiose arches of the garden floor a dull, half-cloudy moon had appeared and from the pool she could hear the splashes of the reptile that was still there, biding its time. She had thought, once upon a short time ago, that she might have come out on top after all. But at the last minute she had misjudged and faltered. The chessboard she had tried to play like an expert had tricked her eye. She looked down at the tiny glass she was holding and it slipped from between her sweaty fingers and, as if in slow motion, fell to the marble flooring. There, in total silence, it exploded into a thousand brilliant shards and the colorless poison inside it turned into bubbles like fragmented mercury. In Pop's eyes there was now a sad fatalism. *What did you expect?* they seemed to say. And as she fell equally slowly to one side, like a top losing momentum and therefore balance, the darkness lit by bonfires beyond the glass-topped walls seemed to sweep over her. Against the lingering sound of rain, she could feel the presence of the bodies of water around her, the rising floods that lurked just below the surface of the city. In their depths was an unconsciousness just like this one, the brief struggle of a drowning.

NINETEEN

Leaving her where she had fallen, laid out on her side and her eyes stilled by disbelief, Pop finished his *gaeng som* slowly and then waited for the fire to subside a little. It was not even late and he preferred to leave the Kingdom, as was his intention, after midnight. Therefore he took his time to enjoy his pipe again and to think over his self-made options. For one thing, he had no intention of reporting to Mrs. Lim. On the contrary, he intended to tell her nothing at all but simply to disappear. For people in his social stratum disappearance was the only weapon they could use to outfox their overlords. Even she would not be able to find him. The building was now entirely abandoned and even the guards at the outer gates had slowly dissolved away, no longer willing to be the targets of vengeful mobs of their own people. It would be a week before the electricity returned. Long enough for an obscure groundsman like himself to quietly erase his own existence.

He had the island of his mother and father to go to in the

south. It was a place called Koh Kho Khao, an island so close to
the mainland north of Phuket that you could swim across to it
if you had a mind to. It had been destroyed by the great tsunami
in 2004 and he had not been back there since the deaths of his
parents. But there was no better place to eke out a retirement,
and he had long planned to recover his father's abandoned house
from which their ghosts could be exorcised. For years he had
planned his flight there as he worked the gardens and repaired
the wiring of the Kingdom, an obdurate patience that had paid
off unexpectedly. Such was the law of life: results came to the
humble and the patient. He had had so long to plan this move
that he didn't need to think much now, it had all been rehearsed
a thousand times inside his own mind. Thus, when he had finished his curry, he didn't fret about the order of the actions into
which he launched himself. He put out his pipe, stored it in the
bag he had decided to take with him, and walked up to the pool
to take a look at the *Varanus* lizard.

He at first was tempted to kill it to avenge the human dead.
One could not pass over their incessant desecrations of cemeteries. But as he watched the beast lazing at the edge of the pool
having tired of the water, it occurred to him that it might have its
uses after all. Its acute sense of smell had alerted it to the presence of two humans and its snout was lifted, aware of him. There
was a terrible symmetry in the way he had told Sarah about the
European girl who had met her end on Koh Tao. But such was
the way things worked under the sun and the moon. Since the
animals had conquered the Kingdom for a few days it was wiser
to step aside and let them have their way. It gave him a quiet
satisfaction. He went back down to the garden and felt the girl's
pulse. It was still there, very faint, fading, but not yet departed.

The paralytic agent he had put into her glass he had obtained from his contacts in a hospital, but he had little idea how to dose it or what its effects would be. He had asked for something strong enough to render someone incapacitated and nothing worse. But he had taken a stab in the dark. She was unconscious, or semiconscious, but completely paralyzed—for how long he didn't know. Nor did he have time to wait and find out. He looked around for a place he could have hauled her out of reach of the *hiia*, but there was nowhere. That was regrettable, if convenient to him, but his own conscience would always know that he had not done it on purpose. It was fate, and that was all. He wondered only if she would be conscious while it was going on.

Taking the traveling bag he had prepared in advance, he went down to the empty lobby and left it on one of the rattan armchairs. He then commenced the arduous climb to the fifteenth floor.

There was no need to have taken her keys, because he had already noticed that she had neglected to lock her door. He rose floor by floor without the flashlight, not wanting to attract any attention, and on the fourteenth he sensed the dogs lying idle on the bridge, exhausted by the heat. By now the bats had penetrated the atrium and were gathered around the penthouse landings, murmuring to themselves. He opened Sarah's landing door and crept into her apartment, turning on the flashlight. It was exactly as Goi had described. It looked like the apartment of a person who had partially lost her mind. There were candles everywhere, clothes hastily tipped into a suitcase, cans of tuna opened in the kitchen swarming with small flies. The windows were open and out on the balcony he could see a table with wineglasses and overflowing ashtrays. The heat was unbearable.

In the spare room, as indicated by the maid, the money was already neatly stored in a suitcase in one of the cupboards, ready for flight. There was little point in counting it, and he didn't care. He simply picked it up, looked once around the empty room for other valuables, and, seeing none, left by the same route.

On the way down the dogs picked up his scent—he had not washed that day—and one or two of the larger ones followed him at a distance as far as the lobby. Picking up his own bag he went out into the parking area, where his motorbike was parked, and he stored one bag under the seat and the other from the clip under the handlebars. The ascent and the following descent had taken half an hour.

Out in the street beyond the gates there was no light at all except what was left in the sky, and as he rode out of the Kingdom for the last time he wondered at the circumstances that had made it so easy for him to do so. If he passed soldiers on the street they would not stop him even though he intended to drive as far as the Sai Tai Mai bus station, far out on the other side of the river in Thonburi. He had heard on the radio that the station remained open and that the long-distance buses were still running. In reality, they were more in demand than ever. And on the main roads, there was almost no traffic; even the great incomplete construction sites along Rama IV had fallen into suspended animation. The cement trucks stood idle in the floodlit open spaces, the cranes were no longer manned. By the junction with Silom the lights flashed red as if they had been set up to malfunction by the army personnel standing under the tracks at Sala Daeng. But there were no cars anyway. From the bridge over the river he saw that the temples were no longer illuminated, that the rice barges no longer flowed upriver. There was not a soul on the sidewalks.

Within the hour he was at Sai Tai Mai, where he left the bike near the flower market and walked with the two bags into the station where the buses to Phuket took their leave. There, too, the crowds he had expected failed to materialize. The night bus would leave in forty-five minutes and he would be almost alone on it. So Lord Buddha had looked after him and protected him in his hour of need. His resin amulets had not been in vain. The police at the station had no interest in him; they were already playing cards by themselves at folding tables.

When the hour came he loaded both bags into the bay of the bus and climbed aboard with two old ladies, it then being past midnight. Ahead of him lay a fourteen-hour voyage. From somewhere near the Sarasin Bridge, which separated Phuket from the mainland and where he would ask the driver to drop him off, he would hire a private car to take him north along the coast. In three hours he would be at the mainland ferry jetty. There was even a hotel farther up the island called the Sunset, which he knew well, where he could stay for a few days unchallenged and undisturbed. It lay on the long strands that the tsunami had leveled and that had revived only slowly. A few Germans and a few half-broke Swedes were the only white faces remaining. To the north were forests with incongruously hilly paths that he had known as a child. It was a landscape of abandoned jetties and estuaries, of lonely hamlets lost in reeds and waterlogged fields, where the buffalo always seemed to be entranced and motionless. The following day, when he was standing on the mainland ferry jetty gazing over at the low dark jungles on the far side, he remembered how his father used to take him across on a long-tail owned by his cousin and how even in ten minutes the sun would burn his face. The roads were now lost in their own dreams and filled with spirits, emptied by the disaster, and he hardly recognized anything from that time. But in his spartan room later that evening, with the money counted out on his bed and showing him the way to a beautiful future, he decided to think not about the past, because it didn't exist—except as a demonic possession. He prayed to Lord Buddha and then walked out onto Sunset Beach, wild and swept by a hot wind, the low-lying plants quivering as if in terror.

The dead were surely there as well, reluctant to leave the place of their martyrdom. But the beach café was open with its palapas, its lights strung out on a few lopsided poles, and he sat there with a fistful of dollars and ordered everything he could. Hours later, the girls attending the deserted tables closed up the kitchen and he invited them for a few buckets of Sang Som and ice at his expense. How long they were there drinking under the stars he never remembered, but, as if the burdens of years had suddenly been lifted, he found himself dancing with them in the surf to the *mor lam* that blasted from the café speakers, and all that filled his mind in that moment was the simple idea that this was life and nothing else, and like karma life itself always went on, unending and unfair in equal measure, like all things that have been ordained and yet are impossible to see in advance.

ACKNOWLEDGMENTS

There have been many guides through the labyrinth of Bangkok, but none more lighthearted and knowledgeable over the years than Cod Satrusayang and Princess Narisa Chakrabongse. You have made fun of my Thai but corrected it all the same.

ABOUT THE AUTHOR

Lawrence Osborne is the author of the critically acclaimed novels *The Forgiven*, *The Ballad of a Small Player*, *Hunters in the Dark*, *Beautiful Animals*, and *Only to Sleep: A Philip Marlowe novel*, as well as six books of nonfiction. He has written for *The New York Times Magazine*, *The New Yorker*, *Condé Nast Traveler*, *Forbes*, and *Harper's*, among other publications. He has led a nomadic life, living in Paris, New York, Mexico, and Istanbul, and he currently resides in Bangkok.